D0065771

A
CRIMINAL
COMEDY

A VIKING NOVEL
OF
MYSTERY
AND
SUSPENSE

Also by Julian Symons

The Immaterial Murder Case
A Man Called Jones
Bland Beginnings
The Thirty-first of February
The Broken Penny
The Narrowing Circle
The Paper Chase
The Colour of Murder
The Gigantic Shadow
The Progress of a Crime
The Killing of Francie Lake
The End of Solomon Grundy
The Belting Inheritance
The Man Who Killed Himself
The Man Whose Dreams Came True
The Man Who Lost His Wife
The Players and the Game
The Plot Against Roger Rider
A Three-Pipe Problem
The Blackheath Poisonings
Sweet Adelaide
The Detling Secret
The Tigers of Subtopia
The Name of Annabel Lee
Bloody Murder

A
CRIMINAL
COMEDY

JULIAN SYMONS

VIKING

VIKING
Viking Penguin Inc.
40 West 23rd Street,
New York, New York 10010, U.S.A.

First American Edition
Published in 1986

First published in Great Britain under the title
The Criminal Comedy of the Contented Couple

ISBN 0-670-80827-X
Library of Congress Catalog Card
Number 85-40543 (CIP data available)

Printed in the United States of America by
R. R. Donnelley & Sons Company, Harrisonburg, Virginia
Set in Baskerville

Contents

Acknowledgements

Sheila Hale, Timothy and Bianca Holme and Antonio Talamini
have been helpful with some of the Venetian details in this story.
They have no responsibility for mistakes, or deliberate bits of
unpoetic licence. I am grateful to them all, and also to Lady Rose
Lauritzen for a party in the ghetto which bore no resemblance to
that given by Guido Morvelli.

A
CRIMINAL
COMEDY

From The *Sunday Banner Colour Magazine,*
December 1979

??? THE VENICE MURDERS ???

by David Devonshire and Sally Simpson

In June of this year two British citizens died in Venice. One was shot through the heart, the other drowned in an offshoot of the Grand Canal, into which he either fell or was pushed. Nobody has been charged in connection with these deaths, the Italian police seem to have given up hope of solving the problems surrounding them, and Scotland Yard just aren't interested. It appears to have been accepted that one death was accidental, the other suicide, yet the two cases are certainly linked, and as our researches have revealed in both there is strong suspicion of murder.

The story ends in Venice, but as we quickly found, the roots of it are in the very English town of Headfield. All sorts of rumours are circulating among Headfield people, and several of those chiefly concerned quite frankly told us of their dissatisfaction with the present situation. A full investigation, they say, is the only thing that would clear away the clouds of suspicion. More than one personal relationship has been affected, among those closely involved.

The affair began with the anonymous letters sent to the Porson and Crowley families, and round about a dozen of their friends. The letters began a few days before the tragedies, and ended when they had taken place. Our researches showed that there was something odd about them . . .

(The *Sunday Banner* feature is continued on page ----)

PART ONE

The Letters, The Revolver, The Drink

1

Derek and Sandy and Charles and Gerda. Put the names down on paper like that, and they sound like characters in some consciously light and bright American film. And the affair – a word that is particularly appropriate – must surely be regarded basically as a comedy, even though it involved two deaths. Those four might be called the principal actors, again an appropriate word, yet it could be said that Jason Durling was the central figure, for it was Jason's curiosity that prompted the eventual solution. The story might be started at several points, the arrival of the first anonymous letter, the revolver shot at the play rehearsal, the body floating in the water at Venice. Yet upon the whole the symbolically right occasion seems to be the dinner party at which Jason heard the first whisper of Derek's affair.

It was given by the Dixons. Norman Dixon was a producer of TV documentaries, a big man with a lopsided face. When he gave his dogmatic documentary-producer's smile during an argument, his face looked rather like that in a distorting mirror. The other male guests were an American TV executive named Rorker, whom Norman was anxious to impress, and a local doctor called Grayson. Both were accompanied by wives, Mrs Rorker a cachinnating horse-faced lady, Mrs Grayson small and almost speechless, eyes rarely raised from her plate. The party was completed by a red-haired militant woman novelist of twenty-five or so called Biffy, and by the hostess. Caroline Dixon had a cat's face, triangular, with greenish eyes and a pencil line for a mouth. She was not pretty, but many found her attractive.

Jason was a neat smallish bachelor of forty, who dressed

always in quiet dark suits, but allowed himself the single extravagance of brightly coloured bow ties. He was known to have a job in the civil service, and was understood to be interested in literature.

On this evening the conversation resembled that at many similar dinner parties. Norman talked at length about the merits of his last production, in which he had filmed for several months the lives of a factory worker's family in Lancashire and a stockbroker's family in Surrey, cutting in each programme from one group to the other.

Rorker seemed unimpressed. 'What was the point?'

'The different life styles. What do the boys say when they take out girls, where do they take them, what's the parental reaction when Billy brings a girl home, different reactions to schooling. In Lancashire it was all push, upward mobility, you've got to do better than Johnny, in Surrey just the opposite, couldn't care less, as long as Billy's happy what do school results matter?'

'Interesting, maybe,' Rorker said. 'But what does it prove?'

'I don't think TV should be trying to prove things all the time.'

Mrs Rorker gave a defiant neigh of laughter as she said, 'I think your TV's just wonderful.'

Biffy sat next to Jason. She told him at length the plot of her novel. It was what she called a realistic fantasy, in which all the women in the world turned into wolves and all the men into sheep, with predictable results. She seemed to regard this as a happy outcome. Jason nodded his neat head, but said little. Their conversation languished. Caroline said, 'Jason is a novelist too.'

Biffy showed no interest, but Rorker said, 'Is that so? What have you written?'

'Caroline should have put it in a different tense. I *was* a novelist, but it was a long time ago, and I committed the offence only once.' Mrs Rorker started a cachinnation but cut it short. 'I am a government servant now, nothing more. As the immortal Max put it when he was twenty-five, "I, who crave no knighthood, will write no more." I gave up page proofs for blue or yellow files at about the same age.'

12

There was silence. Rorker seemed about to ask a question, but refrained. Caroline said, 'Max was Max Beerbohm, isn't that so?'

'Max *Beerbohm*,' Rorker said. 'Beerbohm, right.'

'He took a knighthood in the end, didn't he? And wrote a lot of other things.' Caroline smiled sweetly. 'So there's still hope for you, Jason.'

Biffy left shortly after dinner, saying that she had an article to write for *Under Twenty-one*, and a deadline to meet. Caroline sat with Jason on a sofa.

'Sorry you didn't hit it off with Biffy.'

'Caroline, you know I was provided as a human sacrifice for her.'

'Jason, would I do such a thing?'

'Yes. But I forgive you.'

'Sweet of you. Have you had one of the letters?'

'I don't know what you mean.'

'Then you've not had one. The Mannerings have, and the Bells, and the Graysons. They all say much the same thing. Have you seen Derek lately?'

'Not for a week or two. What are these letters?'

'Norman says it would be wrong to show them around, he thinks I shouldn't have called people to see if they've had one. But it's right to find out, don't you think? I didn't like to call Derek and Sandy, though.'

'Caroline, I simply do not know what you're talking about.'

'It's suggested that Derek has an outside interest, if you know what I mean.'

'I'm not sure I do.'

'Oh now, Jason, I don't mean he's taken up table tennis. The letters say he's having an affair, getting his oats elsewhere, whatever you like to call it.'

'I don't believe it.'

'I do agree they always seem a contented couple.' Her own eyes were brightly discontented. 'But that's what the letters say.'

'Does Sandy know about it? Or Derek? Have they had letters?'

'I said I don't know. Somebody should find out. You're

13

Derek's oldest friend, I thought you might do it.'

'Who is the woman supposed to be?'

'That's the most interesting thing.' She paused for effect. 'Gerda'.

Gerda was the wife of Charles Porson, Derek's partner in PC Travel.

2

Headfield is agreed by those who live in it to be a delightful small town. It is no more than thirty minutes by train from London, yet is by no means a suburb, but a town in its own right. The angel of death that hovers over British Rail has brushed Headfield only lightly with its wing, so that the service to London remains excellent. Recession is much spoken of, but remains almost invisible. There is a shop in the High Street that calls itself a Gentleman's Tailor, others that bear on their fascias the now rare words Family Grocer and Family Butcher. Antique shops proliferate, showing in their windows no more than a couple of Chippendale chairs and an elegant table, or an array of clocks ranging from grandfather to carriage. Supermarkets exist, and so do building society offices, but the town council has kept them out of the High Street. There are a couple of good hotels, a municipal swimming pool, well-kept public gardens. And although in many parts of Britain theatres are closing down, in Headfield the Margaret Thatcher theatre opened last year, and has a repertory company that plays to well-filled houses. It is true that the fare offered, mostly farces and mysteries, sometimes mysterious farces, is not likely to disturb the intellect or the emotions. Not many of the town's residents would be likely to look at Norman Dixon's documentaries.

Headfield is a prosperous middle-class town with pleasant country to be reached in ten minutes' drive, and most of the recent arrivals have come there for that reason. There are advertising and public relations men who came, as they often say, to get out of the rat race, although they return to it for five days every week. There are business executives who wanted to live out of the city, and others who like the Dixons thought it would be a good place to bring up the kids. Those kids can go to Headfield Grammar, one of the few surviving examples of its kind, there are riding schools just a mile or two out of town, people can often be heard talking about the virtues of clean air and wondering why they hadn't come here years ago.

But not all Headfield residents have fled from the great wen. Some, a decreasing number, were born and raised there. Jason Durling and Derek Crowley were two of these.

Jason's father, a Swedish engineer, had come to Headfield when his employers opened a factory on the town's outskirts for the manufacture of a special design of electric heater. He had married Jenny, who was a Headfield girl, and left her when Jason was a small child, returning to his own country and settling down with a Swedish woman whom he married after the divorce. Mother and son heard no more of him until Jason was fifteen, when his mother was sent a newspaper cutting which said that Anders Durling had died suddenly from a heart attack.

Jenny was the only daughter of a local builder. He had paid for the boy's education, after his first years at Headfield Primary, at Whitestones, which is hardly among the first dozen public schools in the country, but has a respectable place lower down the league table. Jason had known Derek at Headfield Primary, when there was the vast gap of two years between them. Then they had both gone to Whitestones and later to King's College, London, from which Jason emerged with a good degree and Derek with an indifferent one.

Did Jason love or hate his mother? He was never sure himself, but perhaps the question was answered by the fact that, fifteen years after her death, he still kept a photograph of her beside his bed. She was deceptively frail in appearance, with a long drooping neck and elegant hands. On the night before his return to Whitestones she would come weeping into his bedroom, saying that she could not bear to part with him, imploring him not to commit sins that she never described, lamenting his lack of a father and adviser. There were, however, men about the flat, men who called in evening clothes to take his mother out to dinners and dances. There had always been men about, so that when he was at primary school she would come into his room, eyes sparkling, and say that Jean, Mary, Elizabeth, or some other babysitter would look after him and give him supper, that he was to be a good boy, and that in the morning she would tell him all about what had happened. In those days Jason was not always good. At times he cried, at other times he wet the bed, and in the morning his mother was often languid, had a headache, said that the whole thing had been a bore and that Frank or Bryan or Harry – who had looked so wonderfully dashing and had said that Jason was a fine little fellow – had been the biggest bore of all.

As the years passed Frank and Bryan and Harry who had, at least in Jason's memory, been young and handsome, were replaced by men who were older, often fat and sometimes ugly, altogether inferior people. At her request he now called his mother Jenny, and she talked to him sometimes about Roger or Gavin or Bobby. 'They were really – crude, darling,' she would say, waving her beautiful hands. 'And crudeness is the unforgivable sin.' His father's chief fault, he gathered, had been crudeness. Sometimes she would say that she had sacrificed her life for her son. 'I could have married, darling, how often I could have married. Do you remember Oswald? A theatrical producer, such a sensitive man, he once sent so many flowers that they filled every room in the flat. But I told him I could never be separated from my darling son.'

One of the people who had sometimes called at the flat in those later days was Xavier Crowley, owner and editor of the *Headfield Express*, and Derek's uncle. Because Derek called him Uncle X Jason did so too, although they were unrelated. Derek's parents had been killed in a car crash when he was twelve, and he had been brought up by Uncle X and his wife Mary, along with their own son Colin. Perhaps the fact that both Jason and Derek were fatherless was a link between them. In any case much of Jason's childhood had been spent at the Crowleys' big mock-Tudor house on the edge of town. In recent years he had wondered whether Uncle X was one of the people with whom his mother had what she would have called a walk out, but of course the idea never occurred to him at the time.

As the years went by, and Jenny's knees and even her beautiful neck became arthritic, she burrowed more deeply into the life of her son. (*Burrowed* was the word mentally used by the adult Jason.) 'Style is the thing, my dearest, a writer is nothing without style,' she would say. Her interest in Jason's student thesis, on Max Beerbohm and the art of parody, was intense. It was inevitable that she should dislike Heather.

Heather was Jason's first, and indeed only, girl friend. She was forthright and downright, a girl from East London who was also reading English at King's College, specialising in the work of Norman Mailer. Was it because Heather was large, with a hockey player's hands and legs and a powerful profile, that Jason had liked her? And because he was so much her opposite, neat, careful and smallish, that Heather had taken to him? Jenny disliked Heather's appearance, was appalled by her accent, could not endure the way in which she publicly combed her hair. 'But poor girl, she is reading Norman Mailer, how could she possibly know how to behave?' she said. 'I fear she is crude, Jason, crude.'

Afterwards he thought she had been right, but at the time Jason had rebelled. It was his mother's disapproval that prompted him to propose marriage. Heather dismissed the idea with a laugh that was almost a guffaw. 'Marriage is a bourgeois institution, didn't you know? And I wouldn't be marrying you, I'd be marrying your bloody mother as well.' The affair, if one called it that, had been brief, but it had prompted Jason to write his novel. *Loneliness is the Name for Living*, published when he was twenty-three, concerned the struggle for a young man's affections between his mother and a girl he met at Oxford. The mother triumphed, the young man killed himself. He showed his mother

17

the page proofs. She handed them back to him without a word, and he asked whether she had liked the book. Her eyes filled with tears.

'How can you ask such a question? Oh, Jason, how could you be so . . . ' He waited for the word *crude*, but she said 'cruel?'

A week after the book's publication he came home from the job he had recently taken in the Comparative Valuation Section of the Vocational Training Department in the Ministry, to find her in the armchair she always occupied, dead. Her heart had come to the end of its flutterings.

In the years since his mother's death Jason's life had not changed. He had remained in the first floor flat at Ponsonby Court, which was in a good residential part of town. There were photographs of Jenny in the living room and the tiny dining room as well as the one beside the bed, the best showing her bare-shouldered, in a long dress, arms cased in white gloves. To her few but good pieces of furniture Jason had added a glass-fronted bookcase said to be by Hepplewhite, which contained collections of books by his favourite authors. Jason's bedroom, which had once been his mother's, was simple and tidy. He put wooden trees into his shoes every night as he had been taught to do, and had acquired an electric trouser press which was in constant use. Suits were hung in one part of a cupboard with sliding doors, there was a special hanger for his bow ties. Mrs Prancer came in three mornings a week to clean the flat, and also cooked on the rare occasions when Jason gave a dinner party. It was an orderly life, fired by one particular resolve, to write the definitive book about the life and work of the neglected novelist and poet D.M. Cruddle.

Such was Jason Harald Durling, the old friend of Derek Crowley.

The Dixons' dinner party took place on Thursday evening. On Friday the telephone rang ten minutes after Jason had returned from the Ministry. Uncle X's voice boomed down the line.

'Jason, me boy, how do?'

'I am very well.'

'Haven't seen ye for a while. Lookit now, can ye come and see an old man this evening?'

Jason looked at his diary, which was blank, and said that he could. He did not ask what it was about, because he knew that it must have to do with Derek. He was aware that Uncle X only tolerated him because he was a friend of Derek.

Xavier Crowley not only owned the *Express*, which was necessary weekly reading for anybody who wanted to know the local news and gossip, but also used the presses for what was said to be highly profitable printing work. He had the reputation of a hard business man, who negotiated many deals while playing golf or tennis. The sporting phase of his life had ended five years earlier, when he fell heavily while on a skiing holiday and broke his pelvis, with the result that for five years now he had been paralysed from the waist down. He could swing himself from wheelchair to sofa or another chair, but was unable to walk. He was taken to the office once or twice a month, but for the most part ruled his empire from a distance, with the aid of a compliant editor.

Jason had not been out to the house for months. Little had changed since his childhood. There was the same gargoyle-faced knocker, the latch that didn't work on the pseudo-monastic door, and below the latch the incongruous modern lock. Mary Crowley opened the door. She was a small pretty woman, with perfectly dressed grey hair, and a gift for discovering potential disaster in most situations.

'Aunt Mary, you look prettier than ever.'

'Oh, Jason.' She patted her hair. 'This weather, you know it won't last. The forecast is for thunderstorms.' There was a roar from the other end of the hall. 'Coming,' she called, but led Jason to a small room off the hall. 'Why does he want to see you?'

'He didn't say. I suppose it's to do with Derek.'

'He's upset. How long is it since you've seen him? Nearly a year, I thought so. You'll find he's changed.'

'Where are ye, then?' Uncle X appeared at the doorway in his wheelchair, and glared at them. 'What are ye doing out here?'

'I was saying hello to Jason, he's such a stranger.'

'Don't blame him, who wants to see a couple of old fogeys, one of 'em stuck in a wheelchair? Come into me sanctum, Jason, have a drink.' Another glare at his wife. 'Things to discuss.'

'I shall be busy in the kitchen,' she said in a tone that implied she would be on her knees scrubbing the floor. As he wheeled himself along the passage leading to his study, she murmured a request to Jason that he should see her again before he left.

The study contained a few shelves of books, most of them about the newspaper business, a row of pipes on a leather-topped desk, leather chairs of the kind found in men's clubs. Uncle X wheeled across to a drinks trolley in the corner, and poured whisky.

'If that's for me I'd prefer gin.'

Uncle X's 'Ha' was a sound of disapproval. He regarded whisky as a man's drink. He gave Jason a large gin and tonic and kept the whisky himself, wheeled over to one of the leather chairs, and levered himself into it, then lifted a book from a small pile on the table.

'Read this?'

The book was *The Three Musketeers*. Jason touched his bow tie, a mark of embarrassment. 'I think perhaps at Whitestones. Some of it, anyway.' Among the other books he glimpsed *The Hero of Hartley Hall, Graham Makes the Grade, Peter's Second Innings, With Kitchener to Khartoum, Treasure Island*.

'At Whitestones. Read some of it. Didn't like it, eh? What about this?' He held up *Peter's Second Innings*. Jason shook his head.

'Cracking good story. Never played cricket, did ye?' He did not wait for a reply. 'What ye doing now, then? Still a pen pusher? Not written any more of those books?'

Jason repeated his joke of the previous evening. 'Only one offence, and that was a long time ago.'

'But still a friend of Derek's?'

'I hope so.'

'Never comes to see me.' His next words were unexpected. 'Lookit now, wouldn't have a biscuit about ye, by any chance? A

20

bourbon maybe, or a custard cream?'

'I'm afraid not.'

'Nothing at all? Pity. She keeps me short, y'know. Haven't seen a custard cream in months.'

'Perhaps you're not meant to eat sweet biscuits.'

'Nothing to do with it, skimps on food, that's all. It ain't starvation, I don't say that, just keeps me short. Next time you come don't forget, custard creams and bourbons, just slip 'em in your pockets. No use showing the packet though, if matron sees 'em they'll be confiscated.'

'You wanted to talk to me. Was it about Derek?'

'Ha, yes, Derek, he's in trouble.'

Before Jason could ask what kind of trouble the door opened. The first momentary impression was that Derek had come into the room, but in the next instant Jason wondered how he could have been deceived. Uncle X's son Colin, who stood in the doorway, had a superficial resemblance to Derek in height and figure, but where Derek's face seemed to Jason instinct with intelligence, Colin's characteristic appearance was vacuous, his mouth was now slightly open, his expression one of surprise. Colin had done all kinds of things unsuccessfully. He had been an advertising man for a film company, a partner in a publicity agency that folded within a year, a journalist on a short-lived monthly magazine. A job had been found for him on the *Express*, but even its compliant editor had complained that he was never to be found when a story broke, and he had been summarily sacked by his father. He had been married and divorced, and was reputedly attractive to women. He had the confiding manner of a friendly dog.

'Jason old man, how's things? Dad, I wanted a word, hope I'm not intruding.'

'Just what ye are doing.'

Colin beamed. 'Sorry, make myself scarce then, have a word with mum. See you later.'

When the door closed Uncle X said, 'Don't know why we have children, get no joy out of 'em. You know what he's doing now? Derek's found him a place in that travel agency, a courier he calls it. A son of mine and he's nothing better than a sort of servant, looking after baggage. Now he's chasing around with that girl, Derek's sister, what's her name, Stephanie. Brought her to tea on Sunday, not much of a tea, just bread and butter and a couple of scones. Plain girl, don't know what he sees in her. She in him, either.'

'You were saying something about Derek.'

'Ah.' He levered himself into the wheelchair again, went to the desk, felt for a key in his back pocket. From the desk he took out an envelope, gave it to Jason. 'What d'ye make of that? Go on, look inside, it won't bite ye.'

The envelope was square and white, and Xavier Crowley was printed on it in neat capital letters. The address also was in capitals, the postmark Headfield. Inside was a single sheet of white paper, once folded. Words were written on it in the same capitals:

YOUR PRECIOUS DEREK IS PLAYING AROUND WITH HIS
PARTNER'S WIFE IS THAT CRICKET

'Well?' Uncle X said impatiently.

'Caroline Dixon asked last night whether I'd received one of these, but I haven't. Apparently several have been sent, all saying much the same thing.'

'Is that a fact? What I want to know is, is it true?'

Jason was aware that his characteristic caution made it hard for him to respond in any way that Uncle X would not find irritating. 'I should think it most unlikely.'

'Derek and that wife of his, Sandy, it's all tickety-boo with them? Always thought so.'

'I should be very surprised if it weren't. Caroline was saying last night that they always seem a most contented couple.'

'Caroline was saying,' the old man repeated, fiercely mocking. 'That bitch never says a word she means. What do *you* say, eh, you're his oldest friend? No smoke without fire, is that it?'

'Hardly even smoke, I should say, just a damp squib.' Jason permitted himself a small smile.

'Ye say there are other letters. Who's sending 'em?'

'I haven't the least idea.'

'Something's up. Seen these?' He opened the desk drawer again and took from it three small pamphlets, each with decorative lettering on the cover. They said *Four Poems by D.H. Lawrence, 1914 by Rupert Brooke, The Convergence of the Twain by Thomas Hardy.*

Jason took the pamphlets, looked at them blankly.

'Forgeries, all of 'em.'

'But that was years ago. When we were at college. It's all settled, forgotten.'

'Ha.' In the stare Uncle X gave him there was anger, confusion, perhaps madness. He snatched back the pamphlets, returned them to the drawer. 'When d'ye say it was?'

'Seventeen, eighteen years.'

'Never mind then, never mind.' Uncle X glared at him. 'Lookit, Jason, never made you out. Don't smoke, don't gamble, don't go in for women. Eh? Asked you to come and work for me once, wouldn't do that. Y'mother put me up to it, said you'd be a writer, lovely woman she was. But ye said no.'

'I wasn't cut out for Grub Street, not even Grub Street, Headfield.'

'Preferred the Ministry of Chit Chat. Matter of taste, I suppose.' His large hands, the fingers white and puffy, gripped the chair arms. 'He never comes to see me, ye know that? Never.' Jason said nothing. 'I love the boy, d'ye hear? He's more like a son to me than that miserable creature who came in just now. Talk to him, will ye, tell him to come and see me. If he's in trouble, tell him Uncle X can fix it. I may be stuck in this damn wheelchair but I still have a little influence in this town. Tell that to him, eh?'

'I'll tell him.'

Aunt Mary and Colin were in the kitchen eating slices of fruit cake. She said, 'He's mad, isn't he?'

'He's certainly rather mixed up about time.'

'You don't know. Some days he won't eat lunch because he says he wants breakfast, he's not had breakfast. And he gets so angry with Colin.'

Colin gave his uncertain smile. 'I come in most days to have a bit of a chat, cheer him up. Sometimes play a game of cribbage, but he tries to cheat. Do you know what he wanted the other day? Made me search the house for old annuals about Billy Bunter and Harry Wharton at Greyfriars. Wouldn't believe it when I said he had thrown them out, and got so angry I thought he'd have a stroke.'

Aunt Mary patted her hair. 'He showed you that letter, the one about Derek? Is there any truth in it?'

'I'm sure there isn't.'

'Try and get Derek to come and see him, that's what he wants. Will you do that?'

Jason said that he would.

3

On Saturday afternoon he talked to Derek at Headfield Squash Club, after he had beaten Norman Dixon. Derek's squash was stylish rather than sound, full of touch strokes and attempted boasts, which looked spectacular when they came off. Today he had been in form.

'Fantastic, wasn't I fantastic?' His voice rose above the sound of the shower. 'Everything going right. Do you ever have that feeling you've got supernatural powers? I don't mean exactly supernatural, just that everything you touch is right, it's all bound to succeed. At the moment things are like that.' He came out, a towel wrapped round him. Beneath a crown of still golden curls his features were delicate but firm, his figure sturdy rather than elegant. 'What's up, Jason?'

'Why should anything be up?'

'My dear man, you're coming to lunch tomorrow, something I hope you've not forgotten, and I know that you detest all games involving physical effort, so if you come round here it doesn't need Sherlock Holmes to deduce something's up.'

'I thought it might be difficult to talk privately tomorrow.'

'Too right. Tell me about it in a quiet corner over a drink.

24

Norman's dashing off, and I'll wave away intruders.'

In the bar Jason said, 'Are you in trouble, Derek?'

'If you could see how you look.' Derek's blue eyes sparkled at thirty-eight as they had when he was thirteen. 'Why should I be in trouble? Business this year is thirty per cent up, and next year I'm aiming to include the Far East. It's untapped, Jason, practically untapped. Colin's been out there for us, and say what you like about him, Colin gets on with people. He's got offers for some amazing things, not just hotels, but tours in Japan that are out of this world. Talk about holding the glorious East in fee.'

'Gorgeous.'

'Gorgeous then if you have to be pedantic. Glorious is better.'

'I hear Colin's going around with Stephanie.'

'Steph's private life is her own affair. But you didn't search me out to talk about Colin and Steph. So what's up?'

'People are talking. About anonymous letters.'

Derek threw back his head and laughed. Jason stared at the smooth white neck. 'Those? We've had one, or rather Sandy did. She showed it to me. Funniest thing I've seen in years.'

'Sandy thought so too?'

'If you have a good relationship, it's the kind of thing you can make jokes about. And that's what we have.'

'What about Charles Porson, does he think it's a joke?'

'I don't know. You have a point. Anybody sensible would know there's nothing in it, but Charles — well, Charles is Charles. He's coming tomorrow, Gerda too. I suppose I might have a word with him about it.'

'Do you have any idea who might have sent them? Caroline says there have been several.'

'I really hadn't thought about it. Truly, Jason, they don't bother me.'

'Uncle X had one. He didn't think it was a joke.' Derek made a face. 'He's a bit mixed up about times, showed me some of those Rupert Brooke and Lawrence pamphlets, seemed to think they'd just been issued. He says he hasn't see you for months.'

'I know, I know.' Derek ran a hand through his curls. 'I've been so damn busy.' Jason merely looked at him. 'All right, you know me better than I know myself. Yes, I hate to see the old man like that, can't bear people who're ill, detest hospital visiting, you know it all.' He held up his hands in mock surrender. 'Bad behaviour, yes. I'll see him next week. But the pamphlets and anything like that, they're all over, I swear. Long, long ago. The look on your face, Jason, if you could see yourself. Talk about Miss Prim.'

Jason flushed slightly. 'I'm sorry you don't like my expression.'

Derek's hand rested for a moment on Jason's sleeve. 'Come on, Jason.'

'But as you said, I know you better than you know yourself. I can see the signs.'

'Signs of what? Sandy's on top of the world, Owen's just had a special commendation for an English essay, everything's fine and dandy.'

'No wonderful plans for the future, no problems?'

'You really like people to have problems, don't you?'

'Once or twice you've been pleased I was there to help solve them.'

'True enough. I'm a dreamer, aren't we all? And sometimes the dreams fall apart, and then I'm grateful Jason's around. Don't think I forget. But at this moment, on this fine afternoon, there's not a cloud in the sky.'

He looked straight into his friend's eyes, and Jason knew that he was not telling the truth. Perhaps Derek was justifying his new and dubious scheme to himself in some way, telling himself that it didn't present any problem, but that there was a scheme Jason had no doubt. He had been given that straight eye-to-eye look by Derek too often not to know that it was a warning.

4

Sunday morning. Derek lay in bed watching Sandy as she came out of the bathroom, removed nightdress, put on pants and bra, sat down at the dressing table.

'Do you know we're against nature?'

She stopped combing her hair. 'How's that?'

'Both blondes. I was always told that blondes were attracted by brunettes.'

'I'm not blonde, just light mouse with freckles. Still, pleased to know I attract you.'

'Come back here.'

'Not possible. All those people coming. You'd better get up.' Derek groaned. 'You wanted to invite them, not me. I hate that damn Porson, don't know how you stand him. I know he's your partner, but do we *always* have to ask him? Or his German wife, come to that.'

'Be nice to him. He's got to agree with the expansion plan.'

'You want me to go to bed with him, the way you do with Gerda according to that letter? One night of bliss with my wife if you sign on the dotted line.'

'You're a devious woman, I've always said so.'

'I shouldn't like it, I can tell you, the sacrifice would be too great.'

'I have *not* gone to bed with Gerda.'

'That's not what the letter said.' She put her tongue out at him.

'And do not wish to.' He jumped out of bed, clasped his arms round her from behind, touched her breasts.

'No, no, no, no,' she said. 'Breakfast.'

They found Owen already downstairs, eating cornflakes, a study of *Ulysses* propped up by the toast rack. Derek and Sandy had been married for six years, and Owen was her son by her first husband. He was a pale spectacled boy of fourteen, who was doing well at Headfield Grammar, particularly in English.

'Cornflakes will make you fat,' Sandy said.

He looked at her solemnly through his large glasses. He adored his mother. 'I burnt two pieces of toast and then gave up.'

'If you'd watched the toast it wouldn't have burnt,' Derek said. He thought Sandy was too indulgent to Owen.

'You're not supposed to have to watch a toaster if it's automatic.'

'Anyway, toast makes you fat,' Sandy said. 'With butter at

least. It's a hopeless struggle.' She patted her stomach. She was a tall woman, only two or three inches shorter than Derek, and not thin.

'What are we having for lunch?' Owen asked.

'Everything fattening. Only fattening foods are nice.'

Charles Porson spent the morning in his shooting gallery. He had two particular interests, women and hand guns. The night had been spent with Gerda, the morning was for hand guns. His collection of these included a large ring hammer Mauser of the kind bought by the Italian Government in the 1890s, two Walther automatics dating back to World War I and one of the famous PP models from the Thirties, a Colt 45 with the arched and checkered grip, and three or four Webleys including the rare 1904 prototype which British Army testers had found at different times quite satisfactory and hopeless. There were guns alleged to have belonged to gangsters including Dillinger and Dutch Schultz, and three or four with elaborately chased butts. These were the historical items. There were also half a dozen revolvers that he used for target shooting, and the tiny model 90 Beretta with a gold-plated frame that he often carried in a specially made side pocket, so that he was able to produce it on occasion with a dramatic flourish.

Porson was president of the Headfield Shooting Club. There were less than twenty members, all of them subscribers to weapons and militaria journals, and some to American gun magazines. The gallery, which was a specially built brick structure at the end of the garden, had been used for several competitions among local marksmen. On this morning, however, the only visitor was a retired Army Major named Metcalfe. They shot against each other at targets of different lengths, sometimes using their own guns, and sometimes exchanging them. Porson outpointed the Major comfortably, and felt the surge of satisfaction that for him was always associated with the exercise of power. The two of them were so absorbed that Gerda had to come down to the gallery to remind her husband that they were going out to lunch.

'Metcalfe fancied himself,' Porson said to Gerda as they drove to the Crowleys. 'I showed him what's what.'

'You did?' she said without interest. 'Good for you.'

Porson was in his fifties, and not in appearance an attractive man. His face was square, flattish and brick red, the small nose pushing upwards, the thick mouth bending down. In spite of the warmth of the day he wore a suit, and what looked a tight-fitting collar and tie. Gerda was not more than half his age, and the unkind said he had found her in a German brothel. Another, and more probable story, was that he had met her when she was a courier for a German travel agency. She was blonde, evidently Teutonic, and the set of her well-shaped mouth and chin was determined. She spoke English perfectly, rather slowly, at times with an accent. The Porsons had been shown one of the anonymous letters, but none had been sent to them.

'I am not sure why we are going to lunch today,' she said. 'I thought you were having problems with Derek.'

His hands on the wheel were thick and stubby. 'We are going because of those letters. I want people to see there's no truth in the rumours.'

'You have arguments with him in business, that is true?'

'That young man thinks he's clever. He needs to be taught a lesson.'

Jason enjoyed Sunday mornings. On weekdays, out of concern for his figure, he breakfasted on a high fibre biscuit and a glass of grapefruit juice. On Sunday he allowed himself a cup of coffee, two slices of toast, and a three-and-a-half-minute boiled egg. The Sunday papers were also a source of pleasure. He had no political views, but read the review pages with interest, making notes on what seemed to him particularly ridiculous observations, as some write in the margins of books. On this morning, however, his thoughts returned persistently to Derek, and what he might be up to. Was it something that would land him in trouble?'

Trouble had marked Derek's youth. It could have been called financial, but Jason preferred to think of it as a romantic protest against the restrictions of his childhood. His parents had both been teachers, Charles Crowley the assistant headmaster of Headfield North Junior School, Phyllis a physical education teacher at a local college. They believed in simple living and high thinking, and were determined to imbue their son with their own ideas. Jason had been in some ways an indulged child. When he found homework difficult Jenny or her current gentleman friend did it for him, and if they could not do it she said that the questions were stupid. If he wanted money to buy sweets, ice cream, toys, it was given to him. Derek, by contrast, was not allowed out in the evening until he had done his homework, received a small weekly allowance of pocket money, and had to account for every penny of it. His end of term reports were pored over as if they had been written in code.

After Derek's parents had died, Uncle X had tried to continue as he thought they would have wished. Derek was still kept short of money at Whitestones. There he soon made a reputation for himself, both as a games player and as a boy always ready to circumvent authority. This expressed itself in odd ways. For more than a term Derek took bets on horse races, cricket matches, and other events quoted by Ladbroke's and Corals. He told boys doubtful about receiving their winnings that his father was a partner in Ladbroke's, and that they would pay out in the event of a big win. His business flourished, but of course Derek spent the winnings, and was unable to pay when somebody landed a bet at long odds. He was beaten up in a mild schoolboy manner, his housemaster heard about it, Uncle X came down, expulsion was narrowly averted.

The gap in their ages meant that Jason had seen little of Derek at Whitestones, and had heard only rumours of the bookmaking activities. That did not stop Uncle X from reproaching him. 'Lookit, Jason, ye're his friend, should have looked after the boy.' Jason had protested almost tearfully that he now saw little of Derek, but Uncle X brushed this aside. 'Ye were thick as thieves back at home, I've had a word with the powers that be, said you'd keep an eye on him.' Afterwards Derek had spoken to him, contrite and apologetic, and said what a fool he'd been, how sorry he was that Uncle X had involved Jason. Then his smile had changed from apologetic to affectionate. 'Wouldn't have happened if I'd talked to my old Jason, would it? I must have been off my rocker. Won't happen again, I swear it.'

It never did happen again. At college Derek was secretary of the Students' Society. There was a fuss about his handling of the bar accounts, and a suggestion – but nothing more – that one or two suppliers had given him a rake off for placing orders with them. At this time Derek had literary interests, mostly inspired by Jason, among them Swinburne, Henley and Scott Fitzgerald. He also became fascinated by the Thomas J. Wise literary forgeries of first editions, and when he left King's and found a job with a secondhand bookseller he essayed a little forgery of his own, of a modern and modest kind. These were the pamphlets Uncle X had produced to Jason. They purported to be the first printings, and hence valuable rarities. The crude deception was quickly discovered, Uncle X again stepped in, money was returned to the purchasers, Derek was sacked.

Uncle X talked to him sternly, and gave him a job on the *Express*. There Derek immediately made a good impression. He wrote lively accounts of Council meetings, interviewed local people with grievances, produced a series of articles about the scandalous conditions at an old people's home, Uncle X was delighted, but Derek found local journalism tame. He produced a story about a man telephoning the office, confessing to a recent murder in the area, and arranging a meeting with the police at which he would give himself up. The man never appeared at the meeting, and under police questioning Derek admitted inventing the story. That ended his career as a journalist.

All this was ancient history. For several months Derek had been out of a job. Then, again through Uncle X, he got a job with Porson Travel, a Headfield firm founded by Charles Porson's father, and his career there had spiralled upwards. In Jason's view this was because Derek was a fantasist, and a travel agent is in the business of selling fantasies. He was thirty-two when he married Sandy Linnet, a divorcee with an eight-year-old son. His career continued to flourish, and the firm became Porson and Crowley, later abbreviated to PC Travel. The only flicker of his youthful fantasising had been when, a couple of years earlier, a local riding school had for some reason refused to accept Owen as a pupil. Sandy had been upset and Derek had become angry, saying he would buy the school, and making a verbal arrangement to do so at an extravagant price. Uncle X, now confined to his wheelchair, had telephoned Jason, and Jason had talked Derek into withdrawing from the deal, although he insisted that it would have been a good investment. Looking his friend straight in the eye, Derek had said that was his only interest in the riding school, as years earlier he had sworn that the forged pamphlets were genuine.

So the frank eye-to-eye look meant that Derek was up to something. What could it be?

Jason dressed with care in a plain grey lightweight suit, a shirt with a grey stripe in it so faint as to be almost invisible, a dashing red and grey bow tie, and shining moccasin style shoes which added what he felt to be the right touch of informality.

The fifteen-minute walk from Ponsonby Court took him through a good residential part of town. The only old buildings in Headfield were in the town centre, and the general architectural style might have been called red-brick ex-urban. On this fine Sunday morning executives disguised in dirty old overalls were tinkering with their Jaguars, BMWs and Volvos, men with hairy chests rushed up and down lawns with motor mowers. Headfield, Jason reflected, is a delightful place marred only by its inhabitants. Hardly Wildean wit, he thought, but pleasing.

The Crowleys' house, Philip and Elizabeth Villa, was in the best part of the best residential section. The road in which it stood was protected from speeding cars by the humps in the road called sleeping policemen. A hawthorn hedge concealed those in the garden from their neighbours, and there were lawns at front and side. The house itself was squarish, deep, and of course in red brick. A double garage, with games room over it, was attached at one side. The neighbouring houses had their own beech or hawthorn hedges. In Headfield it would have been generally agreed that one need not be obtrusively conspicuous to one's neighbour.

32

'Jason, lovely to see you.' Sandy gave Jason both her hands, but did not proffer her cheek. She was bare-legged, in an azure dress deliberately shapeless, with flat-heeled shoes. They were in the garden, Sandy said, and to reach it they went through the living room, on which Jason cast as always a half-amused, half-horrified eye. At college Derek had had taste, an eye for colour, a feeling for symmetry, but what had happened to them? If Jason had seen a picture of the room in a colour magazine supplement he would have written by the side of it 'Contemporary clichés' with an exclamation mark – he greatly favoured exclamation marks. One wall was painted puce and the others off-white, a Bang and Olufsen TV in dove grey stood in a corner, on the walls were perhaps reproductions of Pollock and de Kooning, perhaps original splodges done by Owen. The furniture was Modern Heterogeneous, a teak drinks cabinet, one of the button-back sofas that appear in every TV play, a plush armchair in a colour meant to match the puce wall but just failing to do so. Could it all be put down to Sandy? Jason preferred to think so. The french windows to the garden were flung wide, and people were sitting out there on the filigree pattern white metal furniture. A few feet away stood a barbecue which, mercifully Jason thought, showed no sign that it was to be used. Just beside it Derek was pouring some sangria-like concoction into glasses from a tall jug. He wore an open-necked short-sleeved shirt, old trousers, sneakers.

'Derek,' Jason said. 'I fear I am over-dressed.'

'Is that a delicate way of saying Sandy and I are looking sloppy? If so, you're right. A glass of Crowley Special, which is more alcoholic than it looks without being lethal? And Owen, will you take this Bloody Mary to my esteemed partner? He doesn't trust a Crowley Special, and perhaps he's right. Jason, you know everybody.'

That was true. He saw Charles and Gerda Porson, the Dixons, Derek's younger sister Stephanie, Colin, and the local librarian Miss Hormine, a tall thin woman who had little conversation but a frequent and as it sounded disdainful sniff. Miss Hormine's surprising Christian name was Gladys. Jason sat

33

as far from her as possible, on the basis that they would probably be next to each other at lunch.

The conversation was typical Headfield chat, moving over such matters as the threat of a new road coming into the town as an accompaniment to a by-pass being built five miles away, the Alan Ayckbourn play on at the Margaret Thatcher, the Town Council's permission for a new block of flats on what had been regarded as common ground. It might even, Jason thought, be called a scene typically English in its green serenity, the level lawn with neatly trimmed edges, flower beds without a sign of weeds, rockery providing a splash of colour, butterflies in search of not yet flowering buddleia. English too the voices, gentle but a little high, discussing trivia. Yet he felt something wrong about the scene, a tension that did not belong to the easy gossip.

Derek clapped his hands. There was silence broken only by the buzzing of a bee around Porson's head. Derek stood by the barbecue, facing them all. Sandy, also standing, was beside the French windows, Owen by her side.

'I hadn't intended to say anything about this, but Jason had a word with me yesterday. I always listen to Jason, and nothing but good has ever come of it.' Jason was awarded a bright smile. 'After what he said, it seemed to me I should say something to clear the air. Anonymous letters are floating around. Sandy's had one, so have Caroline and Norman. So has Steph. Anybody else?'

Colin said, 'Dad had one. Damn awful thing to send, upset him.'

'Of course, I'd forgotten Uncle X.'

Miss Hormine sniffed. 'I received a letter. I tore it up at once.'

Derek raised his eyebrows and looked at his partner. Porson shook his head.

'I don't know how many other people have had letters, and I don't much care.' He glanced at Sandy, gave her one of those brilliant smiles, amended his last words. '*We* don't much care. That isn't to say we don't mind about the letters. Of course we do, anybody dislikes having rumours of that kind spread around.' Derek smiling was replaced by Derek serious. How well I know you, Jason thought, how naturally you move into the limelight.

34

'But we think the best thing to do – and Sandy thinks this even more strongly than I do – is to ignore them. We ask all our friends to do the same. Here endeth the explanation.' He put his hands together. 'Amen.'

'Bravo.' Caroline clapped hands, smiled her cat's smile. Owen, who had been looking owlishly through his large glasses, took his mother's hand. Sandy put her arm round him.

If the statement had really been meant to clear the air, it had not succeeded. Porson said, 'What about the police? Calling in the police.'

'Sandy and I don't want that, and I'm surprised you should think of it. They'd be going round the office, interviewing staff, upsetting people. The last thing we want is publicity. It couldn't do anything but harm the firm.'

Norman looked from Derek to Sandy. 'You mean you're just going to let this man . . . '

'Or woman,' his wife said.

' . . . or woman go on sending this stuff out to everyone who knows you? Not a good idea. Don't know if you saw a docufict I made a few months back about a couple whose twelve-year-old son had disappeared.'

'Forgive me, but what is a docufict?' Jason asked.

'Used to be called faction, but docufict's different, much nearer documentary, just the names and places changed.' Norman was not pleased by the interruption. 'Anyway this couple ignored the accusations that they'd been involved and things just got worse, in the end the police were digging up the garden and what have you. Turned out the boy had run away and was living with gypsies, hated his parents, didn't want to go back.' Norman looked round with his distorting mirror smile, his docufict smile. 'I'd suggest you correlate the material, check the postmarks, writing or typing, kind of paper and so on. If there's enough to go on, and with several letters there should be, it's possible to learn a lot. If that's no go, employ a private detective. Some of 'em rip you off, but I know a couple of good ones, used them for programmes. Glad to give you their names.'

Derek looked at Sandy, who shook her head. 'Thank you,

Norman, but we won't need the names.'

'You'll just let it go? Unwise.'

'Even so.'

Sandy and Owen, who had vanished inside the living room, reappeared carrying red and white checked tablecloths. Derek gathered up glasses, the cloths were spread over the metal tables. Al fresco eating, Jason thought with a sinking heart, perfectly acceptable in Italy, southern France, Spain, Greece, but in the English climate the height of folly. As if to justify him a sable cloud blotted out the sun, large drops of rain fell on bare heads and shoulders, the cloths were snatched back to the accompaniment of little shrieks and laughs, the retreat sounded. Within a few minutes the table in the dining room was laid, and Derek was dissecting a whole salmon.

Jason found himself, as he had expected, next to Miss Hormine, but to his surprise Sandy was on the other side. The food was cold salmon with a cucumber salad, sauce hollandaise, thumb-size new potatoes, a firm Alsatian pinot blanc.

'What a perfectly faultless meal,' he said to Sandy. 'Only the weather has betrayed us.'

'Thank you.'

'Derek seems very cheerful.'

'You know how he is, either up or down. Things going well, the sky's the limit. When they're going badly the bottom's fallen out of the travel market, etcetera, and he needs cosseting. You learn to live with it.'

'And at the moment they're going well.'

'I suppose. Derek has *plans*, but I don't suppose I should talk about them, do you?' Her laugh was uninhibited, revealing perfect white teeth. Jason was reminded of a phrase in a Henry James story, to the effect that a girl who had such a lovely way of showing her teeth could never be heartless.

He turned to Miss Hormine, and asked her about the well-being of the public library. The question proved ill-advised. With a preliminary sniff she described at length the way in which the service was starved of funds, the inevitable reduction of purchases, complaints from the public, her struggle to maintain

36

standards. Jason placed his responses on automatic pilot.

At the other end of the table Derek was telling a story about catching the salmon himself during a weekend's fishing. Did he expect the story to be believed, might it even be true? With Derek anything was possible. Porson, sitting on Sandy's other side, paid attention only to the food, concentrating on each separate piece of salmon as he lifted it to his mouth. Colin attempted to cap Derek's salmon story with a typically feeble one of his own. All this Jason noted with part of his mind, as he noted also that Stephanie looked pale and that Gerda seemed immoderately amused by Derek's story, while still making the right responses to Gladys Hormine.

'*That bitch.*'

He was startled to hear the words, which had been murmured *sotto voce*, so that they had not disturbed Porson's attention to the salmon. Had they been uttered at all? He wondered this, then saw that Sandy's face was strained, eyes looking down at her plate. In a low voice he asked what was the matter.

'Nothing. Please, Jason, talk to me about something.'

Jason obliged by telling her of his elaborate negotiations with a bookseller about buying some letters written to D.M. Cruddle in his youth, one or two to Henry James, others to Hugh Walpole, and of his careful checking of dates to show that they were unmistakably fakes. Sandy nodded and smiled.

Colin was talking about his experiences in Japan and China.

'*China,*' Caroline said. 'D'you mean you've arranged tours in Red China?'

'No real problem, you just have to get on with them, y'know. They liked it when I rode a bicycle. It's not Red China any more, by the way, it's mainland China. At least that's what we call it in the agency.'

'And what about Japan? I suppose the tours you've arranged there are more sophisticated.'

'It's wide open for tourists. Yanks go there, of course, but we've given it the cold shoulder. Lots of things haven't been touched by British agencies, gastronomic Japan, Japan by train, Tokyo by day and night.'

'You speak Japanese?'

'I did pick up a bit,' Colin said apologetically. 'Good at picking up languages, got no grammar you know, but manage to make myself understood somehow.' He gabbled a few words, collapsed into laughter.

'Colin's being modest,' Derek said. 'He did a wonderful job out in the Far East, came back with so many good ideas and offers we're still sorting them out.'

Porson's face had been getting steadily redder. Now he said, 'I shouldn't advise any of you to think you'll be booking to the Far East with PC Travel.'

'It's still investigatory, of course,' Derek said easily. 'But the prospects are fantastic.'

'Money down the drain.' Porson turned to Colin. 'Hasn't gone to your head, all that Far East travelling, I hope. You'll be back to work as courier on the Venice trip next Friday.'

'Of course.'

'You'll have the pleasure of my company, I shall be keeping an eye on you.' Colin gave his slightly inane laugh. 'I have to see our Italian associate Guido Morvelli about various matters, and I want to see how well the PC Travel train tour operates.' The words were spoken to Colin, yet they seemed to be addressed rather to Derek. With a feeble attempt at a joke, Colin said that they would be delighted to have the chief aboard.

'You'll have me aboard too,' Jason said. Porson directed his lowering gaze away from Colin. 'I'm going to Venice, and Derek kindly made arrangements for me to go on the train, even though I'm not part of the tour.'

Porson did not comment. Colin said he was jolly glad Jason wasn't on the tour, no doubt he knew everything about Venice, and it would have been pretty difficult to spout his nonsense if an expert had been trailing around with him.

'Colin, you make me mad,' Stephanie said. 'You know an *awful* lot about Venice, I've heard people who've been on the tour say so.'

'Only people who don't know anything.' Colin winked at her.

'In the country of the blind the one-eyed man is king, and all that.'

Stephanie made an irritated gesture. Porson wiped his thick mouth with his napkin. 'Delicious. My compliments to the chef.'

This fine old cliché seemed to have a smoothing effect. The conversation moved as if on castors to another cliché: cheese or pudding first, French style or English? Discussion was terminated by Gerda, who said: 'I like to feel at the end of my tongue something with bite.' Small teeth were shown ready for practical demonstration, some sort of sexual invitation seemed hinted. Charlotte russe was followed by a Stilton to be scooped out.

A true Headfield summer luncheon party, Jason thought, and wondered why a jeering thought should enter his mind when the meal had in fact been delicious. Was he right in feeling that Derek and Sandy were playing at being host and hostess, and the whole thing was a colour supplement luncheon designed to be photographed so that it might enter a million homes as an example of gracious living?

Coffee was taken in the living room. The atmosphere remained uneasy, thunder rumbling not very distantly. Derek sat at Stephanie's feet talking to her in a low voice, and slowly her discontented look faded, once or twice she smiled. When seen together they were obviously brother and sister. Derek had the gift, when talking to anybody, of doing so as if no other person was in the room.

Porson sat on the TV sofa, Gerda beside him. When he accepted a mint chocolate with his coffee she snatched it from him, saying that he ate too many sweet things, he would swell up like a balloon and burst. Porson looked like a pig being stroked with a hard brush on his back.

Owen brought round coffee. He crouched beside Jason's chair. 'I've just finished reading *Ulysses*.'

Jason gave the smile that Derek had called prim. 'Anything may be forgiven to youth.'

'Don't you think it's good? My English master says it's the greatest twentieth-century novel.'

'Perhaps so. Tell me what you think when you've had time to reflect on it.'

'As a matter of fact I've read it three times, I'm attending a seminar about it next weekend along with a lot of Joyce scholars. They've never had anyone as young as me. You must have an opinion. Derek says you know more about books than anyone else in Headfield. You wrote a novel once, is that right?'

'That's right.'

'Why didn't you go on?'

'Not enough people bought it, I wasn't encouraged.'

'He says you're working on something else, your *magnum opus* he called it.'

'I'm working on a book, that's true. I have been for years. It's about the life and work of a very important twentieth-century writer.'

'Who is it?'

'His name is D.M. Cruddle. He wrote novels. And poems.'

'Never heard of him.' Owen departed. Sandy asked if he had been a bother.

'Not in the least. He just made me realise how old-fashioned I am.'

'Come out in the garden. The rain has stopped.'

In the garden clouds were scurrying away, sun appeared fitfully. They walked slowly across to some blood red peonies, looked at them as if they held a vital secret.

'Sandy, what did you mean by what you said in there?'

'What did I say?'

'You said it to yourself, very low, but I heard. You said "That bitch."'

She shook her head and told him he was mistaken, but he knew that was not so. Jason's preference was for a Jamesian indirect-ness of approach in emotional matters, but now curiosity made him unsubtle. 'When you said it, were you thinking about the letters?'

As if the words were a signal, she walked rapidly across to a rose bed where she bent to examine a pink flower, small and delicate. He followed and asked, pitilessly as a prosecuting counsel: 'Is it the letters you were thinking of? Are you afraid there's really something in them?'

'I told you, you're mistaken.' She straightened up and stood on a level with him, awkward yet dignified. 'These roses have mildew, I must spray them.'

They returned to the house, and shortly afterwards the luncheon party broke up. Before he left Jason said to Derek, 'You told me Sandy was on top of the world. I'm not sure that's true.'

'She will be.' In the friendliest possible voice he went on, 'You're a nosy old bugger at times, aren't you?'

On the way home Caroline said to Norman, 'Did you notice one odd thing in what Derek said about those letters?'

'He didn't pay any attention to my idea of a docufict, I know that.'

'He asked us to ignore them, but didn't say whether they told the truth or not. Nor did anybody else.'

'Nothing in that, don't suppose he bothered to mention it. No need when Derek and Sandy never seem to have a cross word.'

Caroline restrained a sigh. No doubt Norman was a good TV producer, but at times he seemed to her just stupid.

5

Jason Durling kept an occasional journal, a notebook of reflections and events, not written every day but when the feeling moved him. Late on Monday evening he sat at his little writing table, a reproduction piece but elegant, and filled some pages of the vellum covered book in his neat hand. Jason wrote:

A nosy old bugger – the uncharming phrase echoed in my mind. It is true that I am inquisitive, I like to know things, especially if they seem to be secret. I had no doubt that hidden meanings rippled beneath the surface of that luncheon party. Why was Sandy driven to murmur 'that bitch' about Gerda, and then deny it? And was it right to assume that the words referred to Gerda, or

41

even to anybody present? I pondered these things on Sunday evening in the course of making an omelette and a cup of caffeine-free coffee. An omelette, an apple, a chapter or two of Gibbon's *Decline and Fall*, which I am reading more for the rolling prose than the history of a collapsing civilisation, and so to bed.

There I was assailed, as happens intermittently, by an unpleasant dream. In it I am engaged in struggle to escape from people who are preventing my movement, although (what is especially disturbing) not by any physical means. They are always men I know – Bruce-Comfort from the Department, Derek, the headmaster at Whitestones. They taunt me, I try to escape by running away but am unable to struggle up. My legs fail to respond to the orders of the mind. The people threatening me come nearer, I try to push them away, but my arms are muffled in some clinging material, and I roll helplessly from side to side. The dream's conclusion is that I wake with a thumping heart.

Monday morning. I face another day. I wash, shave, eat, excrete. I think of Conrad Aiken's Senlin:

> *It is morning, Senlin says, and in the morning*
> *When the light drips through the shutters like the dew,*
> *I arise, I face the sunrise*
> *And do the things my fathers learned to do.*

I put on a discreet blue office suit, a blue and white striped shirt. The mirror shows a round pale face, dark hair with a touch of grey, small ears close to the head. Bow tie in hand I contemplate the face that Jason Durling Esquire is compelled to look at in the glass – how extraordinary that it never varies! Then I flip one end of the tie over the other.

So everything is as it has been ten thousand times before? Not quite. An envelope lies on the carpet in the tiny hall, a white, square envelope. My name and address are written on it in small printed capitals. I slit the top with an ivory-handled paper knife that belonged to my mother, and take out a single sheet of white paper with words written in the same careful capitals. It is identical in style with the letter shown me by Uncle X, and I suppose with the others. It says:

YOUR FINE FRIEND DEREK IS SCREWING HIS PARTNER'S WIFE WHAT PRICE THE OLD SCHOOL TIE?

That is the first unusual event of the day. There are others I think worth noting, although most of the day is like the ten thousand others. Have I described my office in this journal? I think not.

Mr J. Durling, Section Principal is in gold lettering on the door. Within is an oak desk, a filing cabinet the secrets of which are known to my secretary Rhoda, shelves containing Blue, White and Green Papers on vocational training which I never look at, a chair with arms for me and one less comfortable for a visitor. A window gives a sidelong view of a side street. I am a principal in the Comparative Valuation Section of the Vocational Training Unit. The Section is dedicated to making endless comparisons. What sort of comparisons? Between the quality of vocational training in particular areas, the percentage of those trained who obtain jobs, the percentage who keep the jobs for more than twelve months, comparisons between those trained and those not trained at VTUs. Papers are drafted, dozens of papers, conclusions are reached. Has anybody yet acted on such conclusions? I am not aware of it.

Jason Durling, this is your life.

Can it be believed that when Rhoda comes in, she is excited? Excited, I mean, by the figures for Merseyside, which show a thirty per cent rise in something or other. She speaks of VT job aggregations, of balanced gains, of the drag factor. What do the figures mean? What, even, do the words mean? What would Gibbon have said of the term 'job aggregation'? I say that the figures may be deceptive, but agree that she should take them along to Section A for something called pooled discussion. I know that by the time the pooled discussion comes up, perhaps next week, I shall be on leave.

When Rhoda had gone I took out the envelope (yes, I know I am changing tenses), propped it in front of me on the desk,

43

extracted the message, read it again, then telephoned Derek. I
was told that he was in conference, said it was important, heard
his voice. I told him I had received a letter, and he asked what it
said. I repeated the words.

'Much the same as the others.'

'I thought you would wish to know about it. I'm sorry if you
think I am merely being a nosy old bugger.'

He laughed. 'Sorry if I gave offence. No harm meant, you know
you're my oldest and dearest.'

'There is something else. I don't care to mention it on the
telephone. I wondered if you could spare a few minutes tonight to
come round and have a drink. But perhaps you're too busy.'

'Must I? Okay, okay, it's just that we would-be tycoons are
occupied twenty-five hours a day. As long as you don't mind if it
really is only a few minutes. Around nine-thirty? See you then.'

It was hardly a satisfactory conversation.

At lunchtime I went to Giovanni's, which is my Monday
restaurant. I give my custom to five restaurants in rotation, one
for each day of the working week. None is expensive, and in none
is the cooking elaborate. At Giovanni's the saltimbocca is tender,
the lamb with rosemary flavoursome. The same corner table is
reserved for me each Monday, and I sit back in it with a pleasant
consciousness of being somewhere familiar and safe.

As I drank my customary single glass of sherry Colin appeared
in the doorway, in the company of a plump man perhaps in his
thirties, wearing jeans that fitted tightly over hips and buttocks,
an open neck shirt and a slightly grubby jacket. Colin was
obviously less than delighted to see me, and visibly recoiled when
the waiter showed him to the table next to mine.

'Hallo stranger, fancy meeting you.' The inane words were
accompanied by his inane laugh. I smiled and held out my hand.
Colin reluctantly made the introduction to Chuck Waterton,
whom he called a business associate. Chuck Waterton smiled,
revealing some gold teeth, and said it was good to know me, in
what appeared an American accent. Or had he assumed a
mid-Atlantic accent, like thousands of other people in London?

Colin said to the waiter, 'Look here, do you think we can have

44

another table? You know how it is, Jason, talking business.'

'Of course I understand you may have things to discuss that you don't wish me to overhear.' Colin made a gesture both of acknowledgement and dissent, gobbling slightly so that his lack of chin was more than usually apparent. 'I thought you would be in Headfield, arranging our Venetian journey.'

'Oh, that's all laid on. This is just a private affair.'

'You're a friend of the family, come from Colin's home town, you must know Steph,' Chuck Waterton said.

'Stephanie? Yes, of course.'

'Nice girl.' He made a clicking sound and showed the gold teeth again. Colin took his arm and led him to another table. It was clear that he was the host, which was unusual since Colin was almost always short of money. I glanced occasionally in their direction and saw Chuck (to be informal) making points, as it seemed to me rather forcefully. Colin looked relieved when I got up to go. I was not wholly surprised to hear his voice on the telephone an hour after I had returned to files and papers.

'Jason, it's Colin. I say, I hope I didn't seem, well, rude today. Moving to another table, I mean. Thing is, as I said, Chuck and I have a deal going.'

'You did tell me, yes.'

'Thing is, Chuck's got some machines he wants to get rid of, shopsoiled stuff, and I may have a buyer, do myself a bit of good.' One of Colin's laughs. 'Always a good thing to do yourself a bit of good.' I did not say that Colin's varied career had never, so far as I knew, been connected with buying or selling machines. A pause. 'Thing is, this is on the side if you know what I mean. I'd just as soon nobody at PC Travel heard about it, people can get a bit stuffy. No names, no pack drill.' Colin has a cliché for any occasion. I said that I should not think of mentioning it, and also I hoped Stephanie had no connection with the deal. He sounded outraged.

'Steph? Nothing at all, what makes you think so? Oh, Chuck saying she's a nice girl, yeah, I get it, he just met her at a gig one night is all.'

Perhaps so, perhaps not. And since Colin's speech had also

suddenly turned mid-Atlantic, perhaps I was mistaken in thinking of Chuck as an American. It might be that he was impeccably ex-urban like Colin, and had spent his childhood in Watford or St Albans. Upon the whole, however, I thought not. He had more the appearance of a small-time American crook in a minor British film.

The afternoon was enlivened by a visit from Robin Bruce-Comfort. When I saw Robin's long form sidle round the door I wondered which of his hats he would be wearing. Would it be that of Department Secretary (a notch or two above Section Principal) complaining about my failure to return this or that set of figures which were urgently required, or that of my Headfield neighbour who was the Other Cultured Man in the Department? I was not kept long in doubt. When wearing his Department Secretary hat Robin's body writhes like that of a snake under the charmer's pipe. In discussion of artistic or literary matters his natural languor prevails. Phrases drift slowly across the air and, sometimes incomplete, hang like tobacco smoke in an airless room.

'D'you have a moment to spare? That's good, good. I wanted to . . . ' His voice faded as if the smoke were barely penetrable, a few phrases coming through. I slowly became aware that he was talking about the next production of the Headfield Players, our local amateur dramatic company. Derek and Sandy supported it, and were both to be seen on the boards. Porson, surprisingly enough, was also an occasional amateur actor. It was at Derek's persuasion that I had been drawn on to the committee, although I will admit that the envy and jealousy aroused by the choice of plays and allocation of parts held some fascination for me. Bruce-Comfort, the vice chairman, was also eager to appear before the footlights, a passion I really do not understand.

'Really most inappropriate,' he said now. 'We are *not* in competition with Margaret Thatcher.'

'What was that?'

'We are not in competition with the Thatcher theatre. Hence to put on an Agatha Christie play is . . . ' His voice faded again.

'I didn't know that had been proposed.'

'It is what Brenda Wilson wants. She sees herself as Miss Marple.'

Brenda Wilson, wife of the headmaster of Headfield Grammar, was passionately devoted to the stage, or at least to her own appearance on it.

'Brakl,' Bruce-Comfort said. 'Gene Brakl. From California. Latvian originally, of course. The theatre of the informal.' He elaborated for what seemed a long time on the merits of Brakl, whose work had never been produced in England, and was ideal for an amateur company. I temporised, suggested that we should see what the committee felt, and declined the offer to read the text of a Brakl play, sent to Bruce-Comfort by a Californian friend.

When Derek arrived at nine-thirty he laughed at my story of Robin and Brakl. Robin's enthusiasm for unknown and difficult dramatists was known to everybody connected with the group. Then Derek put on his serious look. The phrase is deliberately chosen. Derek cannot help acting, so that it would not be quite right to say he *looked serious*. He assumes the attitude that seems proper for the occasion.

Wearing this look he said, 'Robin's an old fusspot, but he's right, we shouldn't put on the same sort of popular stuff as the rep. When we tried Beckett, though, it was a disaster. Compromise on Priestley perhaps? Shan't be there myself, but I rely on the well-known Durling tact to steer us to a compromise. That can't have been what you rang about.'

I showed him the anonymous letter. He glanced at it, then said impatiently, 'Much the same as the ones I've seen, and you told me about it on the phone. Is that it, then?'

'Not quite.' I told him the words Sandy had murmured under her breath at lunch, and then denied having spoken. Should I have done so? I can only say that I felt it was right he should know about something that was mysterious and might affect him. Derek retained the serious look, then said something that surprised me.

'You don't think much of Sandy, do you?' I assured him that I did, and in any case she was his wife. 'I doubt if you're predisposed to like any wife of mine. And you think she's just an ordinary Headfield housewife, but you're wrong. She gave up a good career in advertising when we married, and she looks over all our brochure copy now, often improving it. I rely on her more than you may think, tell her everything.' He got up, moved round the room, looking at the Beerbohm caricatures on the walls. 'That drawing of Queen Victoria meeting Rossetti, I was with you when you bought it. And the Sickert sketch too. I remember those days, I remember Whitestones. But it's the past, and the past is over, remember that, Jason.' He was drinking whisky, and went across to pour another tot. 'This decanter was your mother's?'

'That's right.'

'Do you suppose Uncle X took her to bed?'

No doubt my face showed my offence. I replied in the same vein.

'You are sure you're not taking Gerda to bed, as you put it.'

Derek serious was replaced by Derek comic but irritable, perhaps in the part of Simon Gray's Butley, which we had put on with success.

'They're all nonsense, those letters. If they'd been written about Charles now, there might have been some point. You remember Jack Sanderson?' I nodded, but he continued. 'Charles not only had an affair with Stella Sanderson but deliberately let everybody know about it, and you know why? Because Sanderson had beaten him in the final of some shooting competition or other. Perfectly true, it was done just to get back at him. He's a vengeful sod is our Charles.'

'You should be careful of him.'

'Oh, I am.' He gave me his brilliant smile. 'Advised by Sandy.'

'I take it he's opposed to your plans for Japanese and Chinese tours.'

'That and other things.'

'And he's the senior partner.'

'Correct. I exercise my powers of persuasion, not very successfully. But say not the struggle nought availeth. We shall survive, we shall triumph.' Another smile. 'About what Sandy said, if she said it. I've no idea what it meant, but I trust her. I

48

shall ignore those letters, and so will she.'

Five minutes later he had gone. Now it is after midnight.

And so to bed.

6

Tuesday morning. Owen ate the last mouthful of his cereal, said 'Got to go,' kissed Sandy, waved to Derek, was gone. Derek said reflectively, 'He loves you.'

'As is right and proper.'

'But only tolerates me. He never calls me anything but Derek, not that if he can avoid it.'

She placed a hand on her heart, said mockingly, 'Died and never called me father. Come on, Derek, he's just shy, that's all.'

'He's had six years to get used to me. Perhaps he misses the rackety life with his real father. When he wasn't in jail.'

Sandy buttered a piece of toast, then said carefully, 'I'm sorry you should say that. I know Dicky lived from hand to mouth, his hand to other people's mouths. When I finally decided he was no good I left him, and I should have left him sooner. And yes again, perhaps Owen remembers the good times and forgets the bad ones. But I thought we'd agreed not to talk about it.'

'So we did, darling. Sorry.'

'Now let me ask something. Who's somebody called Cruddle? Jason was talking about him at length at lunch on Sunday, and I've never heard of him. Apparently he said something to Owen too, Owen asked me who he was, said Jason had told him Cruddle was the greatest living writer or something. Does he exist?'

'Indeed he does. Jason's been working on a book about him for years. Cruddle lives in Venice, and that's why Jason is going out at the weekend with the PC party, to meet him for the first time.'

'But who *is* he? And why have neither Owen nor I ever heard of him?'

Derek took the *Encyclopaedia of Modern Novelists and Poets* from a shelf, found the brief extract, and read it to her.

49

CRUDDLE, D.M. (Dante Milton) (1895-) Blessed by his father, a Yorkshire miner of literary bent, with the names of Dante and Milton, D.M. Cruddle naturally enough began as a poet, although *Songs of War and Peace* (1916) and *Riding Down the Sky* (1919) fully justified his modesty in using only D.M. instead of his full Christian names. Shortly after World War I Cruddle went to live in Greece with his wife Angela, daughter of millionaire shipping magnate Sir James Radley. There between 1921 and 1926 Cruddle wrote three novels about an imaginary country called Borgogrundia which caused some stir at the time, not only because of their fantastic settings, but also through the exaggerated whimsicality and extravagance of their language. One critic said: 'It is as though the Arabian Nights had been rewritten by Mrs Amanda Ros in collaboration with Baron Corvo.' For a short time Cruddle had a small cult following, but this quickly faded as the absurdity of his work was recognised. He has published nothing in recent years.

'They sound ghastly,' Sandy said. 'Have you read any of these whatever they're called novels?'

'I have indeed. If you'd been a friend of Jason's as long as I have, you couldn't avoid it. Jason discovered him when we were at King's, wrote to him. They carried on a correspondence, but Cruddle's a recluse, doesn't see anybody. There was some scandal in Greece, I think he left his wife for a young man. Jason must be the only Cruddle scholar in the world, and now at last he's being admitted to the presence. It's the most exciting thing that's happened to him for years.'

'What are the novels like?'

'Unreadable. But as I said, I've read them. Shows the persistence of youth. Listen to me, something else. Those letters.'

Sandy put down her napkin. 'I'll have to go in five minutes, it's Extractor day.' She worked three days a week as receptionist for a local dentist named Ricecroft, who was unfashionably eager to extract teeth rather than fill them.

'This won't take more than two. I said to Jason last night that we'd do nothing about them, but since then something's occurred to me. They all stress the same thing, the fact that it's my partner's wife. Perhaps the object of the exercise is to damage the firm.'

'Rather a roundabout way of doing it.'

'I don't know. Suppose letters have been sent to people we deal with, ticket agents and so on. They might think, hello, what's up, better be careful about credit. One way the letters make sense is if they're trying to drive a wedge between Charles and me. And that isn't too hard a job as you know. Perhaps we should go to the police, after all.'

'Don't worry.' She went round to him, kissed his cheek. 'And don't go to the police. That will make it public, you'll have them round asking questions of everybody, just as you said when you made that little speech. Leave it, for a few days at least.'

'I expect you know best.' He laughed. 'I'd have liked to be a fly on the wall when Charles talked to Gerda about them.'

A few minutes later they parted. The Extractor's surgery was within walking distance. Derek took the car to the agency's office just off the High Street. He had not mentioned the phrase Jason said he had heard her use, in part because he did trust her, and in part because he knew she would resent the fact that it had been repeated to him.

7

Charles Porson, tightly buttoned into a dark blue suit, black shoes well shined, pushed papers across the desk at his partner. Head slightly lowered, short hair bristling, small eyes glaring over gold half-rims, he looked like a bull ready to charge.

Derek, a faintly disdainful golden-haired matador, sat at ease on the other side of the desk. He glanced at the papers. 'They're outlines of three main tours in Japan and one in China, with possible variations to include specialised trips, an art tour, a historical tour, and so on. All costed.'

'You think anybody will want to go on a Japanese *art* tour, people here in Headfield?'

'I'm not sure, I'd like to find out. And they wouldn't be confined to Headfield. There are such things as advertisements.'

'I'll tell you what I think, what I *know*.' Porson's face reddened as his voice was raised. 'This is the surest way of losing money I've ever seen.' He pointed to the small posters on the wall which said, 'Rimini, the Playground of Italy,' 'Florence the Flower of Cities,' 'Sun and Sea in Sardinia.' '*That's* what the firm's been built on.'

'I know we're specialists in Italy, I'm not suggesting we should give up the Italian end or even reduce it . . .'

'I should hope not.'

'Simply that you can't stand still. Standing still merely means running backwards. You turned down the idea of opening a London office.' Porson snorted. 'But we should extend our operations. Japan and China are two possibilities. There are others.'

'You sent your cousin off to the Far East without telling me. Perhaps you intend to foot the bill personally.'

'If you insist, I'm prepared to do that. I didn't tell you in advance because it would have involved endless argument.'

'And now you produce these figures behind my back.'

Derek's faint sigh was hardly placatory. 'So far from being behind your back they are on your desk.'

'Very clever, very comical. Let me make myself clear. I do not agree to this lunatic project, there is no point in pursuing it. It's finished, do you understand?'

In the outer office Porson's secretary Miss Nettleberry stopped filing her nails, and said to her assistant, 'He's on the rampage.'

'I think you're unreasonable, but yes, you make yourself clear.' Derek seemed not only mentally but physically cool, whereas his partner was sweating. 'Is that all you wanted to talk about?'

'It is not.' Derek expected mention of the letters, but instead Porson asked on the intercom whether Mr Carter had arrived. He had, and was shown in.

Carter was short and dapper. He was a partner in Headfield's largest firm of solicitors, and had acted for PC Travel in the rare but not unknown cases where dissatisfied holiday-makers had threatened to sue the agency. Derek greeted him, then got up and went across to the window. Porson spoke to Carter as a colonel might to an NCO.

'Told you what I wanted on the phone about Morvelli and the shares. Just read the Riot Act to Mr Crowley, tell him what's what.'

Carter raised his eyebrows fractionally, opened a file, took out some papers. 'Perhaps it would help if I outlined the position briefly. When Porson Travel became PC Travel it was as a company with a thousand shares, four hundred owned by Mr Porson, three hundred by Mr Crowley, the remainder unissued. Five years ago an Italian branch was set up, when the firm absorbed the Italian firm of Morvelli Travel. One condition was that Signor Morvelli should have an option to buy two hundred shares in the company, at a price to be agreed. He did not take up the option then . . . '

'Didn't have two thousand lira to rub together,' Porson said with satisfaction.

'And the matter rested until Mr Morvelli, Signor Morvelli, indicated recently that he wished to activate the option clause. The agreement of the other shareholders is necessary, but may not be unreasonably withheld.'

'And it is being withheld. By Crowley here.'

'Not so,' Derek said. 'We aren't arguing about the principle, we're arguing about the price.' Derek had the look of somebody enjoying himself that was familiar to Jason Durling. 'I don't say anything about the fact that Guido Morvelli was brought in by Charles, so that he's in effect Charles's nominee. The point is that when he had the option the shares were worth very little. Now the firm's on the up and up, he should pay the going rate. Is that unreasonable?'

Porson's voice became a shout. 'Yes. Morvelli has worked hard. You're trying to price the shares high deliberately, to keep him out.'

Carter coughed. 'Mr Crowley, your valuation of the shares is more than double that of Mr Porson's. I understand that the higher price has been put to Mr Morvelli, and he thinks it is too much.'

'I would remind you that this firm was founded with my money,' Porson said heavily to Derek.

'Your father's, surely, but never mind. The thing about Guido is he's a great kidder. He's kidding about the shares, he enjoys it.'

'You think so? Then come and tell him that.'

'Go to Italy instead of you, d'you mean? Not possible, I'm afraid. There's a travel agents' conference in London this weekend, and I'm booked for it.'

'Travel agents' conference, just a waste of time and money.' To Derek's objections he said that it was easy enough to make a cancellation, and that the expense would be nothing to the money wasted on Colin's Far East trip. 'And I do *not* mean go out instead of me, I'm not a fool. You'd come back saying he didn't want to take up the option. You come over *with* me and talk to Guido, man to man, tell him what you've been saying. The three of us can work it out together round a table.'

'An excellent idea, if I may say so.' Carter rubbed his little hands together as though washing them. 'This is the kind of problem a solicitor can't solve. There is no such thing as a market price for these shares, because there is no market. They're worth whatever the buyer and seller agree. It's a matter of goodwill.'

'The Lord forbid that should be lacking.' Derek came away from the window, laughing. 'All right, Charles, I'll come out with you on our train. Then we fly back, agreed?'

Porson agreed and said virtuously, 'It was high time one of us went along to make sure the special PC train operation is running smoothly. I shall be interested to see how your cousin copes with clients. My opinion of his abilities is less high than yours.'

'You might be surprised. If Colin can cope with two of us breathing down his neck he's a wonder. Have you ever met our Guido Morvelli, Carter?' The solicitor shook his head. 'Great talker, marvellous salesman, not to be trusted further than you can throw him in the old phrase. But thank you for healing the rift in the lute, showing us the path of righteousness. Or, since no doubt Charles thinks he's never strayed from it, putting *me* back on to the straight and narrow.'

When Carter returned to his office he told one of his colleagues that Derek Crowley was charming but obstinate. Porson was equally obstinate, less charming. It was sad to see two intelligent men squabbling like children.

Derek returned to his office whistling.

8

'Another one.' Caroline turned over the envelope in her hand, her manner that of a cat given an unexpected saucer of cream.

Norman knotted the thin leather tie that was his compromise between bohemianism and orthodoxy, and told her to open it. He watched her as she did so, face alight with anticipation.

'My my. Do you know what this says?'

'Not until you tell me.'

'Writing looks like the other. It says: "Where's the love nest? Try Wallington Apartments, Sallytom Road." So that's where they shack up.'

'I've never heard of Wallington Apartments.'

'Neither have I, but they must be somewhere in town.'

'You sound envious.' She wore a green and white striped dress, the green the same colour as her eyes. Her arms were bare. He gripped them now. 'Caroline, you're not to make mischief.'

'Of course not.'

'You've not got enough to occupy you now the kids are out of the hutch.' Their daughter Nella had recently married a wallpaper designer, their son William had dropped out of university, and was living in a ban-the-bomb commune. 'You should get a job.'

'Don't be ridiculous, I haven't had a job for years.'

'Take pottery classes then.'

'That's insulting. I play bridge.'

'I know you do. That bridge club's a hive of malice.'

'And I have the house to look after. And your dinner parties to arrange. And then I do still have what you might call a regular job, an onerous duty.'

'I've got a train to catch.'

'There's another train. Let TV Centre wait. You know the old proverb, it's never too late to blend.'

Norman caught the later train, but left adjuring her again not to make mischief.

Caroline spent the afternoon at the bridge club. She had a good memory, a clear and logical mind, and a flair for knowing when a finesse should be attempted. Success at bridge gave her particular pleasure, because it proved her intellectual superiority over her opponents. When the rubbers were finished, and she had sympathised over tea and toast with Olivia Drysdale and Amy Melling for holding poor cards, and had mentioned the anonymous letters to see if either of them had received one (they had not, but it aroused their curiosity), she made her way in the direction of Wallington Apartments. She believed that knowledge is power, and it was in pursuit of knowledge that she wanted to find out whether the latest letter told the truth.

There are no slums in Headfield of the kind to be seen in London and other big cities, but certainly West Headfield is the poorest part of town. There is little new building here. Most of the streets are terrace houses, respectable but shabby, and they are all very similar so that the effect in certain parts slightly resembles a miniature maze. One series of streets was put up by a speculative builder who was allowed to name them after his ten children, so that Maryjo Street is opposite Laurabill, with Lennora and Willbert nearby, all of them running off the stem of Sallytom Road. The town's small coloured and Irish population live around here. There are corner shops run by Pakistanis, and West Indian youths can be seen tinkering with beaten-up cars that show no road fund licence stickers. At night these old cars, Mercedes, Porsches, Lotuses, come to life and go roaring down the narrow streets at speeds far over the limit.

Caroline had looked up Sallytom Road on the map, and now took the bus to one end of it. To walk down the road was for her a journey of exploration. She had driven through West Headfield on the way out of town, but had never before been there on foot. Now she took it all in, the sparsely filled shop windows, the black boys who whistled at her, the secondhand store with its sign, 'We Sell JUNK – And It's CHEAP.' Past Laurabill and Lennora the road's character changed. The houses were bigger although not better kept, with flights of stone steps leading up to front doors lined by half-a-dozen bell pushes. These houses were interspersed with dingy little apartment blocks. Wallington Apartments was one of these, a square four storey building in pitted mud-coloured brick on which boys and girls had scrawled graffiti.

She walked into a square hall painted bilious yellow. There was no lift, but a flight of uncarpeted stairs led upwards. A small board held the names of tenants on cards, O'Gorman, Doyle, Krutch, Pete W. Patel, Singer, Fletcher, Miss J. Mead, a dozen others. Some of the cards were old and dirty, others almost new. There was no card bearing the name of Crowley or Porson. Below the cards a notice said: 'All rubbish in bins at back. No dumping. No bicycles in hall. No games on stairs. Trespassers prosecuted. By order. Caretaker in basement.'

She rang a bell in the basement, and was confronted by a wizened pixie-like figure wearing a red and green striped jersey above a flowered apron. A tam o' shanter rested on his head. She asked if he was the caretaker.

'The one and only. Pat O'Brien at your service. You recognise the name.'

'I don't think so.'

'He was a famous man on the fillums in his day, but ah, what's the difference? Flesh is grass and fame is fleeting, isn't it true? Will you come in then?'

She followed Pat O'Brien into a small dark sitting room which held a strong odour of stewed tea. He removed the apron and took off the tam o' shanter. 'I wear it when I'm washing the dishes, it seems more cheerful. I hate washing the dishes, if I could get one of those machines that do it for you I would. Wonderful the machines they have nowadays. You'll be the happy owner of one, I don't doubt, Mrs . . . '

'Smith. Yes, I do have a dishwasher.'

'Just so, Mrs Smith, just so.' A smile revealed teeth too white to be real, the wizened face was clever as a monkey's. 'You'll take a dish of tay now.'

She said that she would, but regretted it as soon as she saw the big brown teapot, and the two cracked cups with a rim of dirt round the edges were placed on the table covered with American cloth. The tea was poured, a tin of biscuits produced, Pat O'Brien sipped with approval. He sat in an old rocking chair, she in an armchair that sagged in the middle. She avoided the dip only by sitting forward in an expectant manner.

'There now, that hits the spot. And what can I be doing for you, Mrs Smith?'

The story she had prepared was thin, but she hoped this would not matter. 'A friend of mine has recently come to live in this district, and I've foolishly lost the address. I know it was Sallytom Road, and almost sure it was these Apartments. I wondered if you could help me.'

'So you lost the address, isn't that a shame now? And your friend's name, what would that be?'

'That's just what I'm not sure of.' She lowered her voice in the manner of one letting him into a secret. 'My friend, you see, is having a little trouble, and wouldn't be using her own name here. I'm sure you understand me, Mr O'Brien.' In a spontaneous-seeming burst she added, 'I think the room or apartment may have been taken by a gentleman.'

'Is that the way of it? And this would be – when did you say?'

'Within the last few weeks.' That was guesswork, of course, but it seemed likely.

'You've hardly touched your tay.' She drank a little, reluctantly. 'Now I tell you what would help me, what I truly need to know, and that is whether your friend is dark or fair, black or white, in the bloom of youth like yourself, or just a little antique and rusty the way I am.' She described Gerda and Derek, and he sighed. 'A lovely young couple they sound.'

'But do you know them? Have they rented an apartment here?'

'Ah, it's possible. I have to get my memory to work, and it's like an old clock, rusty.'

'But you said . . . '

'I'll tell you something, Mrs Smith. I've been on my own down here for five years. I don't complain, mind, I'm what you may call a philosopher, and I take it to be my destiny. What is to be will be, and if Pat O'Brien is meant to end his days in this basement room, so be it. But what if that shouldn't be so? Do you follow me?'

'Not very well.'

His faded blue eyes were sunk so deep she could hardly see them. 'Supposing, you see, I should be able to remember somebody of the kind, who just might be your friend, I should wish to do it. But then again, supposing I was wrong, it was not your friend and I was misremembering. And then Mr or Mrs Whoever it might be complained to the stingy devils that own this place, what would happen to poor Pat? Would it be his destiny to be thrown out in the street, or just the foolishness of his misremembering, do you catch my drift?' Tapping his forehead the little man said, 'What does a rusty clock need? Oil.'

'Oil? Oh, I see.'

'Ah, that's good. Now at the moment I can't bring the name to mind, but I've a book may tell me.' He turned his back on her and picked up a grubby exercise book from a shelf. Caroline took a five pound note from her bag and put it beside her mug of tea. The little man turned, clapped a hand to his forehead. 'It's not in here, but begod it was on the tip of the tongue and now it's gone. I have another book in the cupboard back here, I'll look in that.' While his back was turned again, she reluctantly added a ten pound note to the five. She could have sworn that he did not even glance at what lay beside the mug when he said, 'I have it now. Mead is the name, Miss J. Mead.'

'You're sure? They'd only be here occasionally, perhaps twice a week.'

'I never pry. But that'll be your friend, it's her all right, and no doubt it's the gentleman too but I wouldn't be knowing his name. When you find them now, don't you forget it was Pat O'Brien helped you.'

She said acidly, 'I'm not likely to forget.'

'He was famous, I tell you, a famous actor on the fillums when I was a boy.'

Miss J. Mead was on the third floor. She walked up the stairs, looked at the dark brown door, went down again. She had found the place where the lovers met. No doubt the knowledge was important, and she was pleased to have it. If she could not use it, however, she had paid fifteen pounds for nothing.

9

On these fine summer afternoons Mary wheeled her husband out on to the terrace. The lawn sloped down to a ripple of water at the bottom. There was farming land on either side, not a house to be seen. Stone steps led from terrace to lawn, and at the side a gentle concrete slope had been made, down which Uncle X could wheel himself to the grass. Often he did so, and sat under the shade of a tree or went down right beside the trickling water, but today he remained on the terrace. Newspapers and *Billy Bunter's Greyfriars Annual* lay unread beside him.

'You should be on the lawn on a lovely day like this. We shan't have many more of them, they're predicting rain. Shall I wheel you down to the water?'

'No thankee, could wheel myself over if I wanted to. Too cold.'

He was, she saw, in one of his moods. 'Xavier, you're being naughty, it's a *beautiful* day.' She was the only person who called him by his first name. She had been frightened of him once, but now he was a piece of property to be wheeled about, helped in and out of bed, tucked up at night. She asked who had been on the telephone.

'Jason. Told me he'd had one of those letters, same sort of thing. Something wrong, I can smell it.' He lifted his great prow of a nose as if detecting rottenness in the scent of grass and flowers. 'He's doing something, that boy.'

'Jason? Oh, I don't think so.'

'Jason, who said anything about him? Jason was born an old woman, never has been anything else, never will. Always sticking his nose into other people's business, useful for running messages, nothing else to say about *Jason*. Our boy, I mean, Derek. What's he up to?'

'Who can be writing such awful things? Everything nowadays is so unwholesome. When there are so many lovely things in the world why do people have to write about unwholesome matters, and show them on the television? I wish you'd explain that to me, Xavier.'

His hand, brown and strong as in youth, was held out to her. 'Know why I love ye, Mary? Because ye're so silly.'

'Oh, Xavier.' She blushed. 'But who *can* have written such things?'

'Haven't a notion. Perhaps you did.'

'Xavier!'

'Frustrated wife, husband in wheelchair. Teasing you, m'dear, shouldn't do it. Who wrote 'em, I'd like to know meself. That's why I've called him up, asked him to come and see the old man.'

She patted her hair. 'Is he coming?'

'When he can spare the time,' he said bitterly. 'I'll tell ye something, me girl. Life ain't like these Greyfriars stories, more's the pity. I don't want that boy to go to prison for putting out forgeries.'

'Xavier, that's over long ago. Derek is doing very well now.'

'Is he? How d'ye know? He's coming to tea.'

She thought he might have imagined this, and was half surprised when Derek arrived just after four-thirty. She said in a flustered way that she was making some of the scotch pancakes he had always liked. He sat on the kitchen table swinging his legs, and asked why Uncle X wanted to see him.

'Those letters have upset him. Derek, is everything all right?'

'Couldn't be better.'

'Is Sandy well?' She could not bring herself to ask whether what the letters said was true.

'On top of her form. I say, is anything up? He's usually listening for visitors, wheels himself out here.'

'He often goes to sleep after lunch. Why don't you go and see?'

He smiled, put an arm round her. 'You come too.'

They waited until tea was ready, then took it in together. They found Uncle X asleep, still on the terrace. He opened his eyes, looked at Derek and said, 'Ha, here ye are. Tea interval, is it? Make any runs?'

Derek paled. Mary remembered his hatred of illness, both mental and physical. 'You've been dreaming. Derek doesn't play cricket nowadays.'

'Who said he did? Harry Wharton's been doing well for Greyfriars.' He gestured at the Billy Bunter annual. 'Sit ye down, me lad, we've got things to talk about.' His eye roved over the tea tray. 'No biscuits.' Mary indicated the scotch pancakes and a plate of cream crackers. 'They're not proper biscuits.'

'You're not meant to have sweet cream biscuits. They're bad for you. Dr Grayson said so.'

'What in hell does he know? Will eating biscuits take away the use of me legs?'

She said equably that he ought not to talk like that, poured the tea and left them. Uncle X regarded Derek watchfully, refused a scotch pancake, took a cream cracker. 'What's the truth of it, ye may as well tell me. Will they prosecute?'

Derek said earnestly, 'Believe me, Uncle X, I don't know what you mean.'

'Those damn pamphlets, boy.' He dropped his voice. 'I've got three of 'em in there. In the desk. Locked up.'

'That was years ago. It's all over now. You were very helpful. I could have been in real trouble but for you. I haven't forgotten.'

'Years ago. Sure of that?'

'Soon after I left college. You helped to settle it, you must remember.' The warmth had gone out of the sun, but sweat shone on Derek's forehead, gleamed in his golden curls.

'Ha, was that the way of it?' He looked with distaste at the cream cracker, threw part of it out on to the lawn below. 'Not real biscuits, dry stuff. What about this woman, are ye bedding her?' Derek, his mouth full of scotch pancake, shook his head. 'Ye're not? What about Sandy, how's she take it?'

'Sandy knows it's all rubbish. She agrees with me, the only thing to do is ignore the letters.'

'What about your partner and the German piece, how do they feel about it?'

'You're as shrewd as ever. I doubt if Charles Porson likes it much.'

'Shrewd, am I, the old man's shrewd? I'll tell ye another thing. Ye're up to something, and it means trouble. Eh?'

'You're imagining things.'

'You've given that no good son of mine a job, is it to do with him?'

'With Colin? Most certainly not. I'd never involve Colin in anything . . . '

'Then there is something, eh? Ye'll tell me what it is, me lad, or I'll know the reason why. It was only the other day I paid out money over those pamphlets . . . '

'I've told you, it was years ago, fifteen years.'

Uncle X wheeled his chair very close to Derek, began to shout. 'Fifteen years, ye're a liar, it was just the other day. I brought ye up, looked after ye, and ye just lie to me about everything, always have. Ye're no better than that dirty little toerag Colin. Sitting in corners with your nancy boy friend, laughing and making dirty little plans. Ye're nothing but a cheapskate.'

'I'm sorry you think of me like that. And you're wrong about Jason, you don't understand him.'

'I understand all right. And I'm sick of it, I tell ye, sick of it.'

The big brown hands that had been lying on the rug covering the useless legs suddenly sprang to life, seizing Derek and shaking him. He made no resistance but allowed himself to be shaken back and forwards, his face drained of colour.

'I'm cutting ye out of me will, understand that, like cutting out a canker,' Uncle X cried. Tears ran down his face. 'Ye're no sportsman, Derek Crowley, I'll tell ye that, a thief and a liar.' The hands moved from Derek's shoulders to his throat. Derek tugged at them, forced them away. Uncle X, leaning forwards, over-balanced, and fell heavily from wheelchair to terrace, knocking over the tea things. Mary came running, knelt beside her husband. His eyes were closed, his breathing stertorous. Saliva dribbled from his mouth.

Derek said apologetically, 'He suddenly got very angry. All about nothing, he doesn't know what he's saying. I'll ring Grayson.'

Dr Grayson had a soothing manner under all circumstances, something much appreciated by his patients. He said that he thought no harm had been done, although it was too soon to know, it was possible that Xavier had suffered another slight stroke. In the meantime he must stay in bed.

'I'm dreadfully sorry, but truly I did nothing to provoke him,' Derek said to his aunt. 'Shall I arrange for a nurse to come in, or can you cope?'

'I've been coping for a long time. He's not himself, you know. He said this afternoon that he wished life were like one of those schoolboy books. They're the only things he reads now, hardly glances at the papers.'

'That's what he had in mind when he told me I was no sportsman.'

'He loves you. He was good to you when you were young.'

'Don't think I've forgotten. So were you.' He kissed her. 'The scotch pancakes were terrific.'

10

Wednesday morning. Porson sat in Carter's little office.

'I thought we should have a private word about the implications of what is proposed in relation to Mr Morvelli's purchase of shares,' the solicitor said. 'At present you hold the majority shareholding. With the issue of a further two hundred shares, however, the voting balance would be held by Mr Morvelli.'

Porson lighted a cigar before he replied. Carter, a non-smoker, thought what a pity it was that one could not choose one's clients. If that had been possible, a man who set fire to one of those weeds without so much as a by-your-leave would have come very low down on a list of those he cared to work with. As it was he smelt the noxious fumes, watched the look of self-satisfaction on his client's face, and smiled. Porson was a man of importance in Headfield.

'Eleven ack emma, first of the day. Grayson says don't smoke until after lunch if then, but it's a pleasure, and what's life without pleasure?' Smoke curled about the office. 'I'm not a fool. Crowley may think I am, but I'm not. I knew perfectly well what he was trying to do when he suggested a few months back setting up an employees' Trust Fund with a hundred and fifty shares allocated to it.'

'Something of the kind is quite usual in a firm of your size.'

'I daresay. But when he suggested that just as a *matter of convenience* he should have voting powers on the employees' behalf, did he really think I'd agree to it? I soon put paid to that one. When I said he was very busy and it would be just as convenient for me to have the voting powers, we heard no more about it. Derek's a clever lad, that's why I took him into partnership, why do all the work when you can get a dog to do it for you? But he needs watching.'

'Perhaps so.' Carter's little cough might have been meant as an oblique reference to the cigar smoke. 'I repeat my point. Mr Morvelli, Signor Morvelli, will hold the balance when he takes up the shares.'

'And Guido's my man, or why d'you think I'd agree to it? I've known him a long time, he'll do what I tell him. When he said he'd like to take up the shares I called him straight away and said I was in favour, but Derek might drag his feet. Sure enough he's trying to put a ridiculous price on the shares, because he knows once Guido's taken 'em up there'll be no chance he'll get control. But he can't hold it up for ever, can he?'

'Not indefinitely. Provision is made in the articles for an independent adjudicator if necessary, but that's most unlikely. I'm glad Mr Crowley's going out with you to Venice, personal contact is so much better than communication through the telephone. I wanted to make sure you understood the position, and I'm happy that you do. My own situation is a little delicate, because I have acted for you personally, and also for the firm, but never for Mr Crowley.'

'He can look after himself. Or thinks he can. Very well then, let him do it.'

'No doubt he has his own solicitor.'

'He'll have his job cut out to stop this little deal going through. Mind you, Derek is the know-all type who doesn't think he needs advice from anybody.'

Carter felt a little sorry for Derek Crowley. He said with relief, 'Tea and biscuits.'

The girl who came in had large breasts and buttocks. Porson's gaze was on her as she bent to put down the tray on Carter's desk, lingered on swinging buttocks as she turned. When the door closed he gave a satisfied nod.

11

Norman was interested by Caroline's account of her investigation, even though he disapproved. What was she going to do now?

'I've already done it. I'm taking Gerda to lunch.'

'What's the excuse?'

'You know Gerda flatters herself she's got wonderful colour sense?' He shook his head. 'It's a fact. I told her we're redecorating the hall and lounge, can't decide on the paper, will she advise. Of course she will. So we'll spend an hour in Baxter's looking at papers, then to lunch.'

'And at lunch?'

'I shall drop various hints, ask if she's ever drunk mead, say I had a dream and woke up saying Wallington Apartments, that kind of thing. Very subtle. When she looks alarmed, blushes, runs from the restaurant in panic, I shall *know*.'

'Caroline, you really are too much.'

Did the phrase imply distaste? She felt sure that her too muchness attracted him.

Clarabelle's is a newish restaurant in the Market Square. Headfield no longer has a market, but the square is a traffic-free precinct, and is generally agreed to be one of the town's attractions. Gardens have been made, in the centre of them a small fountain plays, there is a bookshop, an art gallery selling bad original pictures and good prints, clothes shops with French names. The residents of Headfield, or the more prosperous ones, are pleased that supermarkets, building society offices, takeaway food shops, have been kept out of the Market Square.

'I have not been here before.' Gerda looked at the tables, the tops in some light wood, the legs dark green, at the small lamps with dark green shades on each table, the young waiters who wore dark green cutaway jackets, white frilly shirts and black trousers. 'I like it very much.'

'I thought the colours might appeal to your artistic sense.' Gerda had recommended a purple and black Regency striped wallpaper for the lounge, a grey and white stripe for the hall. 'I'm grateful for your help. Of course I may not be able to persuade Norman, he's so stuffy.'

'Husbands are stuffy.'

That seemed a promising opening. 'Norman's no worse than most, but do you know I'm really glad he's up in town all the week. I couldn't bear it if he had a job here, and came home for lunch every day.'

'Charlie sometimes comes home.' She said nothing more, but it was almost (Caroline said that evening to Norman) like being taken into the bedroom. The same look was given to the young waiter, who seemed to return it as he took in Gerda's breasts prominent in the scarlet blouse that matched her fingernails. It was also odd to hear Charles Porson called Charlie.

'I suppose I'm just selfish, and Norman is too in a different way. The other day he insisted, truly insisted, that I should go into the dingiest part of town on an errand for him. You'll laugh when I tell you why.'

Gerda took a forkful of her *oeufs florentine*, and looked questioningly at her companion.

'He collects cigarette cards.' Gerda showed no inclination to laugh. 'Has done for years, and there was an ad in our local rag put in by a man with a collection to sell. Norman was specially excited about some sets of cards of old motor cars the man advertised. He was going himself, but he'd had to work late on a programme, so he asked me. Do you know West Headfield?' Gerda shook her head. The story was a total invention, but provided a reasonable basis for what she had to say, and Caroline was rather pleased with it. She was a little disconcerted when asked what day she had paid her visit, and busied herself with her *salad niçoise* while considering any possible difficulty in naming a day. She could see none.

'Friday evening. It was a really run-down block called Wallington Apartments, no carpet on the stairs, awful paint, you know the kind of thing.' Gerda shook her head. 'No, of course you don't know, how should you? I looked at the names on the board in the hall, mostly foreign or Indian, only one or two that might have been English, like Mead . . . '

She paused. Gerda seemed unmoved. She finished her eggs, took one of the toothpicks that the Clarabelle provided, and began to probe in her mouth.

' . . . but the name of the advertiser, O'Brien, was not there.'

Gerda removed her toothpick. 'Irish.'

'What's that? Oh, Irish, yes. In the end I found him in the basement. He was the caretaker. But he had sold the cards that afternoon, could have sold them several times over he told me. And would you believe it, Norman had the audacity to say I could have bought them if I'd gone in the morning. As if I had nothing else to do with my time. Men!'

'Yes. The *Express* is published on Wednesday. You left it too late. No thank you, I will not have pudding, just coffee.'

What more could Caroline say? She felt herself quite infuriatingly frustrated. Gerda *knew*, she said to Norman that evening, knew exactly what she'd been talking about. It was almost as if Gerda had been laughing at her.

'I don't see what business it is of yours.'

'Don't you want to know the truth?'

'I thought you'd found out that Gerda's having an affair, why

68

do you want to know anything more? I'll tell you what *is* interesting. The effect of rumour in a small town, the way it spreads and affects the lives of a group. Might make a good docufict. A town's too big, you need a village really. Poison pen letters, people ignoring them, the poison spreading, some recluse suspected, the whole thing ending in an act of violence, the suspect's house burned down and him with it. Perhaps it wouldn't do, too fictional, not enough that's documentary about it.'

She gave up Norman as hopeless, but did not abandon the idea of somehow confirming the truth about the love nest. Later in the evening she rang Lucy Langley, a dim woman who did part-time social work in West Headfield, and asked if she could possibly call on Miss Mead when she was passing.

'I think she's somebody I used to know, but whenever I call she's out, and she isn't on the phone. If it would be no trouble to you . . . '

'No trouble, I'm often round in the area. I'll say you want to see her.'

'Don't do that, it might not be my Miss Mead. She was a girl when I knew her, the daughter of an old friend.' She described Gerda, and said that was her Miss Mead. 'Don't mention me, if it is her I'd like to call and surprise her.'

'What *shall* I say, then?'

Caroline said impatiently that she should say she had come to the wrong flat. Deception was so natural to her that she took it for granted it must come just as easily to others.

12

Discussion of the winter catalogue for holidays in the Italian Alps and the Austrian Tyrol, in the company of two English and two Italian representatives, occupied the whole of Derek's Wednesday afternoon. He was in the midst of it when Stephanie rang up and said that she must see him. She sounded more distracted than usual, a sign of impending trouble.

'Steph, what's up?'

'I've lost my job.' Stephanie was an expert audio typist and so never found difficulty in getting jobs. She stayed in none of them long, however, because of traumas in her emotional life that led her at times to take days off without notice, while at others her problems became mixed up with the audio typing, and she put down on paper what she was thinking instead of what she heard. 'Derek, darling, I'm so miserable. I must talk to you.'

He did not ask what she wanted to talk about. Since it was Stephanie it must be a man, and the current man was Colin.

'Are you in the office?' When under stress Stephanie carried on half-hour telephone conversations from her office, a practice that had ended two or three jobs.

'No, no, I'm at the flat. Can you come round now?'

'Not now.'

'I'm going crazy, Derek, I must talk to you.'

'At the moment I'm up to my eyes. I'll be round at six, or as near as I can manage. And Steph, don't start drinking.'

When he had put down the receiver he rang Morvelli in Venice.

'Derek, hallo. How did the meeting go about the new programme? Splendidly, I guess. We found some pretty hot things for you, eh? My boys did some real hard bargaining.'

'The meeting was fine, the winter catalogue looks good. Guido, you may know this already. I shall be there when you talk to Charles on Saturday about taking up the share option.'

'I understood you would not be coming.' Morvelli's voice had less than its usual enthusiasm.

'Charles wanted us to work it all out sitting round a table. He thinks it's the best way.'

'If you both think so.' His voice picked up enthusiasm again, as a car gathers speed. 'It will be good that you both come out. We settle our business, then we go out on the town, have a little party. How long can you stay?'

'Not long. You know we're coming by train? There's a PC cultural travel group coming that way on Friday, and Charles thought we should see how it all went, grace it with our presence. So we arrive on Saturday around dawn, have our meeting in the afternoon, fly back on Sunday.'

'Saturday night we celebrate our deal.' A pause, then Morvelli said, 'The beautiful Gerda is coming? And the beautiful Sandy?'

'I understand Gerda's coming. I haven't spoken to Sandy yet, but I think she'll flinch from the train trip. And Guido.'

'Yes?'

'I'll be a hard bargainer.'

'I should expect nothing else.'

'There's some fairly filthy white wine and these rather mouldy cheese biscuits, nothing else. I'm disorganised.'

'Fairly filthy white wine will do very well. I'll pass up the biscuits.'

Stephanie's flat was in an apartment block near the station. The flats were identical boxes, each providing a small bedroom, tiny bathroom and slit of kitchen. The living room was square, with a window that looked out over the railway line. It was filled with the impedimenta of Stephanie's life, which was always disorganised. Records were littered about the floor, two pairs of shoes lay where they had been cast off between sofa and bedroom, an ashtray was filled with a damp mess that had been cigarette ends, an old treadle sewing machine stood on a table with material beside it that might be transformed into a dress but would more probably be discarded as hopeless, crumbs were sprinkled liberally on floor and sofa. Derek had seen several similar rooms occupied by his sister.

'This place is a mess, don't say it. So am I.'

'Steph, you've been drinking.'

'There was some gin. Now there isn't.' He said nothing. 'I'm in love with Colin.'

'How does he feel about it?'

'The same way. He wants to get married.'

'Hurrah for you both.'

'But Derek, it would be like incest.'

'Nonsense. You're first cousins, but nobody worries about that

71

kind of thing any more.'

'Colin says he's done well with the firm, you're pleased with him, OK?'

'Perfectly true. People like him, he's one of the best couriers we've ever had. And he came back with a lot of good stuff from that Far East trip.'

'People like him,' she repeated. She sounded perfectly sober, and nobody who knew her less well than Derek would have realised that she was not. 'He says get married, settle down, be a contented couple like you and Sandy. It's what he needs, what I need. It'll never happen.' She began to weep. He put his arm round her, felt her body shaking against his. 'Sorry to bother you, got nobody else, no mother, no father.' Unlike him, she felt the loss of their parents deeply, and had always found Uncle X and Mary inadequate substitutes.

'Of course it will happen, why not? I don't see the problem.'

'I'm a mess.' He made a slightly impatient gesture. 'And then there's the incest. And Colin's a crook.'

'Colin!' He did not say that he felt Colin would lack the nerve to do anything criminal, although that was what he thought.

'And he's so nice,' Stephanie wailed. 'He's the nicest man I've ever known. Nobody else has ever been so good to me. But he knows his father hates him, only likes you.'

'Steph, pull yourself together.'

She said miserably, 'I'm as together as I ever shall be, and look at this place.'

'What did you mean when you said Colin's a crook?'

'Oh, I don't know. P'raps I'm wrong, I expect so. It's just that he said he might be making a lot of money soon, and he'd never make a lot of money honestly, would he?' Derek agreed with her, but did not say so. 'There's some deal he's got on, I don't know what. He admires you, you know. "Derek's got it made," he says sometimes. "Derek's going to be rich."'

An idea occurred to him. 'He hasn't said anything to you about the letters, has he?'

'What letters? Oh, *those*. No, why should he?'

'Do you think he might have sent them?'

'*Colin?*' The suggestion stopped her tears. She looked at him in astonishment. 'He'd never do anything like that. Oh, Derek, I can't make up my mind, shall I marry him?'

'Is he living with you here?'

'For the last few weeks, yes, of course. What do you expect?'

He said he thought she should give life with Colin another month or two, and if they still felt the same way he was sure everybody would give the marriage their blessing.

13

In spite of Robin Bruce-Comfort's desire to promote Brakl and other European dramatists, the next play to be produced by the Headfield Players was *Murder Most Informal*, a vintage piece which provided parts for a cast of more than a dozen, even though three of them met early deaths. Bruce-Comfort himself was excellently cast as an amateur investigator in the Peter Wimsey style, Porson almost equally well as a no-nonsense Detective Chief Inspector. The principal suspect, an autocratic lady who had good reasons for murdering almost everybody else on stage, was played by Brenda Wilson. The actual killer, however, turned out to be her secretary, played by Sandy. An insistent professionalism was provided by the direction of Norman Dixon, who began every rehearsal by saying that nobody should worry too much, they were just there to have fun, and ended by shouting at those who forgot their lines or moved into the right place at the wrong time.

The rehearsal on Wednesday evening had wound through its course, and by ten-thirty had reached the last scene. Bruce-Comfort and Porson had gathered the suspects together, and then taken turns in switching suspicion from one to another, in accordance with ritual. A case was built up against Brenda and speedily knocked down, and then attention turned to Sandy. The other characters moved slowly away, leaving her isolated in the centre of the stage. Porson ended his combined analysis and denunciation, and stood with forefinger pointed at Sandy. She opened her handbag, fumbling with the clasp, and drew out a blue-bodied revolver. A comb came out with it, and dropped to the stage, Sandy bent down and picked it up, Norman put his face momentarily in his hands, began to speak and checked himself.

'Stop,' Sandy cried. Porson, who had not been moving, advanced slowly. 'Don't come any nearer. Stop there, I shall shoot.'

Porson said, 'Don't let's have any trouble. Just you hand over that revolver nice and quiet now.'

Then it happened. Porson advanced another step or two. Sandy cried out 'Stop' again, raised the revolver, fired. The sound was loud. Porson fell, clapping a hand to his shoulder. A glass vase of flowers to the left of him also fell. Bruce-Comfort sidled rather than ran across the stage, grappled unconvincingly with Sandy, and took the revolver from her.

'Charles,' she cried. 'Charles, what happened? Are you hurt?'

Porson looked up to say that he was perfectly all right, why shouldn't he be, at the same moment that Norman came storming up on to the stage and asked Sandy what the hell she thought she was doing.

'First you drop a comb, then you start talking to Charles. You've got another couple of speeches before curtain, perhaps you'd get on with them.'

Sandy pointed to the vase. 'The shot broke it. That was a real bullet.'

Norman said nonsense. Porson stared at her.

'It was a real bullet,' she repeated. 'I might have shot Charles, I might have killed him.'

Gerda, who was sitting next to Jason among the dozen people in the stalls, giggled briefly.

'You're imagining things.' Norman went across to where the vase had stood, bent to look at the bits of glass, returned looking shaken. He had a small piece of metal, the bullet, in his hand. 'You're right. What a damned silly joke.'

Porson took the revolver, broke it. 'The rest of these are blanks.'

'It is not my idea of a joke,' Bruce-Comfort said. 'If Sandy had pointed the revolver directly at him as she should have done, Charles would have been shot. I don't think we should finish the rehearsal, I think we should find out who could have played this dangerous trick.'

'OK, OK.' Norman waved a hand. 'The gun's just a prop, been used often enough. Edna looks after the props, how about it, Edna?'

Edna was a teacher at Headfield Grammar. Like the rest of the audience she was now on stage. 'It was in the prop box until half an hour ago, when I gave it to Mrs Crowley. Anybody could have picked it up.'

'A Baby Browning,' Porson said. 'Must be five years ago that I gave it to the company. And there's just the one live bullet. Can't tell when it was put in.' He explained. 'This gun doesn't get used that often, only when it's needed as a prop. The live round may have been put in six months ago, longer still. Perhaps there were four blanks to be fired before it.'

Robin writhed so that his whole body seemed pliable. 'It's a matter for the police.'

There was a chorus of dissent. Porson said it was obviously a stupid practical joke, Brenda pointed out the undesirable publicity likely to follow any police enquiry, Norman said if they wanted to wreck the performance by having the police tramping round the whole time, this was the way to do it.

Sandy had been silent. Now she spoke. 'As Charles said, we've got no idea when the bullet was put in. Since he's prepared to take it as a practical joke I think we should too.'

The suggestion was greeted with relief. Afterwards Jason took Sandy aside. 'Do you really believe it was a coincidence?'

'Just somebody's stupid joke.'

'The anonymous letters involved Charles, now he might have been killed. Surely the two things must be connected?'

'I don't see why. The letters have been aimed at Derek. I don't know why you think I'd want to shoot at Charles.'

Jason fingered his bow tie. 'Sandy, of course I didn't mean you shot deliberately. I think the bullet must have been meant for

Charles. And whoever put it in knew you'd fire the gun in that scene.'

'It's an idea.' She stood considering it. 'You do have some ingenious ideas, Jason.'

14

Derek had been at a Rotary Club dinner, such business being one of the means by which PC Travel throve. When Sandy asked what it had been like, he said: 'It was Rotarian. I made Rotarian jokes, slapped Rotarian backs, laughed at Rotarian speeches. May the Lord forgive me, for I know Jason wouldn't. He'd have said it was unendurable, and he'd have been right. I need another whisky.'

'Pour me one too. You think a lot of Jason.'

'He's my oldest friend. I know you don't like him much.'

'I don't mind him, but he's malicious. Not about you, about everybody else. Me in particular, I shouldn't be surprised.'

'Sandy, my love, I swear with my hand on my heart that we never . . .'

She burst out laughing. 'No need to put on your serious look, I don't mind whether you did or didn't. I know what boys in public schools get up to. By the way, I nearly shot your partner tonight.'

He listened fascinated, but did not seem to take the story seriously.

'Of course it was an accident, any other idea's ridiculous. There are lots of people who don't love Charles, but nobody would try to kill him like that. Listen, love, I've got to go to Venice on Friday.'

'I thought you were away at some travel conference.'

'I've had to scrub that. Charles was insistent that we should settle the share deal at what he calls a round table conference. We're going on a PC train package, Charles wants to see our clients' reactions at first hand. Typical of him. Interested in the nuts and bolts, turns down any genuine ideas for expansion. We go out on Friday, fly back on Sunday. Like to come?'

'No thanks. Sitting in a train for twenty-four hours isn't my idea of bliss, and then there's Owen to look after. Sunbathing in the garden is more my line. So thanks, but no thanks.'

'Gerda will be on the trip.'

'Will she now? I see.'

'What does that mean?'

'Oh, nothing. I wouldn't be surprised if she's going just to see what sex is like on a train. But forget Gerda, let's talk about you.' Her wide clear forehead was wrinkled. 'Is it all going to work out?'

'It was your idea in the first place . . . '

'Refined and improved by you.'

'So it's bound to work out. We've been very clever. And really it's in everybody's interest.'

'Especially in yours. You're a tricky devil.'

'And you're the wife for a tricky devil. But darling Sandy, I'd never play any tricks on you.'

15

Headfield citizens are respectable middle-class people, decorous in their public behaviour. Yet even in Headfield odd things go on behind closed curtains.

'Just hand over that revolver nice and quiet now,' Gerda said.

'I won't.'

'You will.' She knocked the toy revolver from Porson's grasp with a smart tap of her plastic truncheon. 'Hold out your hands.'

'Oh please, no.' Hands were held out, handcuffs snapped over them. Gerda wore a policeman's uniform, and a helmet which said that she was PC 007. Porson was naked.

'You are a dangerous man.' She went to a cupboard, took out pieces of rope. 'I think you must be tied down. Lie on the bed.'

Porson's chest was hairy, his stomach large. He lay on the bed. 'And what will you do then?'

She made a loop round one ankle. 'Perhaps we shall shoot you – yes? – like this.' She put the toy revolver to his head. It snapped harmlessly. 'Perhaps other things. We shall see. Turn over.'

Porson wriggled with delight. He turned over. Gerda's face wore an expression of acute boredom.

16

Thursday morning. Robin Bruce-Comfort sidled into Jason's office, wavered in front of the desk, looked disapprovingly at Arthur Machen's *The Hill of Dreams*, which was open in front of his colleague, but forbore to comment.

'That was a bad show last night. I mean, Porson might have been shot.'

Jason put away the book. 'Yes, he might have been.'

'It's not something one can just leave and do nothing about, don't you agree?'

'What do you suggest? Nobody seems to care for the idea of calling in the police.'

Robin coiled his long body into a chair. 'There's something I didn't mention. It was said the live bullet might have been put in some time ago, but that isn't so. I borrowed the revolver last weekend, and filled it with blanks when I put it back.' He shifted about in the chair. 'It was Barry's birthday, and we had a cops and robbers party. He wanted it to be fairly realistic, not just cap pistols, he watches a lot of those American thrillers on TV. There was no harm in it, no reason to look like that.'

'I was just reflecting that both you and Eldred disapprove of violence on television.'

'Of course, but even so. I suppose you never watch anything except educational and artistic programmes.'

'I don't possess a television set.'

'Oh,' Robin said defiantly, 'As Eldred says, one can always use the off switch.'

'Yes, but does one?'

'Anyway, you see what I mean. I put it back on Monday filled with blanks. Somebody put in a live cartridge, and it must have been one of our members. They knew it would be fired at the rehearsal. It doesn't bear thinking about.'

Jason fiddled with the figure of a Chinese mandarin on his desk. 'Have you received any anonymous letters in the last few days?'

Robin looked alarmed. 'Good heavens, no. Do you mean they're being sent in *Headfield*?'

'Even in Headfield.' He told Robin about the letters. 'So you see, there might be a link, even though Sandy thinks otherwise. If you feel you should tell the police, then you must tell them. It's likely, though, that they'll regard it as a stupid joke.'

'You think I should go to them?'

Jason smiled in the way that many people found annoying. 'I didn't say that. I have no opinion.'

Robin was annoyed. He uncoiled himself from the chair, bent slightly forward, spoke with emphasis. 'I have been waiting two weeks for sets of comparison figures relating to training schemes in the South East, There is a planned development for the area which is held up until we know the viability of the scheme in terms of comparative accessibility and achievement. When will the comparison figures be ready?'

Still faintly smiling, Jason said: 'I am on leave next week. Shall we say Wednesday in the week following?'

'You can't let me have them tomorrow?' Jason shook his neat head. 'Wednesday week then, without fail.'

'Without fail.'

The air of disapproval remained until Robin Bruce-Comfort reached the door. Then he turned and said in a different tone, 'Eldred and I hope to see you this evening.'

'I much look forward to it.'

When the door closed Jason rang for Rhoda, and repeated what had been said about the figures. Rhoda said he could have them on the following morning. Jason said he would not feel equal to looking at them in detail just when he was going on leave, the Monday after his return would be time enough. When she left the room he returned to *The Hill of Dreams*.

17

The Dixons had guests coming at the weekend, and Caroline spent the morning preparing a dish called Jonathan's chicken with cullis, which she had found in a Jane Grigson cookbook. Whether because the dish was difficult to prepare – the removal of thigh and drumstick bones ('make as neat a job as you can,' the recipe said encouragingly) produced a dismally unattractive-looking result – or because she was preoccupied by the desire to discover the facts about Wallington Apartments, the final product didn't look promising. In the end she shoved the dish, cullis and all, into the freezer, and settled down with the *Guardian*.

Of course the odds were against the door being opened to Lucy – perhaps the lovers would not be there or would ignore the bell, in which case she would have to try another approach – yet she felt that the telephone would ring, and that it would be Lucy with exciting news. She snatched at the receiver when the bell rang at three o'clock, and heard Lucy's faintly aggrieved voice.

'I'm glad I got you. A lovely day like this, it's no good for making calls, everybody's out. I mean, you can't blame them, can you? Why should they wait in to see a social worker, you can't expect it.'

'I suppose not.'

'And yet, do you know, one of my clients was in bed with flu. In this weather! I said to her, you're the first case I've ever come across in flaming June.'

'Lucy, do you have something to tell me? About Miss Mead?'

'Of course, that's why I rang. You're wrong, you know, it's not your Miss Mead.'

'What do you mean?' She was about to say that it must be her Miss Mead, but checked herself. 'Can you tell me what happened. Please.'

'That's just what I am doing. I was paying a call on a family in Maryjo Street this morning, and what do I find? Taken the car, gone to Chessington Zoo for the day, at ten o'clock mind you, they certainly made an early start. So I thought, I've got a few minutes to spare and it's near Wallington Apartments . . . '

'And you called on Miss Mead.'

'I did. And she was out. No reply. So then I called on . . . '

Caroline realised the uselessness of interruption. Lucy's narrative unreeled slowly, like a tape. She absented her mind from the account of calls made and clients seen or not seen, switching on again at the words ' . . . your friend Miss Mead'.

' . . . one o'clock, and I thought I'll give your friend Miss Mead another call, then one more later on. So I rang. And the door opened. And I said "Can I speak to Miss Mead?" and she said, "That's me, I'm Miss Mead." She'd come home for lunch. But she wasn't your Miss Mead.'

'She wasn't blonde, you mean? Grotesque thoughts of Gerda wearing a wig crossed her mind.

What might have been a laugh came down the line. Lucy was not a great laugher. 'She certainly wasn't. She was black.'

The conversation continued for another half-minute, but when Caroline put down the telephone she had no idea of what had been said. Bewilderment, a feeling that Lucy must have made a mistake, was succeeded by fury. She had no doubt, after the lunch on Wednesday, that Gerda knew exactly what she was getting at. She had been deliberately conned by the caretaker. The thought was unbearable. An hour later she was back at Wallington Apartments, in the bilious yellow hall, then ringing the basement bell. Pat O'Brien opened the door wearing his tam o' shanter.

'Mr O'Brien, on Tuesday I came here and saw you. I asked some questions about a friend of mine. I thought she might be staying here.'

'Ah, me memory's not what it was.'

'This wasn't last year or even last week. It was the day before yesterday.'

'You misconstrue me, madam. I remember your coming, no problem about that, it's the name – ah, I have it. Smith, you're Mrs Smith. And your friend's name now, what was that?'

'I told you I wasn't sure. You said it was Miss Mead. That wasn't true. Miss Mead is black.'

'So she is.' A fleeting smile crossed the wizened face. 'Black as your hat, as the saying goes. Bless her heart.'

'Then why did you give me her name?'

'Why I must have misremembered, Mrs Smith, misremembered entirely.'

'So which flat is my friend in?' He shook his head. 'Mr O'Brien, you took money from me under false pretences. I shall not leave without getting an answer.'

'Isn't it a terrible thing when your memory's gone? Because I cannot remember a word of it. As for the money now, you'll have a receipt, a bit of paper to show.'

'You know perfectly well I haven't.'

'Ah well, then, Mrs Smith, I'm afraid . . . ' And he shut the door in her face. She rang the bell again but got no reply. Upstairs in the hall she looked at the names, and for a wild moment contemplated coming back one evening and ringing every bell, O'Gorman, Patel and all. Then commonsense returned, and she reluctantly walked out of Wallington Apartments. She did not doubt that Gerda and Derek were having an affair, but her curiosity with regard to the small print of the liaison remained unassuaged.

18

It is said that the class system in Britain has broken down in the past half century. Perhaps in big cities this is true, but in towns like Headfield distinctions still exist, although they may be somewhat blurred. The Bruce-Comforts were conscious of their position in the community. Robin was the Honourable Robin, the younger son of a hereditary although impoverished peer, with a family tree that he traced back as far as the Wars of the Roses. Eldred sat on the local magistrates' bench, and was a governor of schools. The invitation list for their occasional At Homes included the local bohemian painter Oliver Spaceley but not the town mayor, who by the law of seniority happened that year to be a Labour man and a train driver.

It was not the mayor's political preference that caused his exclusion, for Eldred had once voted Labour in her youth, but his occupation. As she said, he would simply have felt hopelessly out of place. Most of the Headfield Players were invited, but not Betty Jones, whose husband was a butcher. Democracy, as Eldred also occasionally said, must have limits.

This particular occasion was not called an At Home but a Summer Party, and it took place on a Thursday only because Eldred had confused the dates. The invitations had been sent out for Saturday, but that was the birthday of Robin's mother, an occasion on which the family always gathered together. A hurried telephonic change had been necessary, and the numbers were smaller than usual, forty people instead of the usual sixty.

The Bruce-Comforts lived out of town in a rambling seventeenth-century manor house with some later additions, including a wing added a few years back by an architect who thought it merely cowardly to attempt a blend of ancient and modern. He had accordingly added a structure of gleaming glass and mock-marble to the original dull red brick, producing an effect which was certainly original. Beyond this modern wing, screened from view by a box hedge, was a swimming pool with chairs and tables round it, and a structure that might have been a surrealist cricket pavilion, containing changing rooms, shower rooms and a bar. Caroline Dixon said it looked like a bit of Torremolinos transported to Headfield, but still she was pleased to accept invitations to the Bruce-Comfort parties. On this fine evening she made her way to the pool, leaving Norman behind talking to his host about the next Players production. A few people were in the pool, Sandy and Derek among them. As she watched, Derek swam after Sandy, caught her, there was playful struggling and shrieks of laughter. She felt a twinge of envy and a moment of wonder. Could one partner of this contented couple be cheating on the other?

Eldred Bruce-Comfort was tall, with dark eyes, and an air of command conspicuously lacking in her husband. She was in no doubt of her standing as a woman of culture, and greeted Jason with warmth.

'Dear Jason, it is so nice to see you. Do you know what I miss here, dearly though I love Headfield? Somebody one can talk to, somebody who really knows. About important things, I mean.' Jason bowed his head appreciatively, and she suddenly tittered. She was given to occasional words and gestures inappropriate to her majestic bearing. 'Do you know, I've never seen you wearing anything but a bow tie?' She herself was in a flowing blue silk dress, short-sleeved, with long jet earrings.

'I have one for every day of the week, and others that I keep for particular occasions, like this one.'

'I never know whether you're joking.'

'Certainly not. I should no more think of wearing the same tie on consecutive days than of eating at the same restaurant.'

'Now I *know* you're joking. Tell me, have you read Kingsley Amis's latest? It really is the most outrageous thing he's done.'

'But then we should all be distressed if we couldn't say that about each new book by Kingsley Amis, isn't that so?'

She was saved from reply by the arrival of Oliver Spaceley, who kissed her hands and said that she looked magnificent. The artist was small and hairy, a quality emphasised by his open shirt which showed more than a glimpse of black wire sprouting upwards, and by the sandals that revealed bits of hair emerging from his toes. He viewed Jason's appearance with reciprocated distaste. Eldred repeated her remark about Kingsley Amis.

'No time to read, too busy painting. What's this I heard about old Porson nearly getting shot? The amateur dramatics might be worth watching if they're getting a bit of realism into it.'

Jason said coldly, 'Somebody put a live bullet into the property revolver.'

'Robin takes it very seriously,' Eldred said reprovingly. 'There is Helen Jameson, I must say hello to her.' She almost hurried to greet Helen and more particularly her husband Sir William, a property speculator whose recent knighthood had been linked by some to contributions made to Conservative Party funds.

'Taking a dip?' Oliver Spaceley asked. Jason shuddered. 'I'm getting changed. Not much point in coming to a do like this if you're not putting a toe in the water.'

Derek and Sandy were out of the pool. Sandy had gone off to greet the Extractor, who had recently been put on the Bruce-Comfort guest list after the discovery that his wife had been at Eldred's own famous girls' school. Derek lay back in a chair beside the pool, a Tom Collins by his side. When Caroline took the chair next to him he greeted her by lifting his glass.

'Don't you think it's perfect? Warmth and peace and pleasure, and all done with discretion and style. It's the essence of England, Caroline, the kind of thing foreigners envy us for, something we take for granted because it's customary. If somebody asked "What's civilisation?" I think I'd direct them here. Not culture, mind you, not like Athens, but a good way of life that it would be foolish to throw away. "Gentleness, in hearts at peace, under an English heaven." Something like that. Nobody thinks about Rupert Brooke now, but he wasn't so bad. He loved England, and so do I. I sound horribly like a travel agent, don't I? Pity that it's abroad I have to sell to people, not Britain.'

'You'd do it well, but are all the hearts at peace? Those anonymous letters. We've had another.'

'Ignore it.'

'I don't know how you can be so calm. They've been sent by one of our friends, or at least someone we know.'

'I'm not sure of that. I believe it's quite possible the letters have nothing to do with any individual, they're directed somehow against the firm.'

She hesitated, as she might have done before diving into the pool. 'I went to Wallington Apartments the other day.'

'You did?' He had the naughty smile of a boy. 'What did you find?'

'What would you expect me to find?'

The smile became a laugh. 'Caroline, I haven't the least idea what you're talking about.'

'You really don't know?'

'Kiss my hand and hope to die, I don't. But I'm eager to learn. What and where are Wallington Apartments?'

'Since you don't know, it's no use my telling you.'

Eldred and the Extractor's wife Fiona spent several minutes in recalling the pleasures and miseries of school, their voices growing higher as they did so. Sandy drifted away to talk to the Porsons, who had recently arrived. The Extractor listened apparently enthralled to the birdlike chatter. Jason, also present, was less enthralled but felt unable to move without impoliteness. Eldred switched her attention to the Extractor, and said something about the anguish she associated with dentistry.

'When I was young I was taken to see *You Never Can Tell*. Shaw, you know.' The Extractor showed fine large teeth in acknowledgement of his knowledge. 'It's supposed to be a comedy, but I could never get that first act out of my mind. The terrible instruments that young man used, was his name Valentine? I'm truly a coward in the dentist's chair.'

'No need, Mrs Bruce-Comfort, none at all. With modern technology pain need never be felt.'

'I wish I could believe it. At the very sound of the drill I begin to tremble. And then the injection.'

'I use a technique that makes an injection unnecessary.'

Fiona said, 'Darling, this is getting rather shoppy.'

'No, I'm interested, do please go on.' Eldred made the words sound like a command. 'It's ridiculous to be as frightened as I am, and I know it.'

'Not at all.' Whatever might be the Extractor's practice, his manner was certainly soothing. 'Fear of pain is worse than pain itself. An injection eliminates the pain, but what if the injection is painful? A chorambazine tablet makes you feel perfectly calm. You are almost but not quite insensible, and face the drill with equanimity.'

'A drug. I abhor drugs.' Eldred spoke as if an insult had been offered.

The Extractor showed his fine teeth. 'They are devices, dear lady, for avoiding pain.'

Jason could bear no more. Muttering an excuse, he moved on.

Drinks were served by a barman beside the pool, and also in the garden, where a large tray of glasses already filled stood on a bamboo table. Beside glasses containing gin, whisky, white and red wine, stood a single Bloody Mary, which Jason took just ahead of Porson, who favoured him with a glare.

'He *loves* Bloody Marys,' Gerda said confidingly to Jason. 'Shall I get you one from the pool bar?'

It was not clear whether she was saying this to her husband, or suggesting that Jason should give up his drink. Porson evidently thought the former, and said irritably, 'Never mind, don't fuss.' He took a glass of whisky, added water.

'I hear you are coming to Venice with us on the train. Don't you find it *exciting*?' Gerda wore a shoulderless and almost backless dress marked with green and black arabesques. The effect was to make her look more than usually like a fruit ready for plucking.

'One should arrive in Venice at the railway station, as Henry James says. But I'm bound to say that I also go by rail because of the special terms offered by PC Travel.'

'Derek is coming too,' Gerda said to Sandy. 'What a pity you are staying at home.'

'It hardly seemed worth going when it's such a short business trip,' Sandy said coldly. 'That's right, isn't it, Charles?'

'Yes, there is a little business to discuss.' Porson spoke absently, his mind apparently elsewhere.

'But to be travelling by train the whole way, I think that is exciting,' Gerda persisted. 'You know I used to work for travel firms before I was married, doing all kinds of jobs all over Europe. Always by air. And I tell you all the places look the same, whether it is Stockholm or Rome or Paris or Munich, there is the airport, the food seems made of plastic, and then the city perhaps is beautiful, but how much do you see of it? Nothing at all. People think it is glamorous, but that is not so.'

'You were glad to get out of it,' Porson said.

'I did not mind so much. But you had money, so we got married.'

Inside the house a bell rang to say that supper was served. The summer food at the Bruce-Comforts never varied. There was chicken mayonnaise with almonds, potato salad, another salad made with endive instead of lettuce, strawberries or raspberries with cream, and cheese. Some of the guests ate in the large room which the modern architect had designed for dances and receptions, others outside on the lawn. The Bruce-Comforts liked their guests to answer the supper bell promptly, and the pool was left deserted, the barman coming up to pour red and white wine.

One of the good things about these summer parties was that there were enough chairs and tables to accommodate the guests, so that no juggling with plates, glasses and forks was necessary. Sandy took her food to a table topped with black glass, and found herself next to Barry Bruce-Comfort, who at sixteen was almost as tall, thin and chinless as his father, and had also Robin's dim yet inquisitive look. His voice had broken, but remained occasionally piping.

'I say, is it true that you almost shot old Porson last night?'

'Yes. Some idiot had put a live bullet in the property revolver.'

'What fun.'

'I don't know that I'd call it fun. Certainly not if I'd shot straighter.'

Barry choked slightly on a piece of potato salad. 'I didn't mean fun exactly, it's just that life here's so awfully boring, don't you think? I'd rather be at boarding school, but the old man wouldn't send me because he says they do all sorts of frightful things, put your head down the loo, make you eat stuff at initiation ceremonies, and then say – oh, I beg your pardon.' He coloured deeply. 'I'll tell you one thing, it was really a miracle you didn't hit him. Suppose you had and, you know, killed him, would you have been charged with murder?'

'You do think of interesting questions. I hope it would have been thought an accident.'

'I wish I'd been there.' He sighed. 'I say, the old man's jolly good, isn't he? For an amateur, I mean. And he says you are too.'

'For an amateur.'

'No, he says you really are good. I'm hopeless, I dry up the moment I'm on the stage.'

Sandy expressed her sympathy.

'Brakl,' Robin said to Norman Dixon. 'What do you know about him?'

'Not much. Fantasy stuff, isn't it? Demons and fairy kings meant to symbolise something or other. Not my line.'

Robin writhed. 'I'm sure you'll agree that we want to get away from some of the rather trivial stuff we do.'

'I'm all for getting away from plays where people nearly get shot.' Norman's face went lop-sided to show that this was a joke. 'But put it this way, I wouldn't want to do anything by most of these modern Europeans. There are a couple of productions done by the Make It Real group, fringe theatre in the States. From what I hear on the grapevine, they're interesting.'

'American accents, I suppose. I don't think many of us could manage them. Our *Streetcar*, you'll remember, was a disaster.' He brightened. 'Perhaps we might have another go at Beckett. After all, he's Irish, not European.'

Gerda was at one of the tables on the lawn. Her neighbour was a youngish bearded estate agent named Rex Harris, who wore a blue blazer and white trousers, rather as if he were on a yachting trip.

'Old Charles seems to be enjoying Emily's company, wouldn't you say?'

She looked across to where her husband was talking with animation to Emily Harris, who was young, dark and pretty. He would hardly have been recognisable to those who knew him only in the office. Occasionally his hand brushed her arm.

'What's sauce for the goose is sauce for the gander,' Rex Harris said. 'And when the cat's away the mice will play, or so I've heard.' She felt his knee touch hers under the table.

She said untruthfully, 'I do not quite understand your English phrases.'

'Don't you now? If I said little birdies have been whispering things into my ear, would you understand that?'

'I am not sure.'

'Things about naughty little girls.' She removed her knee from contact with his. 'Headfield may seem a bit stuffy, but we're all broad-minded nowadays you know, anything goes.'

'Does it?'

She felt the pressure of his foot. 'You're German, aren't you? Always liked German girls, especially beautiful ones. You said you don't always understand English phrases, how about this one? Actions speak louder than words.'

'I am not sure,' Gerda said again. Somebody passed behind her, and he must have jogged her arm, for the glass of red wine she was holding suddenly tilted so that its contents were spilled over Rex Harris's tight white trousers. He sprang up. 'Oh dear, I am so sorry.'

Eldred noticed Jason's absence halfway through supper, and sent the pool barman to look for him. They returned together, appearing through a gap in the hedge dividing the pool from the house. Jason lurched unsteadily across the lawn, occasionally shaking off the barman's attempts to provide a supporting or restraining arm.

Eldred rose and went to meet him. Jason's bow tie was limp, his hair plastered to his head, his clothes dripping. 'Jason, what happened? Did you fall in the pool?'

He raised an arm in an uncharacteristic flourish. '"I have in the destructive element immersed." Conrad, Joseph. Overrated.' His voice was thick. Eldred took a step backwards. She was afraid of drunks.

'He was lying down by the pool, half asleep, after having a dip,' the barman said. 'If you'd like to come along, sir, and just dry off.' The diners on the lawn watched, spellbound.

'I will not dry off. Where is my dear friend Derek, where is

Sandy?' He blundered forward, tripped over the leg of the table at which Porson and Emily Harris sat, lost his balance, sent the table flying, and ended on the grass tangled with Emily.

Porson said angrily, 'The damn man's drunk.'

Jason lay where he had fallen. Eldred said they should call a doctor. Derek, who had been inside the house, came out, knelt down, felt heart and pulse, shook Jason. He did not stir. 'He's out like a light.'

'Dead drunk,' Porson said.

'Looks like it. But Jason doesn't drink much, I don't understand it.' Eldred repeated her suggestion about a doctor. 'I don't think so. His heartbeat's normal, pulse seems a bit erratic, can't smell his breath. He'd be upset by any fuss, I think we should get him home, put him to bed. I'll volunteer. Where's Sandy?'

'Here.' She stood looking at him with no particular expression.

'Don't you think we should take Jason home?'

The lack of expression changed into her warm smile. 'Of course. Poor old Jason, in the morning he'll wonder what hit him.'

Robin had come out. 'It's awfully decent of you, Derek. Jason, of all people, I'm truly amazed. Can we help?'

'You've got a party to look after. Let's disturb it as little as possible.'

Jason was put into the back of Derek's car, taken back to his apartment, undressed, put to bed. He remained asleep almost throughout, breathing comfortably enough. Derek left a note beside the bed, and when they were back at home remarked again that he could not understand what had happened.

'He's always been a moderate drinker. If he got drunk he must have been upset.'

'Perhaps he was excited by the prospect of meeting his favourite writer in Venice. Or perhaps he did it specially so that you'd take him home and tuck him up in bed.'

'Darling, you're *jealous*, I'd never have believed it. And of poor old Jason. Come here.' She came into his arms. 'You're the only one, you know that.'

PART TWO

Venice: The Deaths

1

From Jason Durling's journal.

Venice, Venice. The time is just after midday on Saturday. The sun is shining. My clothes are neatly hung up or put away in drawers, my shoes well polished and firmly treed. I sit on the balcony of my room in the Albergo Pacifico ('specially selected for clients of PC Travel' as the brochure says), looking down on a little rio leading to the Grand Canal, of which I can catch a sideways glance. I feel the compound of delight and astonishment roused in me by this mixture of muddy water, ancient decaying buildings – and of course the prospect that the object of my Quest through many years approaches realisation. But before saying anything about that prospect I must recount the ardours and endurances of the past twenty-four hours and more.

I woke at eight on Friday morning, with a bad headache and a dreadful taste in my mouth. I made my way to the bathroom, brushed my teeth, took two aspirin, returned to the bedroom and saw Derek's note: 'You passed out, Sandy and I brought you back. Don't know how you managed it so quickly. See you tomorrow. D.' I sat on the edge of the bed for ten minutes, pondering what had happened, because I knew that what Derek thought – what anybody might naturally have thought – was not true. I had drunk that single Bloody Mary beside the pool, no more. Only one conclusion was possible: I had been poisoned by the drink. But had the poison been meant for me or for Porson? There had been just one Bloody Mary on the table, and Gerda had said he loved Bloody Marys. Had I taken the drink intended for him?

No doubt *poisoned* is an exaggeration, *doped* would be a more accurate word. The drink had stupefied me, I had fallen into the shallow end of the pool, wakened with the shock, and managed to scramble out again. Or so I supposed. If the doped drink had been meant for Porson and he had taken it, was it possible that the doper would have been on hand to hold him under water?

I felt too ill for the speculation to take root in my mind at the time. With an aching head and a distinct feeling of dizziness I washed, dressed, drank two cups of black coffee, packed my clothes, together with all the notes I had made over the years for the Quest, and made my way to the rendezvous for PC travellers. I must have been poor company, sitting in the railway compartment with head back and eyes closed. The sea breeze across the Channel proved curative, however, and with feet on French soil at Calais I felt suddenly much better. Derek was on the platform talking to a French railway official. When he had finished I made my apologies for the trouble I had caused, and offered my thanks.

'Think nothing of it. You fairly tied one on, unusual for you.'

'Derek, I was poisoned. By a Bloody Mary.'

'Is that so?' He did not bother to hide his scepticism. 'Here's our train.'

In my ignorance I had supposed that our special train would run from London and go straight on to the Channel ferry, but those days are gone. Here now, however, came the train, with 'PC Travel' showing boldly on each *wagon-lit*. As it drew gently to a halt, uniformed stewards opened the doors and stepped out. There were first and second class compartments, and of course I had booked first. I checked the number of my *voiture* and went to the steward, who took my case and led me along the corridor.

The compartment was very small. At one side was an ordinary carriage seat which I assumed would open into a bed, and on the other a shaving mirror above what would (I again rightly assumed) open into a wash basin. There was a luggage rack, and hangers for clothes. But the whole was seven feet by five, smaller than a prison cell, with no room for cupboard or table. I reflected that this was not going to be the luxurious journey I had hoped, stepped out into the corridor again, and saw the card pinned outside the door. With disbelief and horror I read two names on the card, my own and another. I went to the end of the carriage and spoke to the steward. No mistake, he said, two passengers to a sleeper in first class. I got out on to the platform and there stood Colin, smiling.

'You look a bit put out. Anything I can do to help?' When I said it was essential for me to have a compartment to myself, he shook his head. 'No can do. First class is two to a carriage, sometimes three. You're lucky.'

'Then what can second class be like?'

'Couchettes, four or five people, bit of a crush, you wouldn't want them.'

'I must speak to Derek.'

'He's in the HQ, end coach, nearest the barrier. Have a word by all means.'

On the way up the platform I passed Porson, who stood talking to a grey-haired man and woman. The man greeted me as I passed, and I realised that he was the owner of a local shoe shop. Porson gave me the briefest of nods. 'What we feel at PC Travel is that there's no substitute for the personal touch,' he was saying. 'Either my partner Derek Crowley or I make a point of coming out at least once a year so that we know just what the journey's like . . . ' I wondered whether Porson and Gerda were in one of those prison cells. The question was answered when I reached the end coach. It had been divided into two and there was no corridor, so that the carriage covered the full width of the train. Derek, with one of the stewards beside him, was bent over a table on which lay a chart of the coaches, with names and numbers. The door to the other half of the coach was open, and inside I saw a comparatively spacious room with two single beds.

'That's all right then, Joe, problem solved.' Derek looked up with a smile. 'Jason, this is our food steward Joe Sibbles, very important man. Joe, this is Jason Durling, my old friend and valued passenger.'

'I'll make sure you don't starve, sir.' Sibbles was a square-headed man with close-cropped hair. Like the other stewards he wore a brown uniform saying PC Travel. When he had gone, I asked what the problem had been.

'We almost always keep a few spare places for people who want to book at the last minute, and no food provision had been made for them, but Joe got hold of some extra boxes. He's a resourceful fellow.'

'Boxes? Is there no restaurant car?'

'You're living in the past. Competition is the name of the game, and a restaurant car would put costs way up. You'll find the boxed meals are very good. You don't look happy, what's up?' When I told him he gave me the disarming Derek smile I remembered so well.

'Oh dear, you *do* live in the past, don't you? A *wagon-lit* coach is enormously expensive, the rationale of it is at least two to a compartment if not three.' I said I was willing to pay infinitely more to have a compartment to myself. He bent over the chart, looked at it again, shook his head.

'I'd do it if I could, you know that. There simply isn't a compartment vacant.'

'I notice you seem to be quite comfortable.'

'That's special, something Charles had fixed up for himself and Gerda. Charles is the boss.' I could detect no irony in his expression. 'If you're thinking about Colin and me – Colin, or the courier in charge, usually does all the stuff I'm doing – we're spending the night on those.' He pointed to ordinary railway seats, one on either side. 'Just take off jacket and tie and catnap, not like you lucky people in first class. We'll be all set for handling complaints during the night, not that I expect any.'

'Why not leave it to Colin, and share a first class compartment with me?'

'My dear old Jason, I've told you there isn't one vacant.' He gave me the smile again. 'I'm sorry, I truly am. But remember, the longest night is shorter than you think, and you'll wake up in Venice.' One of Derek's weaknesses is that he has little interest in anything that doesn't affect him personally, and I was surprised when he said: 'This does mean that the biography's really coming off?' I said that it certainly looked like it, and that anyway I should be meeting D.M. Cruddle for the first time. 'I'm so glad for you. This demands celebration.'

He went through to the inner bedroom, and returned with a bottle of champagne and two glasses. I drank only one, sipping it rather fearfully, but will admit that afterwards I felt more cheerful. I was about to leave when Porson came in with Gerda. He looked from one of us to the other, then at the bottle, as if suspecting a plot. More glasses were brought, the rest of the champagne poured. Few words were spoken, but I had an odd feeling that all three of them were nursing some private reason for satisfaction. Porson's thick lips were pushed out as he sipped the champagne in a manner unpleasantly sensual, Gerda had what was perhaps a customary air of expecting something exciting to happen, and Derek – well, I know when he is congratulating himself on his own cleverness, and that was the case now. There was a whiff of sulphur in the air as though some unpleasant trick, or perhaps more than one, was to be played. Then I made my way back to my prison cell, casting an envious glance on the way at the comfort in which Porson and his wife were to spend the night.

I was walking along the platform when I heard my name called. It was the steward Sibbles. He was in a small compartment, a kind of miniature guard's van, standing beside a pile of metal containers.

'Wondered what you'd like to eat, sir, been down your end of the train already taking orders, wouldn't like you to miss out. It's breast of chicken and potato salad, or salmon with ditto, and if you take my advice you'll go for the salmon.'

'Do I understand that the meals are in those containers?'

'Right you are. Take 'em on at Calais, unload at Venice and get another lot for the return journey.'

'Like an aeroplane meal? Plastic cutlery?'

'That's the ticket, sir. Will it be the salmon then?'

I said it would be the salmon, and passed on with a heavy heart. I remembered reading that Henry James had come to Venice by train for preference, not only because it was important to catch one's first glimpse of the Grand Canal from the station.

No doubt he had passed most of the time in a sitting room provided for first class travellers, and taken his meals in a restaurant car where attentive waiters guided the diners to tables laid with white cloths and gleaming silver. Now it was plastic cutlery, and food in metal boxes. What a mark of our civilisation's decay! I wondered whom I should find in the prison cell.

When I opened the door he was sitting beside the window, and got up to greet me. He was a small man, several years my senior, with features that seemed never to stay still, and quick, jerky movements. Eyebrows shot up and then down again, mouth twitched, an occasional tic appeared in his cheek, even his pointed chin seemed to slide about. He extended a small hand.

'Pleased to meet you, beginning to think you'd disappeared. Richard Linnet's the name, you can guess what they call me, Dicky Bird. Are you on pleasure bent, in search of art and culture?' I said I had private business in the city. 'Me too. Most of 'em have been bitten by the culture bug, but it's as good a way of getting to old Venezia as any other, if you don't want to fly.'

'I dislike flying, but if I had known how cramped our accommodation would be, I should have flown.'

'Not quite Wembley Stadium, I agree. Much the same as other trains though, except the Orient Express. As for the couchettes . . . ' His brows lifted, eyes rolled, nose quivered, mouth twitched, chin shook. 'Toss for it?'

'I beg your pardon?'

'Upper or lower. You know the drill? There's a ladder stacked up above, they put it up when they make the beds, then one of us climbs up to bye-byes. I'll spin, you call.' When I had called correctly he said cheerfully, 'I'll be the sky rider then.'

There was a knock at the door. It was Sibbles. He pushed down the central seat so that it became a kind of table, and deposited two boxes. When opened they revealed a meal, with everything wrapped in plastic – tinned pâté, the main course, cheese in tinfoil, plastic-wrapped rolls and butter.

'Did he recommend the chicken?' Linnet asked.

'No, the salmon.'

100

'He told me the chicken. Just a matter of which he had most of, they all do it.' He pushed the top off the pâté, spread some on a roll, giving me occasional glances rather as if he suspected me of watching him. Fields and villages unreeled outside. 'From Headfield?'

'I live there, yes.'

'Know a man named Crowley, Derek Crowley? His firm are organising this do.'

'Yes, he's a friend of mine. As a matter of fact he's on this train. Do you know him?'

His features did their shivering act. 'Never met. Used to be married to his wife.'

I stared at him, hardly able to believe the words. I vaguely remembered hearing that Sandy's name had once been Linnet, but could not have imagined her married to this jaunty little man with the air of a commercial traveller. 'Hard to take in, I daresay. True, though, she was Mrs Linnet, Owen's my boy. Partly why I'm on this train. Had to go to Venice, saw the PC Travel ad, thought why not travel with the family firm. Didn't ask for a concessionary rate though. Haven't seen Sandy for years, how is she? And how's the lad?' I said they were both well. 'Wish them luck when you see them. HMG, that was the trouble.'

'I don't understand you.'

'Official work, took me away from home. Nothing vital, just a cog that helped to make the machine move, but not my own master, servant of HMG. Sometimes away for quite a while.' Again one of those darting glances. 'Made things difficult, impossible you might say. You know Sandy?'

'Of course.'

'I could a tale unfold.'

With all the austerity I could summon I said, 'Not to me, please. I don't wish to hear tales about my friends.'

After that we hardly spoke. Another steward came and collected the remains of the meal, put up the ladder, opened out the seats below to form a bed, and let down from the wall a bunk above. When this had been done there was hardly room to move without touching each other.

101

And then – then the frightfulness of undressing one at a time in
that tiny cell, Linnet's facetiousness about going first, his trousers
and underclothes on a hanger plainly visible to me, his jeering
mirth when I put the wooden trees into my shoes – I can say no
more about the horror of it. My aversion to undressing in front of
another human being was increased tenfold by the fact that he
sensed it and said with a little hoot of laughter, 'I won't peep.'
The window blind rattled, I could hear Linnet's snores above the
noise of the train, uneasy sleep was made horrible by the dream of
struggle and escape. This time it was Linnet and Porson who
confined me, and were saying something which I strove
desperately to understand. A hand pressed my shoulder, and I
knew it to be Linnet's, I saw his face.

'All right, are you? You seemed to have the screaming
meemies. Just gone through Milan, shan't be long now.'

We reached Venice just after nine-thirty in the morning. It had
been one of the worst nights of my life.

Guide books to Venice talk about the Tintorettos and the
Titians, the Bellinis and Carpaccios, the churches and palazzos,
but none that I have seen says that the most indispensable item
for a visitor is an umbrella. Why is it indispensable in Venice
particularly? Because when it rains you are likely to find yourself
five minutes or more away from the water bus, the vaporetto, and
you cannot hail a taxi. Venice is a city where walking is not
merely desirable but inevitable. When we disembogued (in the
stress of describing that appalling railway journey I have been
neglecting my style) and stood awaiting the motor boats to take
us to our hotel, it was raining. With a slight sense of satisfaction I
put up my umbrella. Colin was dashing here and there
shepherding the flock, who showed that tendency of travelling
sheep to stray. Derek was helping him. Porson wore his habitual
expression of lustful discontent. Sibbles the steward held a large
striped umbrella of the kind seen on golf courses over Porson and
Gerda. Everybody else was getting wet.

The delay was short. Within minutes several water taxis had
pulled up – I suppose the party was between thirty and forty –
and we were chugging down the Grand Canal. We passed

vaporettos full of sightseers wearing mackintoshes, other water taxis came churning up the dirty green canal. I looked at the magnificent but mouldering façades and thought of Henry, the divine Henry, saying that in Venice the only noises were human, that the sound of the gondolier is the sound of the city, and I could have wept for the way in which the internal combustion engine has vandalised beauty. Then I looked at my companions, listened to their baaing approval as they looked at the palazzos they mostly misnamed, and reflected that Henry James had also observed that nothing else in Venice is as disagreeable as the visitors.

But misanthropy must not prevail. The hotel, in Canareggio rather than the more central and fashionable part of the city, has a flavour distinctively and pleasantly Venetian. There is, as I have said, a glancing view of the Grand Canal from my room. I feel the excitement of one who has an assignation with a lover. In a few hours I shall meet Dante Milton Cruddle for the first time.

I have laid out on the dressing table some of the papers relating to the Quest. They are in one file. In another is the material I have gathered bearing on Cruddle's years in Greece, the great years. There was an interview he had given on parting from his wife, when he had said that his whole life had been spent in search for the One Friend all human beings need, and that this search was the inner meaning of the Borgogrundian novels, there was another file concerning the accusations – which he had always denied – that he had written propaganda for Mussolini . . .

So there were many questions to which I hoped to find answers. Our correspondence had lasted now over nearly twenty years, and I can remember the excitement I felt as I opened the first letter with the Venetian postmark, and saw the crabbed, angular writing. I recall the exact words of that first letter. 'I am much gratified by your appreciative remarks about my work, but regret that I can give no answer to questions which verge on the personal, and hence the impertinent. No answer, that is, further to that given in my books, which will tell you that my whole life has been spent in looking for that One Friend whose existence may be regarded as either corporeal or symbolic. I can tell you nothing more.'

Perhaps that might be regarded as discouraging? I did not find it so, but still it was not for years that I dared to mention the possibility that he might appoint me as his critical biographer, and that if he did so a meeting – even a number of meetings – would be desirable. His replies – for the question had been discussed, deliberated, considered and reconsidered in many letters – had varied. At times he said that he almost agreed with the herd that his work was properly neglected, and if there was no interest in his work there could be none in his life. At other times he said that any secrets in his life were of purely personal interest, at others still that my belief in his genius had been the only thing that made him wish to go on living, and might even make him pick up his pen again. I felt that he had accepted me as his biographer, but he had consistently refused a meeting.

'I am too old, too unwell, to contemplate the nervous excitement raised by such a prospect . . . the desire for the One Friend must now be symbolic only . . . the dubious wisdom of years tells me that a truly civilised relationship must exclude not merely the physical but anything approaching the personal . . . ' Those were phrases typical of many in the letters. But now, now, only a few days ago a letter had come, signed as always with the familiar initials at the bottom. It was brief, saying only: 'It seems, after all, that the time has come for us to talk. If you can make it convenient to pay a visit here in the next month I shall be obliged.' Cruddle's letters varied in tone from delightful expansiveness to occasional brusqueness, and I paid no attention to the tone of this one. The matter of those few lines was the important thing. I answered immediately, and made plans to come to Venice.

2

When the telephone rang Jason felt an almost sensual thrill as he picked it up. Was he about to hear Cruddle's voice for the first time? It was almost a disappointment that the voice was Derek's.

'Jason, when's your appointment with the great man? Five o'clock, good. You're free for lunch then? Can you meet me in the lounge in ten minutes.' It was not until they met that Jason learned he would not be lunching with Derek alone. 'Charles will be there, and Guido Morvelli. I wouldn't be surprised if they're at the restaurant now.'

'Shan't I be in the way, if you're discussing business?

'Just why I'd like you to be there. Don't worry, I told Guido you'd be coming, he expressed himself enchanted.'

Derek's eyes sparkled, his skin had the healthy freshness peculiar to some English males, a kind of glow under the skin. 'Guido's a character, a bit like a stage model of an Italian but quick and clever. Also extravagant, living beyond his means is a matter of principle for him. We're likely to have a long, long session of argument this afternoon, and I don't want Charles arguing at lunch as well.'

'Will Gerda be there?'

'Certainly not. In Charles's eyes women and business don't mix.'

'You two don't seem to be on the best of terms. Are you sure it has nothing to do with Gerda?'

'Nothing at all. Charles thinks I'm after control of the business, that's why he's so put out.'

'Derek, *something* strange is happening. I believe that drink I took was meant for Porson, the one that made me pass out.'

'You had too much to drink, that's all. I was pleased to see you had some normal failings, my old Jason. Mind you, if somebody *has* got it in for my partner I wouldn't be surprised. He's what the teachers in our old days at Whitestones used politely to call a satyr, or in plain English he pokes anything that moves. Where are we? Over that little bridge and down that unlikely looking alley, except that they don't call it an alley, and we should be there. How was the train journey?'

'I had the most uncomfortable night of my life. My companion in the so-called first class sleeper was Sandy's first husband.'

Derek stood still on the bridge. 'Linnet? On the train?'

'As I've said, not only on the train but in my compartment. He said you hadn't met. He also hinted that he did some kind of hush-hush job for the Government.'

'The only times he's worked for the Government are when he's been in prison, as far as I know. He was in jail when I met Sandy. I haven't met him and don't want to. I wonder what the hell he was doing on our train.'

'He said he had to come to Venice, and thought why not travel on the family train. You seem very put out.'

He stood staring down the narrow canal where lines of washing hung out from upper floors. 'He's a villain. Sandy's not seen him or had anything to do with him since she left him. He wrote her a couple of letters which she didn't answer. He's a swindler, once got subscriptions from people named Nelson which were supposed to be used for the recovery of a non-existent fortune belonging to a newly discovered heir of Admiral Nelson. Can you imagine people falling for that kind of thing? Sandy married him when she was nineteen, Owen was born within the year, then a couple of years later he was caught for some company fiddle, went inside for eighteen months. He got money to her while he was inside, and she stayed with him when he came out. Then he was caught again for something or other, fraud or forgery, and she made the break, set out to support herself and Owen, carved out a career in advertising. She was still very bruised and battered when she met me.'

'You've never told me this.'

'It's a closed chapter, we don't talk about it. Now it's been told to you, forget it. Here we are.'

In the restaurant they were led to an alcove where Morvelli greeted them with outstretched hands. He was a large man with thick dark hair, a white face, a blue jaw. He wore a thin light grey suit that shone like silk.

'Derek, my friend, you look more youthful every time I see you. Mr Durling, I am delighted to meet you. I wonder if you are related to my old friend Sture Durling, who once broke a casino bank by persistently playing the *trasversale*?'

'I'm afraid not. Indeed, I am so ignorant that I don't even know what a *trasversale* is.

'I am sorry to hear it. You know what Talleyrand said was the greatest pleasure in life? To gamble and win. And the second greatest pleasure? To gamble and lose.'

Porson leaned back on the banquette, his face brick red. 'You've enjoyed that second greatest pleasure pretty often, Guido, from what I hear.'

'You don't believe everything you are told, I am sure. It would have been a pleasure to see the lovely Gerda here today.'

'She thought we were going to talk business which would have bored her. I thought so too.' He looked hard at Jason.

'I must plead guilty. When Derek told me his friend's name was Durling I remembered my old friend Sture, and said that I must meet him.'

Porson grunted, Derek smiled. Jason wondered whether Sture Durling had been invented as an excuse for his presence. Morvelli clapped his large hands, a genie summoning a waiter. Derek and Jason drank *Punt e Mes*, Porson a Bloody Mary, Morvelli Perrier water.

Jason prided himself on his sensitivity to nuances of speech, shifts of feeling, changes in the atmospheric temperature. As they ate their risotto and fish some stringed instrument seemed to be playing warning notes within his skull, the sounds clangorous and jarring. There were moments when Porson's glance rested on Derek with an almost gloating expression, others when Morvelli looked from one partner to the other like a man calculating the odds at a roulette table. And in Derek Jason sensed, as he had in the train, the excessive animation that marked him when about to

107

attempt some dramatic coup. When he thought of the troubles attendant on projected coups in the past the idea was disturbing.

He detached himself deliberately from the scene around him, and dwelt instead on what lay ahead. What would be the first words spoken when he met Cruddle, what secrets of Greece or Italy would he reveal, was it possible that he had completed some new work and was ready to discuss it? He could not remember afterwards what had been said at lunch, and it seemed that in no time at all it was over, Morvelli was taking his hand again, calling him Jason, saying that he must come to the party he was giving that evening. Porson nodded, Derek gave him a wink. As he strolled back to the hotel the sun was shining.

In the hall he found Colin, and a dozen members of the party. Colin left them, and greeted him with characteristic enthusiasm.

'I say, you know your way around Venice a bit, don't you? Wouldn't care to trail along with us, I suppose? Nothing laid on this afternoon, but some of 'em are eager to get going, never happy unless they're wearing out shoe leather. Be terrific if you came along too, take a bit of weight off my shoulders.' He made his shoulders sag comically and Jason agreed, conscious that he had still two hours to put in before the appointed time for his visit. Colin told the little flock loaded with cameras and raincoats that they were lucky to have with them somebody else familiar with Venice.

They had been walking for only a few minutes when Jason realised that Colin's knowledge of the city was much greater than his own. He led the way with assurance over bridges, down unpromising calles, through sottoportegos and down fondamentas. All the while he discoursed fluently on the features of this or that church or square. Was what he said accurate? Neither Jason nor any of the men and women trailing after him was in any position to correct him. He briskly dismissed the church of the Santi Apostoli and one or two others, and did not pause until they were in the Campo SS Giovanni e Paolo, when he led them up to a monumental figure.

'The greatest equestrian statue in the world.' His raised brows invited a question. Somebody duly asked who it was. 'Bartolomeo

108

Colleoni, a *condottiere* – which for your information means somebody who fought for money – who paid for the building of his own statue in advance.' There was the proper ripple of amusement. One or two people fumbled for guidebooks. Colin staved them off. 'Just look round you. After San Marco this is the most spectacular square in Venice, yet it's off the beaten track.' The sheep duly murmured appreciation, oblivious of the fact that the square was well filled with other tourists.

There was a vague move in the direction of the church. Colin touched Jason's arm. 'Just take care for five minutes, old man, will you?' he said, and walked briskly across the square.

A couple whom Jason vaguely recognised as Headfieldians spoke to him, saying something about the splendour of the statue, to which he returned a non-committal reply. 'Our friend seems to have disappeared for a moment,' the man said. 'Perhaps you can tell us what that building is behind the statue.'

'The Scuola Grande di San Marco,' a voice said behind him. 'Or that's what it was originally. Now it's the city hospital. You don't recognise me, Mr Durling, do you?'

The voice belonged to a short stout woman wearing glasses with mauve frames, decorated with small butterflies. 'Dolores Makins. One of the cashiers at the bank. We know each other over the counter. I go away every year with PC Travel, and one of the pleasures is you meet such unexpected people. I've been to Venice so often I sometimes think I should be a guide.' When he said he thought so too, she tapped him playfully on the arm. 'You're joking.'

'Not at all.'

'Do you mind if we use Christian names, Jason? On these tours we never stand on ceremony.'

'By all means.' He looked round desperately. There was no sign of Colin. 'I think it would be wonderful if you showed the group round the church until Colin returns.'

'I take that as a compliment.' She raised her voice, 'Shall we go and look at the church? There are lots of interesting things to see. We seem to have lost our Colin, but I'll do my best to stand in for him. I'm sure he won't be long.' The sheep baaed enthusiastically, and trailed obediently across the campo. As he moved away Jason heard Dolores' voice raised. The words 'apsidal chapels' came through with startling clarity. What an escape!

He left the square by a different calle from the one through which they had entered, and suddenly saw Colin. He sat at a café table with the man he had introduced as his friend Chuck Waterton. Coffees were in front of them, and on the ground beside Waterton stood three large packages. For a moment Jason contemplated stopping, then decided against it lest Colin should ask what had happened to the sheep. The two seemed to be engaged in argument or warm discussion, but this ended as Colin got up and left his companion. Waterton remained with coffee cup in front of him, packages still at his side. Jason quickened his step. Like many who try to fill in time before an appointment, he had been struck by a sudden fear that he might be late for the most important meeting of his life.

3

Back at the Pacifico Jason put on a plain light blue shirt and a dark blue spotted bow tie, used liquid shiner on his shoes, and set out with the folders under his arm. There was, after all, plenty of time.

He had looked at the apartment half-a-dozen times on earlier visits to Venice, speculating behind which of the shuttered second floor windows the great man was hidden. Once, indeed, he had advanced to the door and stood with finger raised before the bell that said 'Cruddle', before turning away in obedience to the interdict on a meeting. The house was in the eastern part of Dorsoduro, sometimes called the artists' quarter, although the quiet streets of mostly undistinguished houses seemed humdrum enough. This house stood with two others in one of the little cortes with only a single entrance, that may be found throughout the city. At the appointed time, precisely five o'clock, Jason extended his finger and pressed the bell.

He was answered by silence. No step sounded on the stairs, no window opened. Should he press the bell again? Or go away, take a turn round the streets and return, assuming that he had mistaken the time? But he knew that he had not mistaken it. Then a shutter above was thrown open, an old man holding a dustpan and brush leaned out and shot at him a volley of Italian. Jason could understand simple phrases spoken slowly, and grasped that the man was asking what, or perhaps whom, he wanted. He replied slowly in English.

'My name is Durling. I have an appointment with Mr Cruddle at five o'clock.'

The man let loose another volley, of which he understood hardly a word, then the shutters were banged to. He was contemplating the awful possibility that he might not be admitted, when the door opened. The man stood before him, an apron round his waist, the brush and dustpan still in his hand.

'Come.'

Jason closed the door, and was aware of the dankness characteristic of Venetian interiors, as if the water below the building had impregnated the brick. A faint light showed on the landing above, and he groped a way cautiously up the narrow stone stairs. The iron rail was damp and on the other side the wall, when he happened to touch it, gave a slightly crumbly feeling to the fingertips. The cleaner moved ahead of him, and to his surprise opened a door on the first landing. He had been deceived by the difference between English and American notation. Although he named it the second floor, Cruddle was housed on what in English terms was the first. In the past Jason had been looking at the wrong windows.

The light was not much better when they entered a tiny hall. Then the man opened a door, and stood aside to let him enter. 'Wait,' he said. The door closed, and he looked eagerly around.

The room was no bigger than his sitting room in Ponsonby Court. It was still dim in spite of a small window with a rather dirty near-white curtain over it, but as his eyes became accustomed to the light he saw that he might indeed have been in an English flat, although one hardly prosperous enough for

Headfield. Two worn armchairs stood on either side of a small fireplace, a vase of wilting flowers rested on what looked like a kitchen table, there were two glass-fronted bookcases with a collection of Toby jugs on top of one, glass ornaments above the other. A nondescript carpet, in places very worn, covered the floor. Jason's first thought was to wonder how a great writer could live in such surroundings. It was quickly banished. Of what importance were his surroundings to such a writer as Cruddle, whose concern was with fantasy, the spirit, the interior life of art?

There was a door between the glass-fronted bookcases, and now a figure was framed in it. Jason had seen no recent photographs of the great writer, and was momentarily in doubt about the identity of the small old man who shuffled towards him. He knew of course that Cruddle was very old, yet the image in his mind was of pictures taken in Greece many years ago. They showed a man waving his hat in the air, perched on a rock chin in hand, sitting on a terrace with a glass in front of him. Could that be the same person as this figure with bags under his eyes, a moist underlip, withered ears and fingers? It seemed to Jason that a slight musty smell hung about him, the smell of advanced age, perhaps even of the graveyard.

It needed a conscious effort to remember that this was the artistic saint who, with the Borgogrundian novels written, had in his last collection of poetic prose pieces *Finale* considered great cities and civilisations in turn, and dismissed them all in favour of 'the true Nirvana, the endless cultivation of that art realised by Narcissus in the pool of the self,' as he had put it. When he remembered such phrases Jason could have knelt and kissed the withered fingers.

A gesture indicated that he should sit and he did so, on a small sofa which gave a *ping* that made Jason uncomfortably aware of a spring emerging through the upholstery. He shifted slightly to make himself less vulnerable to its effects. The folders containing those papers that were the fruit of many years' research were at his side.

'I expected you tomorrow, it was tomorrow you said in your letter.'

The voice too had the thin piping tones of age. Taken aback, Jason murmured something to the contrary. A box file stood beside Cruddle's chair and he picked this up, put it on his knees, and began to go through it, making a sound between a whistle and a hum as he turned over papers. Then he seemed to give up, closed the file.

'At any rate, you're here. It can't be helped.' His voice was raised, the effect not powerful but like the cry of a bird. 'Juan.' The man Jason had seen put his head round the door. 'Juan, tea.' The man nodded, the door closed again, Cruddle rubbed his hands. 'Now we shall soon have a cuppa.' He looked intently at the empty grate, as if expecting to read a message in it. 'Oh, yes, we shall have a nice cup of tea, nothing like it.' He continued to stare at the grate, apparently oblivious of Jason's presence, then said, 'You like tea, don't you? It's an English drink.'

Jason said that he liked tea, and that he was delighted by this meeting after their years of correspondence. Cruddle's gaze remained on the grate. 'There are questions I should like to ask. Not today, perhaps, but during my visit. A biographer . . . '

He did not finish the sentence, in part because of Cruddle's curt and as it seemed dismissive nod, in part because Juan entered with a tray containing a teapot, two cups, a little dish of cakes. He poured the tea, handed a cup to each of them. Cruddle looked up, spoke in a language Jason recognised as Spanish, and Juan replied at length in the same language.

Jason, cup in hand, was struck as though by a Pauline revelation. Juan, Juan. Of course that had been the name of the handsome boy for whom Cruddle had left his wife, after what had apparently been scenes of violent recrimination. Jason had assumed that the affair was brief, but here Juan was in Venice, apparently Cruddle's partner through the years. It had been no doubt natural, but was still unfortunate, that he had mistaken this devoted friend for a cleaner. Cruddle sensed something of his surprise, and said in his piping voice, 'Yes, Juan Tenoso, the same Juan. My companion and faithful friend.' His hand went out, but Juan made no attempt to take it, simply stood staring at Jason with distrustful black eyes.

113

Cruddle was nibbling one of the cakes, drinking his tea. Jason asked what Juan had said.

'He says what is over is over, he does not wish to talk about it.' Evidently Juan understood English even though he did not speak it, for he nodded angrily and went out. Jason was offered, and refused, a cake. He felt oppressed by the room's dimness, its air of being some relic of a lower-class English suburb transported by misadventure to Venice. He was oppressed also by the apparent unexpectedness of his visit.

Cruddle gave a brief cough and spoke, but only to say that if Jason would like another cup of tea he should pour it. He declined, and they sat in silence, Cruddle sipping his tea, looking for the most part at the grate but giving his visitor occasional glances. Jason feared that in a few minutes he might say it was time for him to rest, and excuse himself. It seemed urgently necessary to speak, although when he did so the words came out in bursts, and he hardly recognised the voice as his own.

'You asked me to come here to see you. We are to discuss my work on my critical and biographical study. I have already done a great deal of research, you will remember our letters. I am hoping you will be able to show me other materials, papers or letters, give me information. Especially about the past, of course, and your abandonment of writing.'

'That was a good cup of tea, yes, a good cuppa.' Cruddle rose slowly out of the chair, put cup back on tray, returned to chair, hunched back in it. 'That letter, the last one I wrote. Do you have it with you?'

Of course Jason had it with him and he produced it now, although he knew the brief contents by heart. Cruddle read it, making that sound between whistle and hum. 'I see nothing about discussing a book.'

It was then that Jason had the intimation, even the knowledge, of disaster. He began to talk rapidly, like a man who hopes by speech to avert an avalanche or earthquake. 'You say in the letter that the time has come to talk, ask me to come out here. What else does it mean except that we should get to know each other, co-operate, the biographer and his subject . . . '

'Is there anything among our correspondence saying that you have been appointed as my biographer?' the piping voice asked. 'I think not.'

The avalanche was descending, the earth trembled. 'For years I have been gathering material, you know that. I wrote letters, you replied, we had an understanding.'

'An understanding. Is that what you thought?'

'How could I think anything else?' The other did not reply, but now looked directly at Jason. Beneath the drooping eyelid he detected pleasure. 'I don't understand why you sent for me.'

'*Sent* for you? Perhaps my phrasing was less exact than I might have wished. I said that we should talk, nothing more.'

Somewhere in the apartment a door closed, there were voices. 'What could it be for, except to meet and talk about the book? I don't understand.'

'Well, hello.' The door through which Juan had brought tea opened. A young man stood there, a man in his late twenties. He wore jeans and a T-shirt, his hair was cut with military neatness, grey eyes looked keenly through rimless glasses. 'You'll be Jason. My name's Dwight Eidelberg. Glad to know you, Jason.' He made for the tea tray, took a cake, ate it in two mouthfuls. 'Very good. Hope you didn't let D.M. eat too many, one's supposed to be the limit.'

Cruddle said gleefully, 'I had two.' Jason was reminded of Uncle X and the biscuits.

'Naughty, naughty.' He looked from one to the other of them. 'Has D.M. broken the news? Doesn't look like it. You've been an admirer for a long time, Jason, right? The same with me too, not as long as you of course, but it was a thesis on fantasy and reality in the Borgogrundian novels that got me my Masters. Then I came over last year, met the great man . . . ' his large capable hand hovered over Cruddle's little one as though about to pat it, ' . . . and we came to an agreement.'

'What kind of agreement?' But of course he knew.

'Why, D.M. here's had an amazing life, and I'm going to write about it. A critical book too, mind, but one that's got the human story in it. *The Genius They Forgot*, how about that? I know the objection, no name in it, but there's a sub-title: *The Timeless Art of Dante Milton Cruddle.*'

Jason moved on the sofa. The spring dug vengefully into his backside. 'You mean you have been appointed as official biographer?'

'Contract signed with an American publisher six months ago. I've been digging in fifty libraries, found stuff even D.M. didn't know existed, started writing a couple of weeks back. Expect to have it wrapped up by the end of the year.' Jason shook his head, without knowing why he did so. 'I see this comes as a bit of a shock.'

'I don't see why it should,' Cruddle piped. 'You can't pretend you were getting along very fast. Dwight here is . . . a live wire. Yes, a real live wire.' Now the American did pat him, not on the head but the shoulder.

The monstrous injustice of it all stung him into speech. 'Why not tell me by letter, why bring me out here? That was . . . ' He was lost for words.

'Well now, I have to say I'm responsible for that.' Behind the rimless glasses Dwight Eidelberg's gaze was direct, friendly, appealing. 'No point in two people working on D.M., agreed? Now you've been going at it for years, right? Not writing but gathering material, I know it, I acknowledge it. Now, here's what I wanted to say. Maybe I should have made the approach in a letter, but it seemed to me it would come better direct, and if D.M. was here to OK it. Would you be willing to hand over the material you've gotten together to me? It's no use to you now, and it will likely fill some gaps, especially in the critical sections. I'll be frank and admit I'm stronger on the human interest side. Fullest acknowledgements made, naturally. And if you feel you should be recompensed for your time, I daresay that could be managed. Within reason, mind, within reason.'

The insult of those last two sentences was too much for him. He stood up, screamed something about betrayal – he could not have said what the words were – and threw the folders at Cruddle, who shrank back in his chair. The letters, the correspondence he had brought and the details he had gathered painstakingly over the years, flew away as the folders opened. They flew like paper birds, his labours of love, on to the floor, the table, into the little grate, on to Cruddle's lap. Dwight caught a couple of the papers and looked at them with interest, Cruddle pushed away those that had landed on him as if they were unclean. Jason pulled open the door, shoved past Juan in the narrow hall, half ran and half stumbled down the worn stone steps. Then he was in the little corte. He turned before leaving it, and saw the curtain partly raised, Dwight's earnest face looking down at him. Then the curtain dropped, the play was over.

4

Jason could not have said himself exactly what he did in the two or three hours after he had left the withered little writer, his once-beautiful boy friend and the genial businesslike American in that dingy apartment with its Toby jugs and glass ornaments and smell of decay. Afterwards he remembered crossing the Accademia bridge, standing in the middle of it, and wondering what would happen if he threw himself into the Grand Canal. He imagined the body striking the water, a gondolier fishing him out, the sympathy of passers-by. 'Poor fellow, he must have been desperate.' He remembered also the locations of some of the bars he entered, one just off the Campo Francesco Morosini, another in the Calle Mandola near the Campo Sant' Angelo – those were the first two, but afterwards he lost count. It was a long time since he had drunk whisky, on an evening when the trouble about the bar accounts at King's had seemed likely to be serious, and he drank it again now, the taste strange in his mouth. Then the effect had been to remove the alarm and dismay he had felt at Derek's problems, and now it had something of the same soothing quality. Yet of course the pain remained, removed into some part of the mind where it was dulled, as analgesics may turn the fierce drum-beat of an aching tooth into a still menacing but distant throbbing.

Certain moments in those despairing hours were etched deep in his memory. One was that of standing talking to a barman in the Campo Manin – he remembered the statue of Daniel Manin in the centre of the square and children playing ball round it – when a voice behind him said, 'Hallo hallo, if it's not my sleeping partner. Remember Dicky Bird?'

Alcohol loosens the tongue. Jason remembered what Derek had told him and said, 'Here on Government business, no doubt.'

'How's that?' Mouth twitched, eyebrows moved.

'HMG was the trouble, you said, jobs that took you away from home. You didn't say the work was in a cell.'

'Somebody's been telling tales, I can see. I've had a bit of bad luck here and there, it's true, but not a word of a lie in what I said, I've done a good many jobs for the Government.'

He commented, with what he felt even at the time to be disastrous facetiousness, 'Selling them a nice line in forged passports perhaps.'

'Now that *is* naughty, anything I did was to help other people. He who is without sin should cast the first stone and all that. Mr Crowley's been talking, has he, handsome Derek.'

'I thought you'd never met him.'

'Just going on the description of my ex. Handsomest man she'd ever met, she said, and nobody ever said that about me. What are you doing in a dive like this, I'd have thought you'd be living it up in Harry's Bar?'

'I suppose you're expecting to meet a Government agent now.'

The little man took this with apparent seriousness. 'Not a bit of it, just a business associate, no mystery about it.'

All the while they talked he had been looking round, eyes glancing, mouth twitching, body making occasional jerky movements. 'And there he is. Hallo there, Shunya. This is Shunya Inoki, Jack Durling. Jack and I just happened to meet here, travelled out from London together.' He repeated the joke about sleeping partners.

Inoki bobbed his head and smiled. He wore a business suit with a waistcoat, and carried a briefcase. 'Delighted to make your acquaintance. We are perhaps arranging for Dicky to visit Tokyo.

Do you know Tokyo, Jack?'

He said that he did not know Tokyo, and his name was not Jack. Linnet gave his face-splitting laugh.

'My mistake. Shall we adjourn, Shunya? Bit of confidential business, old man, know you'll forgive us.'

Outside the café he looked back. The Japanese had taken out some papers, and seemed to be checking them with Linnet.

That was one picture that remained with him very clearly. Then there was a blank until he found himself sitting at a table at Florian's in the Piazza San Marco. He remembered saying aloud, 'Pigeons and people,' and indeed the square was full of both. The pigeons swooped about in clusters looking for and receiving food, small armies of tourists meandered meaninglessly, led by guides bearing banners that proclaimed their allegiance to various travel firms. It was easy, he thought as he sipped a different brand of golden whisky, easy to distinguish the Germans by their Tyrolean hats, the Americans by their silver-haired matrons, the British by their shabbiness, the Japanese by their colour. This last seemed to him such an excellent joke that he laughed aloud, then spoke. 'A scene of unrelenting vulgarity,' he said. 'A century ago the divine Henry said that Venice was a peep-show and bazaar, with the barbarians in full possession. Little he knew.' The effort of speech exhausted him, and he closed his eyes to shut out the red raw knees, the garish clothes, the cameras eagerly pointed by the ignorant at the historic. Somewhere within, the deep wound caused pain.

'Mr Durling. Jason.' He reluctantly opened his eyes, and saw without at first recognising the woman who stood before him, wearing a bright green dress, with a green chiffon scarf and shoes of a slightly different green. On her nose were glasses with frames that were again another shade of green, decorated with small butterflies. It was these butterflies that made him remember her name. He wondered whether she had different coloured frames for all her clothes.

'Miss Makins.'

'Isn't it beautifully warm? But my feet are killing me.' She sat down and fanned herself vigorously with one hand. 'We've been looking at the most wonderful pictures by Carpaccio. St George and the dragon, and St Jerome in his study, and a lion who had a thorn in his foot and Jerome took it out. Colin knew all about them. I do think he's wonderful.'

'But Miss Makins . . . '

'Dolores.'

'Those pictures are famous, you must know of them, you are so well-informed.'

This attempted irony was a mistake, for she took it seriously. 'Oh, Jason.'

He would always have been too polite to get up and walk away, but only on this evening of total catastrophe would he have been foolish enough to ask her what she would like to drink. The service at Florian's is often slow, but now it seemed that a waiter was beside him in a moment, and in another moment a vermouth and soda appeared.

'Isn't this the most romantic place you ever saw? The lion of St Mark's, those lovely arcades, the pretty shops?'

' "A peep-show and bazaar, with the barbarians in full possession." '

'I'm afraid you're a cynic. I love it all. What are you drinking?' When he told her she said, 'Oh, Jason.'

He tried to tell her that the golden drink was a magic potion. Behind or beneath it the pain endured, but on the surface life rippled easily, gently. The incongruities of Dolores Makins' various greens seemed attractive, her toothy smile charming, the amplitude of her person took on Junoesque power and grace.

The magical effects went further. He saw the crowds now as simple people with voices no longer vulgar but tuned to some celestial rhythm that made them fall dulcetly on the ear. Around the Moorish figures about to strike the hour at the top of the clock tower little people scurried, insects all. He viewed the insects with benevolence.

'Why, you're smiling,' Juno cried. 'You look quite different when you smile.' She flung her arms wide. 'I could sit here for ever watching life go by.'

The Moors struck the clock, the ants scurried about ever more eagerly. It came upon him that it was time to go. He rose, gave some of the flimsy notes with large numbers written on them to the waiter, waved away change, took Juno's arm. Did he call her Dolores? Perhaps he did. When she asked where they were going he replied instantly: 'Harry's Bar.'

'Isn't that terribly expensive?'

'Live it up in Harry's Bar, that was Dicky Bird's advice. Dicky Bird the villain, the forger. But he did not steal my papers.'

'I think we should go back to the hotel.'

'Not at all.'

Harry's Bar was always crowded, but on this evening the mass of people seemed impermeable. Waiters struggled in the press, men sweating in T-shirts shoved and swayed, bare-armed and bare-shouldered women shrieked as if under torture. He could see nothing of Juno except her green butterflies turning this way and that, but the need for escape became suddenly urgent. Ignoring whatever might be her plight he used elbows and fists, shoving at the soft bodies until they seemed momentarily to part, and he was suddenly ejected to the pavement. He leaned against the wall beside the Calle Vallaresso gasping for breath. In front of him was the San Marco vaporetto station, beside it a water taxi and gondola rank.

He no longer saw things clearly. They had turned mysteriously hazy, as if a slight mist lay between him and the world. Through this mist the landing stage wavered slightly, but that was natural enough because the stage was on the lagoon. On the landing stage stood a square-headed man who seemed familiar, with some boxes beside him that he seemed to recognise. Where had he seen them? He moved in that direction, and found his arm clutched. It was Juno. He turned to her and said 'Sibbles.'

'Come away, you'll be in the water.'

Sibbles showed no sign of recognition. He picked up one of the boxes, gave it to a man waiting in a water taxi. The man looked up as he took the box. It was Colin's friend Chuck.

'Come *away*, Jason.' He was perfectly clear-headed, but recognised that there must be something erratic in his judgement of distance, for it was true that he was now within a couple of feet of the lagoon. As he stood there, with the landing stage swaying uneasily beneath his feet (or was he swaying?) Sibbles jumped into the boat, and it moved away in a swirl of foam.

The hand on his arm tugged again, and he suffered himself to be led away, even to return to the Pacifico, insisting only that they should go back in a gondola, not on the vaporetto. He recalled nothing of the journey back up the Grand Canal except Juno's face opposite him in the gondola, at once excited and alarmed. At the reception desk she asked for his key, saying that he felt unwell. Then in the lift another transformation occurred. Before his eyes voluptuous Juno, seductive in various greens, changed back into Miss Makins the bank clerk, a person acceptably anonymous on the other side of the counter. But what extraordinary train of events had led to their sharing a gondola, and now a lift? He looked at her with horror as they reached his bedroom door. Was she proposing to come in?

'Can you manage the key, Jason?'

'Perfectly, thank you.' He was pleased with the reply, cool yet polite. She moved away reluctantly, and he stood waiting until, hazy as everything else, she vanished at the end of a corridor. Then, with a little trouble, he let himself in. The room wavered. It was with pride that he remembered Morvelli's party. He looked at his watch, but could not clearly distinguish what it said. Had Derek said something about collecting him? In any event there was time for a nap. He removed his shoes, put the trees into them, hung up his jacket. Then he lay down on the bed, and within seconds was asleep.

5

The train at Santa Lucia station was the one that had brought PC travellers to Venice on the preceding day, but those now returning had been lying in the sun at the Lido, playing golf at Alberoni, riding at Ca' Bianca, or immersing themselves in the lagoon's tepid water rather than in the deep culture bath of the city, so that they now looked bronzed and fit, ready to face the English summer. Sibbles supervised the loading into his miniature guard's van of the metal boxes containing four-course dinners, in which the main course was either turkey or a dish of beef in red wine called *stracotto*. The three boxes from the water taxi stood in a corner of the van, along with some of the sports equipment and presents that passengers had not been able to take into sleepers and couchettes. When the boxes had been loaded he went down the train taking orders. Chuck Waterton was in one of the first class sleepers, his door open on to the corridor, a cigar in his mouth, his fellow traveller a young accountant from Bromley.

'The turkey or the *stracotto*, gentlemen? That's beef, Italian style.'

They both ordered the beef, and agreed to share a bottle of Bardolino. Waterton asked what time they were due at the Swiss frontier.

'Around midnight, sir, but you won't be disturbed. Anything else I can do for you?'

'Not a thing.'

'I'll be round later to make up the beds.'

Waterton closed one eye in a wink.

There was another traveller in the same *wagon-lit*, one who like Waterton had not been with the PC party going out. This was a cheerful little man with a clown's face, who was inclined to be chatty. He told Sibbles that he worked for a computer firm in Turin, had been on holiday in Venice, and was now going to a conference in London. 'Another holiday really,' he said. 'Life's a holiday to me.' Sibbles did not comment on this, but asked if he would have the turkey or the *stracotto*. He chose the turkey.

6

Morvelli's apartment was on the ground floor of a tall house in the ghetto. The ghetto is rarely looked at by tourists, and indeed there is not much to see except the tallest buildings in the city, although at one time it was truly a ghetto with gates that closed at night to shut in not only Jews but all foreigners. If you take a vaporetto going down the Canareggio canal, get off at Ponte Guglio and turn left off the busy Rio Terra San Leonardo where many Venetians shop, you will find yourself in the Ghetto Nuovo, which is actually the old ghetto, or in the more recent Ghetto Vecchio. You can also reach the ghetto a little less directly from the San Marcuola stop on the Grand Canal. The ghetto houses have no special architectural distinction, but they date back to the sixteenth century, the rooms are large, and the ghetto is now a fashionable place to live.

There were forty people at the party, in a large drawing room with a mosaic floor and a painted ceiling showing the labours of Hercules. Double doors had been opened into a smaller room prepared for dancing. One end of the room looked on to a little canal, and french windows at the other opened on to a patio with white metal seats and twisted iron statuary.

Morvelli wore a tight-fitting blue suit, and a wide tie in dazzling stripes. He was talking to Porson when Derek arrived. Then he stood between them, an arm round each of their shoulders.

'The three musketeers, isn't it so?' A flash went off. 'You know my lovely Elsa, the light of my life.'

Elsa was sharp featured, dark skinned, with short black hair. 'He talks like that always, it means nothing, I'm his third wife.' She said to Derek, 'I know Charles, but we haven't met.'

'That's right. I'm the other partner.'

'I have heard a lot about you. Where's your wife?'

'At home, looking after house and son.'

'She doesn't keep you on a leash? She should.' Her look was frankly appraising.

Gerda said 'Derek darling', and kissed him. She was wearing a white and gold lamé dress. 'Your meeting went on a long, long time. I've been walking round the city getting fearfully bored, one old building is the same as another to me. I feel like dancing, I love this schmaltzy music.'

'What is schmaltzy?' Morvelli asked. 'I hope it is nice.'

Derek said 'Very nice. Melts in the mouth like the best chocolate.'

'Enjoy yourselves, it is my dearest wish. You have not brought your friend Jason.'

'I knocked on his door, but got no reply. I hope he'll turn up.'

'I thought him charming, but one of those who remain on the sidelines of life, isn't it so? A little detached, a little . . . ' He made a wave of the hand serve as a substitute for words.

'Guido, you should have been a psychologist.'

'There is Mario.' He moved away.

Elsa asked, 'Did you have a lot of trouble at your meeting?'

'No more than we expected.'

'And you reached agreement?' He nodded. 'You don't give away many secrets.'

'Only to my wife. It should be Guido who tells you secrets.'

'He tells me nothing, just says always not to worry. But why shouldn't I worry? He has lost millions of lire at the casino in the last six months, you know that? First roulette, now baccarat. When we married he was supposed to give it up, but I was a fool to think he would. You know what he says are the greatest pleasures in life?'

'The quotation from Talleyrand? He used it at lunch. In fact I'd heard him use it before.'

'You don't think much of him, do you?'

'Guido is the best salesman I've ever met, whether it's at a conference or one to one.'

'I'll tell you something. When we bought this apartment there were stone flags on the floor, some of them cracked, but at least four hundred years old. Guido had them taken up and that mosaic laid. He likes everything to be shiny, expensive, new.' Derek said nothing. 'I love him, that's the trouble.' She laughed, tapped him on the arm, left him.

He danced with Gerda. Concealed lighting shone on niches in the walls containing enormous animals in Venetian glass, ruby bears, golden wolves, multi-coloured elephants. She asked whether he or Sandy had had any more letters.

'No. Have you had one?'

125

She shook her head. 'Do you think Charles might have sent them?'

'What put that idea into your head?'

'You don't know what he's like.'

'I'm sure it wasn't Charles. I can make a guess at who it might have been.' When she asked him to explain he refused, saying it was only a guess. He became aware of Porson standing between the rooms watching them. Then Morvelli came up to introduce another man, and his partner turned away.

'This is Mario Salvemini, absolutely the greatest expert in the country on every kind of gun,' Morvelli said. 'He is consulted by everybody from the police to the Red Brigades.'

'I don't find that amusing,' Salvemini said. He was a small man with a pompadour of perfectly white hair and a neat white beard.

'Forgive me, Mario, all my jokes are bad, I must give up joking. Mario my friend, this is Charles Porson my partner, who has a passion for firearms.'

'I don't know about a passion. I collect hand guns. And I was nearly killed by one the other day.'

'Nearly killed!' Salvemini echoed in astonishment.

'Perhaps an accident, I don't know. Next time I shall be ready.' He reached into his jacket and the toy revolver lay in his palm, gleaming blue and gold.

Salvemini bent to look at it. 'The Beretta 90. The ladies' revolver, they call it, very suitable for the handbag. I have not seen one before with this gold plating.'

'It will handle gentlemen as well as ladies. My rule in life is tit for tat, and I apply it to everything.' He was looking at his wife dancing with Derek in the other room.

'Tit is slang for breast,' Morvelli said. 'But I do not understand tat.'

'You permit?' Salvemini picked up the little revolver. 'I have never seen one that is prettier. This tit for tat, I think it means an eye for an eye, isn't that so?'

'You see?' Morvelli was delighted. 'I have invited tonight only

126

those able to converse in English, Charles, don't you congratulate me? Although to tell the truth it was Elsa's notion. Jolly good, don't you think?'

Porson slapped him on the shoulder. 'Jolly good, Guido. You're a fine fellow. And tit for tat, an eye for an eye, Signor Salvemini's got it.'

Morvelli beamed. He loved praise. He left the two men discussing something called the Spandau Luger. Apparently only a hundred had ever been made, and Salvemini owned one of them.

A little before nine o'clock the last guest arrived. Derek, who was standing on the balcony talking to Elsa and an Italian journalist, saw him step out of a smart little motor boat painted blue and white, which said Polizia on its side. That was, Elsa told him, Commissario Francesco Farinella of the Squadri Mobili. 'But Francesco comes as a guest, not on business.'

The detective was fleshy and urbane, with an almost permanent slight smile. He wore two large rings, a single diamond gleaming in one, a ruby in the other. He told Derek that when he had visited England with his wife five years ago Guido had arranged it all, and everything had been perfect.

'So you can understand I have the highest opinion of your firm. And of your country. England is a place where everybody is polite, people say please and thank you, and wait their turn in queues. Italy is not like that.' Derek said he had found Venetians polite. 'Venetians, yes, commercial but polite. In Venice, you know, we have little serious crime, but alas Venice is not Italy. Ah, there is Mario, who has a whole arsenal of weapons none of which is ever fired in anger. A true Venetian, concerned with commerce and not war.' They embraced, and Salvemini said something about Signor Crowley's English partner, who was carrying a revolver.

'He fears attack? Here in Venice?'

'I think he may have brought the revolver tonight to impress Signor Salvemini.' Derek explained about the incident at the rehearsal. Farinella smiled, and said that he must meet Signor

Porson and assure him that in Venice he had less need for concern than on the English stage.

Signor Porson, however, was not to be met. One of the waiters thought he had seen somebody resembling Signor Porson go out of the door just before the Commissario's arrival. Perhaps he had found the heat of the drawing room too much for him, and gone for a stroll. In the meantime supper was served.

It was almost ten o'clock when Morvelli took Derek aside, and told him that Charles Porson had not come back.

'I have spoken to Gerda. She says he had no appointment. Surely nothing can have angered him? About the agreement we signed this afternoon, I mean.'

'He was happy enough when he signed it.'

'And you have said nothing since then that might – eh?'

'Of course not.'

'Is he perhaps what you call on the razzle?'

Derek's smile had its usual confidence. 'I doubt it. I'll go out and look around. If Charles did step out for a few minutes he may be lost.'

'My friend, it is possible that you also may be lost.'

'You know my infallible rule for getting back to base in strange cities? Keep turning left. Marvellous how it works. I'll be back in twenty minutes. If he hasn't turned up I'll call our hotel. He may have felt unwell, and gone back.'

'Be careful. Venice is the most lovely but the most deceitful of cities.'

'Talleyrand?'

'Morvelli.'

When Derek returned just thirty minutes later by the clock, he said ruefully that Morvelli was perfectly correct about the deceitfulness of Venice. He had lost himself, and not found his partner. He telephoned the Pacifico, but the reception clerk said that Signor Porson had not asked for his key.

Gerda had been dancing with Farinella. She said impatiently, 'I've told Guido he said nothing to me, but there's nothing surprising about that. Charles does what he wants.'

'And leaves his beautiful wife alone among strangers?'

Farinella said. 'That is ungallant.'

'That's Charles. Besides, they're not all strangers. Derek is a friend.'

'Of course. It is your husband who was carrying the revolver in case he was attacked?' He looked from one to the other of them, smiling.

Derek said, 'We're getting this out of proportion. Charles must have had an appointment, and didn't tell us about it. He'll be back.'

The Commissario clapped his hands gently. 'That is the English calm, what you call phlegm.'

'Nice of you to say so. I don't know that I've heard anybody use the word before.'

'But it is a true English word? Then I am delighted to have used it.'

Just before eleven people began to leave. Derek told Gerda not to worry, and she said that she was not in the least worried, although he saw her looking at her watch.

Elsa said to Derek, 'Did you think it was a good party?'

'Very good. I enjoyed myself.'

'It cost a lot of money. Can that be charged to PC Travel?'

'I must have notice of that question.'

'I do not understand.'

'Sorry. It's the reply ministers make in Parliament when they want to avoid a straight answer. I suppose the answer's no, Charles wouldn't agree. But don't worry, Guido will be all right.'

'Do you have a special arrangement with Guido?' He smiled, but did not reply. 'Charles Porson has a special arrangement also, you know that? Guido is perhaps making trouble for himself. Or perhaps – do you think? – he is making trouble for you?' Derek did not comment on that either.

It was nearly eleven-thirty when one of the waiters spoke to Morvelli, who spoke to Farinella, who went out. When he returned he was wearing black gloves.

'That means there is trouble,' Elsa said. 'Francesco does not like to get his hands dirty.'

Morvelli and Farinella came over. Morvelli's face had the

strained expression often assumed by cheerful people when they hear bad news. It was the Commissario who spoke to Derek.

'My assistant Vincente Gardo has telephoned. A body has been taken out of the water near the Fenice Theatre. There is a possibility that it is your friend. Guido will come with me to make identification if it is needed. I think you should take the signora back to the hotel.'

Gerda, however, was uncompliant. 'If you think I'm happy to sit in a hotel room waiting for a telephone call, you're wrong. I shall come with you.'

They all went in the blue and white motor boat, speeding down the Grand Canal, under the Rialto Bridge, then turning off and threading through the network of waterways. In not much more than five minutes they had slackened speed. 'Teatro la Fenice,' Morvelli said. 'Why should Charles have come down here?' They turned left into a little canal, left again into an area dark except for a single street light. A voice hailed them, torches were waved. They drew to the side near to another police boat, and got out.

In his teens Derek had once been hiking alone on the Yorkshire moors, and had lost his way. Ever since then the glimmer of an unexpected light in darkness, like the light seen long ago after hours of wandering, had affected him powerfully. The street lantern threw only a faint glimmer on the scene. More light came from lamps on the ground that made a hissing noise. They illuminated a group of people standing round something covered with a tarpaulin. Arms were waved, a lot of what seemed argumentative talking went on, much of it coming from a slight figure wearing a raincoat. Derek asked Morvelli what they were saying.

'It is about the circumstances in which the body was found. A young man and his girl were here – this little fondamenta leads nowhere, you would come here only to make love – and the girl saw something in the water. They telephoned the *questura*.'

'So what is the argument?'

'It is whether the body went into the water here or somewhere else, so that it drifted here. It is a matter of the tides, and how long he has been in the water. They await the doctor.'

'I thought I heard "*dottore*".'

'That means nothing, every professional man is a *dottore*, teacher, accountant, policeman. I meant the police doctor.'

Gerda said in a high voice, 'Why the hell don't they lift that cover and let us see who it is? I'm getting cold.'

Farinella had his back to her, but now he turned round. 'Signora, are you prepared to look? If you would prefer that Guido . . . '

'It's what I'm here for. I'll look.'

The Commissario bent over the body. Somebody shone one of the hissing lights. Morvelli and Derek bent forward also. The light showed Porson's face, puffier than usual but perfectly recognisable. Gerda exhaled with a sigh. She said, 'Yes.'

'You identify the body as your husband?'

'Yes.'

Now the light was held so that it illuminated her face, white and strained. It shone also on Farinella, who was looking at her with curiosity. 'It is the English calm again, so admirable. An Italian must have shown emotion.'

'I am German, not English.'

He turned back to the rest of the group, and discussion continued. Morvelli said, 'Now they know it is Charles, Francesco is telling them the body must have entered the water here, or somewhere very near, because of the time. He has been absent too short a time to have drifted far.'

'They'd have saved some argument if they'd let us see the body at once.'

'They like to wait for the doctor. Here he is.'

A third boat with blue and white markings drew up, two men jumped out. There was hand shaking, excited conversation, then one of the men went over to the body, the cover was removed again, he knelt beside it. Farinella turned quickly when Gerda said, 'I should like to go home now.'

'A thousand apologies. We shall need to speak again tomorrow, but tonight – of course I understand the shock you have suffered.' The gloved hand waved. 'You shall be taken instantly to your hotel, but you will please make yourselves available at ten o'clock tomorrow morning. Thank you. For me it will be, as the phrase is, a hard day's night.' A pause. 'Another body has been found, also of an Englishman, in the Emperor Napoleon hotel. I am told it may possibly be a case of suicide. There was a revolver beside him, a Beretta. I think you said Mr Porson carried a Beretta. It is not on his body. The gentleman at the Emperor Napoleon was registered as Richard Linnet.'

Derek was standing close to Gerda. She did not speak but he felt her body shudder and stiffen, like that of one who has suffered an electric shock.

7

The train made a long halt at the Swiss border. Customs men came on board but the travellers were not disturbed. The little clown-faced man had gone to the lavatory, and put his head in Sibbles' van in an unsuccessful search for aspirin. The stewards had collected all the passengers' passports and travel documents, and these were cursorily checked. Sibbles showed the young Swiss customs officer the heterogeneous collection of things in his little van. The three boxes he had brought into the train were no longer to be seen. The customs officer shook his head as he saw the golf clubs, tennis racquets, underwater equipment.

'Sometimes I think the English who travel are mad.'

'Plumb loco,' Sibbles said. 'That's what we call it.'

'The English are plumb loco. Very good, I shall remember it.'

Whistles blew, they started again. It was, Sibbles thought, a piece of cake.

8

'One am,' Grado said. 'And I didn't get to sleep until four this morning. Indigestion, acute indigestion. Mussels.'

132

'You should not eat them.'

Grado sighed. He knew himself to be more intelligent than Farinella, so why was he merely an assistant, not a Commissario? The rank of Commissario in the PS or Pubblica Sicurezza cannot be reached without taking examinations. He had been too lazy to take them when he was young, and now it was too late. Grado's view of life was partly ordered by his gastric ulcer. He was thin and yellow, his expression sad.

The were in a bedroom at the Emperor Napoleon. Dottor Tardelli had just left, after certifying that the dead man had been killed by a single shot through the heart. The gold-plated Beretta was in his right hand. Had he killed himself? Tardelli had been maddeningly inconclusive.

'It is possible.'

'But not likely?' Farinella had asked.

'Not many shoot themselves through the heart. They prefer the temple, regard it as more certain. But of course it is a matter of choice, some do one and some the other, one cannot be dogmatic. The shot was fired from close to, not across the room, I can tell you that.'

'Thanks for nothing, we saw the scorchmarks,' Grado had muttered. Tardelli had not heard or had affected not to hear

The time of death? Again the doctor was not prepared to be precise. Not less than an hour, not more than three, which meant between nine-thirty and eleven-thirty. Might something more be learned after a post-mortem? Perhaps, they would see. After reminding them that he had another post-mortem to do on the other Englishman, and that tomorrow was Sunday, Tardelli had left them to it. The photographers had been and gone, the fingerprint boys had said that only the dead man's prints were on the revolver, there was no sign of a struggle. The contents of the man's pockets and wallet lay on a writing table. They included his passport, which said that he was Richard Edward Linnet, forty-eight years old, a company director. There were credit cards, a set of keys, a hundred pounds in lire and sterling. The set of keys opened a case and briefcase that contained nothing more than clothes and magazines.

Farinella sat in the room's single armchair. He had put away the black gloves, revealing the beautifully kept hands of which he was proud. Grado sat on the bed.

'The other man who died had one of these.' Farinella picked up the tiny Beretta. 'And it was not with him. It cannot be a coincidence.'

'Why not? Berettas are fashionable, small and handy.'

'This one is unusual. Salvemini was at the party, saw Porson's revolver.'

'We can speak to him tomorrow.'

'Why not now? Ask them to find his number, call him.'

Grado sighed, but did what he was told. One of his virtues in Farinella's eyes was that although he often complained, he always did what he was told.

'Blue with gold plating, very unusual, almost unique,' Farinella said when he had put down the telephone after making elaborate apologies for disturbing Salvemini at such an hour. 'And Porson had it at the party. So the two men must have met.'

Bravo, Grado thought but did not say, you are a master at stating the obvious. He rolled gum around his mouth, saw the Commissario's frown, and said, 'It eases the pain.'

'A disgusting American habit. We must find out if anybody saw Porson in the hotel.'

'Many of the staff have gone off duty. It will be better to leave it until the morning. Porson won't mind. Nor will Linnet.' He gave the congealed cough that was his nearest approach to a laugh. Farinella looked at him. Grado went downstairs.

He returned with a swarthy man wearing a uniform that made him look like a high-ranking officer in the Ruritanian army. There were bands of gold braid on his sleeve, gold frogs on the front of his jacket, gold epaulettes on his shoulders.

'Roberto,' Grado said. 'Not a general. Night porter.'

'He saw Porson come here?'

Grado shook his head. 'Nothing about Porson. Linnet and a woman. Tell it the way you did to me.' The porter looked uneasy. 'Come on, General, you've got nothing to worry about, we're not concerned with morals. You knew Linnet, he'd been here before.'

'That is right. Perhaps two or three times in the last twelve months. He stayed always only a night.'

'And he wanted feminine company, asked you to provide it.' Roberto nodded.

'Prostitutes?' Farinella said with distaste. It was his view that there was no prostitution in Venice. Grado chewed more vigorously, his thin cheeks seeming to grow thinner.

'Girls from Mestre. Other hotels do it, a few. The beauties of our city make visitors randy. I told Roberto there would be no morals charge, okay?' Farinella nodded reluctantly. 'Tonight – you tell it, Roberto, I'm tired.' He closed his eyes. His jaws continued to move.

The porter had a hoarse, thick voice. 'Mr Linnet came downstairs, about eight o'clock. He was smiling to himself, always very friendly Mr Linnet, and he asked if I could fix him up for around an hour's time, he'd be in the bar. It was Bettina, fixed for around nine forty-five. He'd asked for Bettina, liked her. She arrives on the dot, says hallo to me, goes up to his room. There's one thing, though, Bettina's not on the game, she's a housewife. Her husband is an engineer on night shift at a factory in Mestre.'

Grado opened his eyes, looked at Farinella, closed them again. 'Tell us about her leaving.'

'Yes, well. I don't know what happened, mostly they stay a couple of hours, never less than an hour . . . '

'Do any stay all night?' the Commissario asked.

Roberto looked shocked. 'Certainly not, Commissario, the management would never allow it. But Bettina was back in half an hour. I asked her if something was wrong and she said no, he just didn't want her any longer.'

'Did she seem upset, frightened?'

'Pleased if anything.'

Grado said, 'As if she'd got full pay for half time?'

The porter nodded enthusiastically. 'Right, Dottore, that's just the way she seemed.'

'So he was alive at ten-fifteen, perhaps later,' Farinella said when the porter had gone. 'But why did he send her away? We need to talk to her.'

'Tomorrow?' Grado said hopefully.

'Tomorrow her husband will be at home, and she may not talk. Tonight.'

'We have her number from Roberto.' He stretched a hand towards the telephone. Farinella shook his head.

Mestre, which joins Venice to the mainland by a road and rail bridge, has been called the unacceptable face of Venice, or less politely its dirty backside. Behind its blocks of factories and warehouses are almost identical streets of small houses. Bettina, whose other name was Parenti, lived in one of them. On the way to Mestre Farinella complained of the low moral standards of visitors who spent all day visiting churches, and then wanted prostitutes at night.

'You heard Roberto, she's a housewife making a bit on the side. And who said Linnet went inside any churches?'

When they rang the bell that said 'Parenti' a blind on the first floor went up, a window opened, a voice asked what they wanted. Grado said, without shouting it, 'Squadra Mobili.'

Five minutes later they sat opposite Bettina in an untidy living room, with the dirty plates of an evening meal still on the table. She was untidy too, a redhead whose skin and hair had both seen better days. She expressed indignation.

'That pimp Roberto, do you know his cut for picking up the telephone? Twenty per cent.' She said to Grado, 'Why are you chewing like a cow? Do you want a glass of grappa?'

He shuddered. Farinella said, 'We are not here on a social visit, and we are not interested in your private arrangements, only in the man you saw tonight.'

She poured a glass for herself, drank half of it, sighed. 'Little dicky bird? You know that's what his name means in English? Nothing wrong with him, he knows how to treat a woman.'

'You saw him tonight, but you left after half an hour. Why?'

'He had somebody coming, but he paid up like a gentleman. What's he done?'

'Nothing. Tell us what happened.'

She told him. She had seen Linnet before, knew the kind of

thing he liked. They had been together for half an hour when the telephone rang. He spoke, arranged to see the caller, then told her that she'd have to go, they would meet again next time he was in Venice. He had paid her, she had left. 'There'd be some who'd have said half time, half pay. Dicky bird's a gentleman.'

'Did he speak in English on the telephone? He did? And you understand it? What were the words?'

'There were not many words, and yes, I know a little English. He said "Hallo," then listened, said "Yes" a couple of times, and something about being pleased and surprised. Then he laughed, and said, "Of course I'll see you, delighted." And that's all.'

'Could you hear the other voice, to tell whether it was a man or woman?' She said no. 'What about the way he spoke? Men talk differently very often, when they speak to a woman.'

'Not to me they don't.' She drank the rest of the grappa. 'I wasn't paying much attention, why should I? He didn't say "My darling sweetheart" or "Mr so and so," I can tell you that. Now I've been a good girl, answered all your questions, haven't said a word about you coming here in the middle of the night, you just tell me what he's *done*, is he in trouble?'

'Not any more. He's dead. He was shot, or shot himself, soon after you left him.'

'Christ save us.' She crossed herself.

'So it's important to know whether he seemed cheerful, and I take it he was.' She merely looked at the Commissario. 'And you can see why the call was important. But you can remember nothing more about it?'

She shook her head. 'I had nothing to do with it.'

'We never thought you did,' Grado said. 'You're just an unlucky housewife.' When they had left her, he said, 'So Porson did come to see Linnet.'

'Perhaps. It might have been anybody. I have told you already, there is a tale that somebody was perhaps trying to kill Porson. That must be investigated.'

'Tomorrow.'

'Yes, tomorrow.'

9

For a short time early on Sunday mornings Venice is marvellously still. People have disappeared even from the busiest streets, only a few vaporettos ply up and down the Grand Canal, the gondoliers know it is too early to look for business. By midday, especially in summer, the streets have filled up again, but at this hour, just before ten o'clock on Sunday morning, Derek as he stood at the window of Jason's room, looked almost at the Venice seen by Henry James and Baron Corvo.

'I knocked on the door last night, but you must have been flat out. You really are tying them on, twice in a week.' Jason was getting dressed. He did not attempt a verbal denial, but feebly shook his head. 'I know, I know, you say the first time was arsenic or strychnine, a little introductory dose no doubt.'

'Derek, please don't make jokes.'

'I'm sorry. I mean, I'm sorry about what happened to you yesterday. What a bastard that man Cruddle must be. Here, let me.' Jason's hands were trembling so much that he was unable to put together the ends of his bow tie. Derek did it for him. His expression was serious, even grave. 'You're sure you've taken in all I was telling you about what happened last night? Good. The fuzz will be here soon, and they'll want to talk to you. You travelled in the same compartment as Linnet, they'll want to know what was said. You're sure you wouldn't like some breakfast?'

'I couldn't eat a crumb. And I can't possibly talk to policemen, I have nothing to tell them. Oh, Derek, I have never been so miserable in my life. It was my life's work, I would have done it well, and now it has all gone. To an *American*, and so *young*.'

'I said I understand. I don't feel very cheerful myself. I shall ring Sandy as soon as I'm through with the cops, and break the news to her. She ended up hating Linnet, and didn't much like Porson, but I suppose hearing your ex-husband has died must come as a bit of a shock. I don't see that there's any need for you to say Linnet was married to Sandy, it will just complicate things and lead to all sorts of boring questions. Agreed?'

'Derek, at the moment I just can't *think*.'

Derek had returned to the window, and saw the blue and white Polizia boat draw up. 'Then let me think for you. Tell no lies but say as little as possible is my advice. Now they're here. Let's go down and face the music.'

10

'My sincerest condolences on your tragic loss.' Farinella had decided to talk to those involved at their hotel rather than have them brought to the Questura, and for this purpose had commandeered the manager's office. He sat behind the desk.

'Thank you.' Gerda wore a white dress with a touch of black at neck and shoulders. He thought her not beautiful but immensely attractive, like a piece of delicious cream cake. She seemed composed. 'Do you know what happened to my husband? Was he drunk perhaps, and fell into the water?'

'We are not yet sure. After the post-mortem we shall know more.'

'There are things I must tell you, Inspector. Inspector, is that correct?'

'Commissario. But it does not matter.'

'First of all, at home in England at Headfield, there have been anonymous letters sent to our friends. They say that Derek Crowley, my husband's partner, and I are lovers. Also, it is possible that an attempt was made to kill my husband.' She described the incident at the play rehearsal.

'I must ask you, do the letters tell the truth?'

'There is no truth in them at all.'

'And you have no idea who sent them?'

'There are malicious people everywhere. I am German, some do not like that. And some people did not like Charles, he could be very rude. There is another thing I must say. Charles did not trust Derek as a partner, he thought he was trying to gain control of their business. I think Charles had made an arrangement with Guido Morvelli to stop it. He did not talk about such things to me, but I know he was angry with Derek.'

'Are you suggesting that might have been a reason for your husband's death?'

'I do not suggest anything. I wish only you should have the information.'

'I noticed that you seemed surprised, even shocked, when I told you of Mr Linnet's death. Why was that? Did you know him?'

'I did not know him. You were mistaken.' But I know I was not mistaken, Farinella thought, noticing that at times of stress she sounded more Germanic.

'Did your husband know Richard Linnet?'

'Not so far as I am aware.'

'I ask again, why did you look shocked?'

'And I say again, you are mistaken.'

'You are very cool, Signora, I think not only because you are German. Did you love your husband?'

'I was working in a Hamburg night club when we met. I tell people it was a travel agency and I was a courier, but that is not true. I was pleased to leave the club, but I did not love him. He was not a man to be loved.'

'And he knew your feelings?'

'He knew, and they amused him. Sometimes he called me his German whore. It was a kind of attraction for him to think that, even though it was not true. And he had many other women, I know that.'

'But still you stayed with him. And you had no affair with Signor Crowley.'

'Nor with anybody else. I did not love my husband, Commissario, but I loved his money. And besides . . . ' She hesitated, then went on, ' . . . if I had an affair and he had discovered it, in some way he would have revenged himself. He was a vengeful man.'

She might look like a piece of cream cake, Farinella thought, but a man could break a tooth on her.

140

11

Grado had been interviewing Morvelli at his ghetto apartment while Farinella was talking to Gerda, but he had returned by the time Derek was being questioned. They discussed the anonymous letters, and like Gerda he said the accusations were baseless. Then Grado put some notes in front of the Commissario. This morning Grado was sucking peppermints instead of chewing gum, and Farinella recoiled at the smell.

'Mr Porson was the senior partner in your firm. Were you on good terms?'

Derek shrugged, something he did elegantly. 'As good as most partners in small firms.'

'Were you trying to gain control of the firm?'

'We didn't always agree about policy. He was reluctant to expand our operations.'

'Did he propose to allow Signor Morvelli to buy shares, so that you might be outvoted if he thought that advisable? Was it to sign an agreement about Signor Morvelli's purchase of shares that you made this visit to Venice?'

'Ah, ah, Guido's been talking.' Derek gave Farinella one of his boyish smiles.

'Was that the object of the trip?'

'It was Charles's purpose, yes. It wouldn't have worked out as he expected.'

Farinella nodded to Grado, whose voice creaked like an unoiled door.

'That is what happened yesterday afternoon? You had the meeting, Morvelli was allotted shares, there was discussion about the price, you pushed the price up, then all was finally agreed and a document signed. Correct?'

Derek awarded Grado one of the smiles. 'Correct.'

'So Porson had blocked any chance of your gaining control?'

'No.' Derek turned his attention back to Farinella. Jason, had he been present, would have recognised that Derek was in a one-man-of-the-world-to-another role. 'Guido is always short of money. I made an advance arrangement with him by which I would buy his shares at double the amount he gave for them. I argued about the price and pushed it up, to help Guido get a better figure. Besides, I knew if I agreed too easily Charles might have become suspicious. He was a suspicious man. In fact, the effect is quite opposite to what Charles intended. When I buy Guido's shares they give me control of the company.'

Both of the detectives stared at him. Derek looked from one to the other with the air of a conjurer who has pulled off a particularly clever trick. Farinella waved his ringed hands. 'This arrangement seemed to you entirely honourable?'

'It happens every day in business.' Farinella nodded to Grado, who got up and went out. 'I have a flight booked to return to England today. I hope that will raise no problems? There are things to be dealt with at home in Headfield.'

'I shall be pleased if you will stay.'

'What does that mean?'

Farinella spread out his hands. 'I wish to speak to everybody concerned. And you will surely wish to stay until we know the result of the post-mortem on your partner. No doubt you would like to know exactly what happened, just as we would.'

'This will not affect the PC tour, I hope. The tour is being handled by my cousin Colin Crowley, and our tourists know nothing about this affair. Will you need to question them?'

'I should like to talk to your cousin, if he knew Mr Porson, but I see no reason why those on your touring party should be involved. That is, I see no reason at present.'

They sat in silence until Grado returned. He whispered to the Commissario.

'I must tell you that Signor Morvelli denies that he has an agreement with you of the kind you mentioned.' Derek looked at him unbelievingly. 'He says there were discussions with you, but no documents. Do you have documents?'

Farinella, watching the Englishman, thought him genuinely surprised, even shocked. He did not speak at all for a few moments. Then he said, 'There are no documents covering my private arrangement with Guido. The agreement was verbal.'

'And now it doesn't exist,' Grado said. 'The kind of thing that happens every day in business.'

'Guido doesn't deny that we talked about it?'

Derek spoke almost mechanically. Either you are truly shocked, Farinella thought, or you act as naturally as an Italian. He left it to Grado to reply.

'He acknowledges that. And he knows what you wanted from such an agreement. He says, however, that he would have asked much more than twice the amount he was to pay for the shares, before selling them to you.' Grado put another peppermint in his mouth. 'No doubt that also is business.'

'Of course that will now not be necessary,' Farinella said.

Derek's golden curls gleamed with moisture. He wiped his forehead. 'What do you mean?'

'Your partner is dead. Presumably the shares will pass to his widow. Possibly she will sell you his shares. Possibly you knew that.'

'What you are suggesting is ridiculous.'

'Is it? You left the party last night. Where did you go?'

'I was looking for Charles. I wandered around, lost my way, eventually got to the Ponto Guglio vaporetto station, found my way back.'

'You were away for thirty minutes according to the man at the door.'

'I told you, I lost my way.'

Grado made a sound which might have expressed disbelief, or might have been a stomach rumble. Farinella did not lose his faint smile.

'One further matter. As you know, a man named Linnet died last night. He was shot by a revolver, one that belonged to your partner . . . '

Derek stood up. His blue eyes sparkled, he looked indignant, but the Commissario wondered whether the indignation was as genuine as the shock of a minute or two before when he learned that Morvelli said they had no agreement. 'I object to the implication of this questioning. I refuse to say anything further.'

'About the dead man Linnet. Did you know him?'

'I never met him.'

143

12

The train reached Calais at three o'clock, a few minutes late. The PC Travel group gathered round the courier who would take them to the ferry. Chuck Waterton got off the train, and so did the little man with a clown's face. Sibbles helped lift out the metal food containers, loaded them on a trolley, and walked down the platform. Waterton was a few steps behind. As the steward turned to wheel the trolley towards the stores, two men stopped him. One said 'Sûreté Nationale' and showed a badge, the other pointed to the containers. Sibbles protested.

'These are what the meals come in, they're empty, what's it all about?'

The man who had said 'Sûreté Nationale' opened a container, revealed cassettes neatly stacked inside. Sibbles looked astonished. Chuck Waterton, turning to run, found his arm firmly locked in that of the man with the clown's face.

13

From Jason's journal.

Sunday night, and all's ill.

Today I underwent the first police interrogation of my life. It was quite endurable, not at all frightening, but in the end I fear I made the most appalling blunder, although it is not one for which I altogether blame myself.

The questioning took place in the hotel, which I suppose was better than being summoned to police headquarters. There were two policemen, one well-dressed, charming and civilised, his subordinate surly, unhealthy in appearance, sucking an odious-smelling sweet. Happily, almost all the questioning was done by Number One.

He began by asking whether I was with the touring party, a question in the circumstances so poignant that I almost broke down. He was so sympathetic that I poured out to him the details of the Quest that had gone over years, the appalling behaviour of D.M. Cruddle and the young American (although, as I think more about it I almost incline to absolve the egregious Dwight of everything except a coarse eagerness to make capital from a *literary property* – it is Cruddle all along who has played the role of Lucifer, tempting me, leading me on to all sorts of expectations, then deliberately *spurning* me – oh, I must not go on with this). In any case I said something of what had happened to Civilised, told him of my total despair, my bout of drinking, my encounter with the ineffable Dolores, my collapse on to the hotel bed. He seemed to understand my feelings perfectly, and even said that he had heard of the strange English recluse who had once been a writer. I liked everything about him except his two vulgarly sparkling rings.

'So you did not attend Signor Morvelli's party?'

No, I said, my behaviour had been truly shameful, my apologies would be abject.

'I am sure he will not blame you. We Italians understand the emotions. You had "one over the eight", as I believe the saying goes, and then you remained in your room the whole evening.'

I said that had been so, that the first I knew of Porson's death was when Derek told me of it on the following morning, and that I had then felt so ill that I had at first hardly been able to take it in. Civilised nodded understandingly. 'I have been told of the unpleasant anonymous letters about Signor Crowley and Signora Porson. Did you receive one of them?'

I said that I had, and emphasised the absurdity of the accusations. Derek and Sandy were a devoted couple. I added that Derek was one of my oldest friends, we had been at school together. Civilised smiled encouragingly at me.

'But that is wonderful. He seems to me such an interesting personality, so lively, so attractive. Yet I sensed tension, impulsiveness, a rashness at times perhaps. Am I anywhere near the truth, or is this a hopeless misreading of his character?'

I complimented him on his perceptiveness, and told him something of our youth together, mentioning one or two of

Derek's early problems. It was not until I saw the Barbarian, the odious sweet eater, making notes, that I realised the possible inferences they might draw from what I was saying. I then stressed that all this was long ago, and that Derek was now a highly successful businessman. I told them something strange was going on at Headfield, and instanced the occasion when I had been poisoned, as well as the near-shooting at the play rehearsal. Civilised nodded, smiled, and then brought me back to Derek, asking whether I knew of any fresh arrangement planned at PC Travel. Nothing, I said, and confessed that my true interest was in art, not in business. He spread out his hands and said he wished devoutly that his own life had been spent in the pursuit of beauty rather than the unravelling of crime. Then he mentioned the death of Richard Linnet, and asked if by chance I had met the man.

Indeed, indeed I had, I said. I had shared a compartment with him on the train, and he was one of the most objectionable creatures I had ever been unlucky enough to encounter. Civilised expressed sympathy, and said that to be in close company with somebody one disliked throughout a night must have been truly painful. More than painful, I said, tedious as well, since he was a great talker. Had he said anything about his reasons for this visit? He had implied he was working for the Government, I replied, but I had not believed that for a moment. Then (here came my error) he had seen the PC Travel advertisement, and thought why not travel with the family firm . . . I stopped, appalled, and hoping that the phrase would pass unnoticed. Of course it did not. What did that mean? he asked.

'I am not sure. I suppose there was a connection, I didn't ask.'

His smile was a little sad. 'Mr Durling, we have been so friendly, we are *simpatico*, isn't it so? And now I do not think you are being frank.' I repeated that I didn't know. 'The family firm, let me see. Was he related to Mr Crowley perhaps? Or to his partner? No, I think it was your friend, or you would not be reluctant to speak of it.' He leaned across the desk. I disliked the rings and the manicured hands, but they seemed appropriate to his personality. 'I think it is something to your friend's discredit,

146

and you are too loyal to tell me.'

That worried me. I thought perhaps it was better to speak than to stay silent. I told him Linnet had been married to Derek's wife, but they had been divorced for years. Civilised sat back, and Barbarian spoke in a disagreeable voice.

'Crowley says he'd never met Linnet.'

'I'm sure that's true. When I told Derek he said they had never met. And something else. Linnet was a bad hat.'

They both stared at me. 'A bad *hat*?' Civilised said.

I told them what the phrase meant, and what Derek had said about Linnet. Civilised smiled, nodded. The Barbarian, looking as if he had never smiled in his life, growled: 'He tells us none of this, only that they never met. What else does Linnet say?'

I said I had refused to listen to anything more, and by way of proving that Linnet and Derek *had* never met, went on to tell of my encounter with Linnet in the bar by the Campo Manin. I mentioned also the arrival of the Japanese. They made me repeat what had been said, the Barbarian taking notes. Then Civilised expressed his thanks, and said that he would be grateful if I could stay in Venice for the moment.

I returned to my room, put my aching head in my hands. Bright lights flashed before my eyes. I closed them, and saw immediately that dismal living room, the Toby jugs and ornaments, the brash Dwight Eidelberg, the papers that in my agony I had flung away, depriving myself of my life's work. *My life's work* – an ironic phrase, for what had it been but a delusion?

A tap at the door. Derek, asking how things had gone. I told him of my error. For a moment he looked enigmatic, an actor brooding. Then the brooding look was replaced by the actor's smile.

'Not to worry.' (I forgive in him clichés that in any other mouth would make me shudder.) 'I daresay it's all for the best. They were bound to find out.'

'Have you spoken to Sandy?'

'Not yet, but I must call her. She's expecting me back this evening, and our polizia have suggested I should stay on a day or so. How did you find them?'

'The assistant is odious, a barbarian, but the Commissario –
"We are *simpatico*," he said, and that seemed true.'

'That's my Jason.'

14

The bell ringing, the receiver lifted, Sandy's voice.

'Hi, darling. I'm still in Venice.'

'In *Venice*. But I'm just cooking dinner. Duck with orange
sauce, green peas, don't tell me you won't be here to eat it.'

'Afraid I shan't. Listen, and don't interrupt.' He told her of
Porson's death, Linnet's death, Morvelli and the shares. He
never kept things from her. She did not waste time expressing
sympathy, but asked if he would like her to fly out.

'No, why should you? It will be cleared up in a couple of days,
must be.'

'Do the police know about the letters?'

'Yes, Gerda told them. I did too.'

'What do they think happened?'

'I couldn't tell you. One's oily, waves his hands about like a
salesman, the other chews gum or sucks peppermints. I'd say
they're just a couple of bewildered coppers.'

'How is Gerda?'

'Bearing up like a good German. She won't shed many tears for
Charles. Seemed more shaken about Linnet, oddly enough.
You'd not seen or heard of him recently, had you?'

'Not for ages. Sure you don't want me to fly out? I can make it
to Gatwick in an hour, you know.'

'Don't think of it, no point. Kiss kiss, darling.'

'Kiss.'

15

'The English are all liars,' Grado said. 'Men and women alike, they lie. It is best to have nothing to do with them.'

Farinella watched with distaste as his subordinate ate a thick salami sandwich. Soon, he knew, Grado would complain of stomach pains, and then chew gum or peppermints to relieve them. Tonight he would eat something like a *fritto misto* with fried polenta, and suffer pains again. The Commissario's own lunch had been cheese and fruit, tonight his wife would give him a piccata of veal or a grilled chop. What a piece of natural injustice it was that he should grow plumper each year, while Vincente's frame was so lean that clothes hung on him.

Their desks were by separate windows on the first floor of the *questura*, so that they could face each other and also look out on to the Fondamenta San Lorenzo. Not that there was much to see. A bridge led to the little Campo San Lorenzo and the dingy church of the same name. Here Bellini had painted a famous picture, the bridge crowded, people lining the fondamenta awaiting the performance of a miracle with eager expectation. Nobody could possibly say that the place painted by Bellini was recognisable today. Now it looked distinctly dingy, even the stucco on the *questura* building was mouldering. Peaceful enough, if peace was what you wanted, but Farinella craved for fame. One day a famous American film star would die mysteriously in Venice, the problem would baffle the police chiefs who came over from Los Angeles, then all that had seemed insoluble would be made simple by Francesco Farinella. Such was the dream. This problem offered no such prospect of world-wide publicity, but still it had the foreign flavour that Farinella liked. A trip to England opened up before him, consultation with Scotland Yard.

'A complex affair,' he said.

Grado finished the sandwich and belched. 'I do not see it.'

'This makes it so.' Farinella tapped the sheets that contained Tardelli's reports on both Porson and Linnet. The pathologist had been unusually quick in spite of his discouraging remarks, and the results were interesting. Porson had absorbed a considerable quantity of some unidentified but powerful barbiturate. There were no marks of violence on the body, and he had not drowned. He suffered from a heart condition – a little tin containing pills for the relief of angina was in one of his pockets – and had died of a heart attack. So much for Porson. He had entered the water at some time between nine-thirty and eleven o'clock, which was just the limit Tardelli had placed on the death of Linnet. The bullet that killed Linnet had been fired by the little Beretta, and the downward angle of entry made it unlikely that he had fired the shot himself. Tardelli had checked records, and confirmed his remarks of the previous night. It was true not only that comparatively few suicides shoot themselves through the heart, but also that among those few the revolver is generally held pointing slightly upwards. Linnet's death was therefore very probably a case of homicide.

Farinella had called Tardelli to thank him for the speed of his work and the clarity of its expression. The pathologist was not deceived.

'Thank you. What is it you want?'

'One or two questions arise, Piero.'

'Ask them.'

'These angina pills will have been prescribed by Porson's doctor. That means his wife, and perhaps other people, knew of his condition.'

'No doubt.'

'Would they also have known that sudden immersion in cold water would kill him?'

'Not necessarily. And you must say *might*, not *would*. It is likely that the barbiturate he had taken played a part.'

'And then you have given precisely the same time limits for the two deaths. It would be wonderfully helpful to know which occurred first.'

'No doubt. But I am a scientist, not a reader of palms or a star gazer. I cannot tell you with certainty.'

'I do not ask for certainty, Piero. We know that the man who drowned was alive after nine o'clock, and the man shot was alive at ten-fifteen. The body in the water was found after eleven o'clock. Do you think it probable that the man in the water died first?'

'If I bet on horses, that is the horse I should back.'

'Thank you.'

'But I should not put much money on it. And I never bet.'

Farinella sighed. 'How strong was this barbiturate?'

'It was strong. It had been taken within thirty minutes of death, probably with alcohol – I mentioned alcohol being found in the stomach. He would have been sleepy, only semi-conscious when he entered the water. And then within moments he had a heart attack. If he had been on land and taken a couple of pills . . . but of course that wasn't possible.'

'He could have fallen in, not knowing what he was doing?'

'Possible.'

'Or have been pushed.'

'Also possible.'

'The Emperor Napoleon is less than ten minutes' walk from the place where Porson was found. He could have gone to the hotel, shot Linnet, taken this drug in alcohol, left the hotel, become sleepy on the way back to his own hotel, fallen into the water. Possible?'

'An admirable reconstruction, Francesco. But you will not forget my little bet, if I were a betting man?'

'Which bet?'

'That Porson died first.' Tardelli was chuckling when he put down the telephone.

'A complex affair,' Farinella repeated. His large brown eyes had a dreamy look.

'I see nothing complex. We have enough facts to see what happened.' Grado ticked off points on thin withered fingers, the nails of which were horny and unusually long. 'The man Crowley has an affair with the German woman. He wishes also to obtain control over the travel firm. They know of Porson's heart condition. He pays the man Linnet to dope his partner, push him into the canal, make sure he has drowned or is dead. He makes the call to Linnet heard by Bettina, goes to the hotel, shoots

Linnet. That is what happened.'

'How did he get hold of Porson's revolver?'

'Perhaps he asks to borrow it on some pretext. A few hours' questioning and he would tell us.' Grado showed large yellow dog's teeth.

'He was absent for only half an hour from Morvelli's party, from ten to ten-thirty. Linnet was alive at ten-fifteen, when the call was made. Crowley could not have got back to the party by ten-thirty.'

'Not if he walked, that is obvious. We know the city, but we could still not have walked from the ghetto to the Emperor Napoleon in the Calle Larga 22 Marzo, shot a man, and returned in thirty minutes. It would hardly have been possible if he had hired a gondola. But he could have called a water taxi by telephone. Then it would have taken no more than ten minutes either way, perhaps less. Up to the man Linnet's room, and – pop.' He aimed a playful finger at Farinella, who suggested coldly that he should make enquiries of the water taxi service, and was not altogether pleased to learn that such enquiries were already in hand. 'It should not take long, for all the water taxis are radio controlled. There are a few private operators, and I have asked that they should be checked also, but it is likely that he will have used the official service.'

'He says he has only a few words of Italian.'

'On the water taxis they all speak English. It is the curse of Italy, the spread of English.' The internal telephone on his desk rang. Farinella affected not to listen to the conversation, which on Grado's side consisted of monosyllables. When he put down the instrument he sat frowning, nibbling at a horny nail. Then he spoke.

'They have checked the radio water taxis. There is nobody who took a fare from anywhere near the ghetto at that time on Saturday night, or brought one back. The private operators not on radio call have also been checked. Nothing. It is strange.'

'Nothing strange. Simply, you were wrong.'

Grado bit off a fragment of nail, looked at it, dropped it on the worn carpet. 'Somehow the man Crowley did it. You heard he is

152

unstable. He tried to cheat Guido Morvelli, tried to cheat people even when young. The Englishman told us a lot, the one you handled so well. You know the one.' He got up and minced round the room, thin arms flapping, in a manner ludicrously unlike Jason Durling. Back at his desk he opened a drawer, took out some gum.

'You make too many assumptions, Vincente.' Crowley said he did not know Linnet . . . '

'Of course he lied.'

'Perhaps. But we do not know of a link between them, except that Linnet was once married to Crowley's wife. Only the revolver joins the two deaths, otherwise they might be completely separate. We have to find a link.'

As if in answer to his remark, there was a knock on the door, and Enrico Pecorino's head appeared round it. Pecorino was a recent recruit to the Squadra Mobili, an eager beaver looking for early promotion, and perhaps also for departure to a police force where they dealt with crimes more violent and more political than came the way of Venetians. Farinella voted always for whatever party seemed least likely to disturb the existing state of affairs, both nationally and in elections directly related to the affairs of the Serenissima Republic, Queen of Cities. He distrusted Pecorino's interest in politics. Here, however, was the young man, with a characteristic look of self-satisfaction on his face. He ushered in a slick-haired sharp-eyed type, who looked to Farinella eminently untrustworthy.

'This is Jose, the barman at the Emperor . . . ' Pecorino had got so far when Farinella stopped him.

'When you knock on the door, Pecorino, you wait until told to come in, you understand? Then you enter alone, you understand? And explain what has brought you, leaving any companion outside or downstairs, you understand?'

The young man was unabashed. 'I know the drill of course, Commissario, but this one you will want to see. If I'd left him on his own he might have skedaddled. Right, Jose?'

The barman smiled uneasily, and said he wasn't looking for trouble. Farinella felt sanctimonious as he said that the best way of avoiding it would be to tell them exactly what he knew.

'That he will now do,' Pecorino said confidently. 'Tell them, Jose, as you told it to me.'

So Jose told his story. He had been serving in the hotel's cocktail bar the whole evening. The bar's lighting was what the hotel called discreet, which meant fairly dim, with indirect tubular lights round the walls, 'casting a gentle romantic glow on the scene', as the hotel brochure said. At about nine o'clock Mr Linnet had come in and ordered a gin and tonic. He had seen Mr Linnet on other occasions, and was sure of his identity. A few minutes later, he could not say just how long, two men came in together. They stood at the far end of the bar from Linnet. One ordered a Bloody Mary and an orange juice. Jose brought their drinks, and turned to serve another customer so that he was not facing them. He glanced into a mirror behind the row of whisky and liqueur bottles on the back shelves, and saw the companion of the man who had ordered the drinks pouring into the Bloody Mary the contents of a small glass phial or bottle. The man into whose drink it was poured laughed, raised the Bloody Mary to his mouth, drank.

Jose then left the bar to take an order across to a table, and turned back in time to see Linnet raise a hand in greeting, and walk over to greet the Bloody Mary and orange juice drinkers. They had chatted briefly, perhaps for half a minute, and then Bloody Mary and Orange Juice had gone out. Linnet had shaken his head in apparent amusement, and then he too had gone – but the other way, back into the hotel.

That was the story, and Jose did not change it, although he was unsure about details. What did the two men look like? The man who ordered wore a striped jacket, had a red face, and was English. This was obviously Porson. His companion, who had emptied the phial into Porson's drink, wore some sort of light-coloured jacket, had a pale complexion, and had on a cap pulled down over his eyes. Had Linnet gone over to greet them both or just one of them, and if so which one? Jose did not know.

'Which one did he speak to first? The one who ordered the drinks?'

'I tell you I do not know. You understand my interest was just because the liquid had been dropped in the drink. That was unusual.'

'He didn't try to conceal dropping in the liquid?'

Not at all, Jose said. The man in the striped jacket had a smile on his face. 'But one thing I have not said. When Mr Linnet went across and was talking to them, he too had a smile on his face.'

'He was pleased to see them?'

'It was not that sort of smile.' He could not say, however, just what sort it was. It was Jose's impression, he did not quite know why, that the man in the cap wanted to leave.

'Think carefully,' Farinella said. 'Did you see the man who drank the Bloody Mary pass anything to Linnet?'

'What kind of thing? A paper?'

'Something bigger than that.'

The barman shrugged. 'I don't think so, but I cannot be sure. You understand the light in our bar is for lovers, not for detectives.' He looked pleased by his near-witticism.

Jose was thanked, Pecorino told to take his statement. The detective lingered at the door. 'Interesting, Commissario?'

'Yes. You did well.'

'Do you want to talk about it? Shall I return when I've taken Jose's statement?'

Farinella said that would not be necessary. Pecorino looked disappointed.

'That young man is too smart for his own good,' the Commissario said when the door had closed.

Grado had not spoken a word during Jose's interrogation, nor had he ceased to chew. 'You mean he may be too smart for our good.'

'For your good, Vincente. If he were promoted . . . '

'You would not find him a congenial subordinate.'

'True.' Farinella's plump hands waved gently, his rings sparkled. 'He is eager for a transfer. Perhaps it might be arranged.' He dismissed Pecorino. 'This changes things.'

'How so?'

'We can now place the time of Porson's death more exactly.

Tardelli said the barbiturate had been taken within thirty minutes of death. It was administered in the bar at about nine-thirty, or a little before. Porson therefore died at about ten o'clock or, again, a little earlier. And it tells us something more.' Grado shifted gum from one cheek to the other, stared dull-eyed. 'We do know that Porson died first. It was ten-fifteen when Linnet received the phone call and sent away Bettina. By then Porson must have been dead.'

'That is, if the liquid poured into his drink was the barbiturate. Why should Porson have laughed when being given a barbiturate?'

'He must have thought it was something else, what they call an upper perhaps.' Grado shrugged. 'There can be no reasonable doubt that is when the drug was given. And there is another deduction, not certain but reasonable. It is this. The man wearing the light-coloured jacket and the cap, the one who doped the drink, was an agent, acting for somebody else. Does the doped drink provide a link for you, Vincente, with something else we have been told?' Grado shook his head. 'Something our friend Mr Durling said?'

'Him.' Grado rolled his eyes, looked up at the ceiling.

'He said he had been poisoned at a party in England. And that he had taken only one drink – a Bloody Mary. I do not have to tell you, you have hardly had time to forget it, that Porson's last drink was a Bloody Mary.'

'And then?'

'It is again reasonable to suppose that the drink which Durling said poisoned him was meant for Porson, and was drugged. Consider also the incident of the revolver shot that might have killed Porson in England. Is it not clear that there was a plan which failed in England, but succeeded here in Venice?'

'Bravo.' Grado clapped his hands gently, the sound like rustling leaves. 'Very clever. But most of these are speculations, you might say guesses. Perhaps the man Durling was drunk in England as he was drunk here, perhaps the man who doped the drink was an agent, but we shan't know until we find him. And so on. It is better to use common sense.'

'I had intended to do so, Vincente. What particular nonsense have I been talking?'

'Forgive me, Commissario. I do not mean to offend.' Grado's eyes were cast down in mock humility. 'It is just that common sense tells us to ask, Who profits from Porson's death? The answer is: his partner.'

The ringed hands waved eloquently. 'Your common sense is too crude, Vincente, it leaves too much out of account. If Crowley thought the deal with Morvelli was fixed, then he had obtained control of the firm. What need was there, then, to kill his partner? For love? But he does not seem to me a passionate man. And besides, I have shown that Porson was dead by the time Crowley left the party, at ten o'clock.'

'That is all talk and timetables.' Grado nibbled again at his nail. 'The associate acted for him, the man in the cap. Perhaps he was what they call in America the hit man.'

'Why was Linnet killed, does your common sense tell us that?'

'How can one say when they are all liars? What I am telling you is that common sense tells us Crowley must somehow be responsible. The way to solve this affair is to bring in Crowley, and the German woman with him. Put them on the grill.'

'The phrase is "grill them".'

'Whatever. Grill them, burn them on the grill, for two, three days, as long as is needed. Grill them until they are cooked. They will break down and tell the truth, say how it was all done. That is the way.'

Farinella smiled often but laughed rarely. He did so now. 'Vincente, it is easy to see why you have not achieved the position your talents deserve. Perhaps I agree with your conclusions, but I have to answer to a Sostituto. What do you think he would say about such a way of interrogating the English?' The telephone rang before Grado could reply. Farinella spoke briefly, put it down. 'Lieutenant Sollima of the Guardia di Finanza. He says he has information that may be helpful. He will be here in ten minutes.'

16

Many Venetian museums and galleries are closed on Sunday, but the Accademia is open, and Colin had taken his flock relentlessly around its twenty-three galleries, from the Bellinis and the Mantegnas and the Veroneses, through dozens of Saints and Madonnas and Virgins. The group emerged dazed, as though struck lightly but often by hammers, and there was an appreciative murmur at Colin's much-used joke that there were more virgins in Venice than anywhere else in the world.

They returned to the Pacifico for lunch, and there Colin saw Derek, Jason and Gerda sitting together drinking coffee. He asked Derek if he could speak privately, and they went into one of the lounges.

'About the tour,' Colin said in his usual over-confident way. 'Do you think it should be called off? The tragedy and all that.'

'Certainly not. Very few of them knew Charles at all well. What's on your mind, Colin?'

'Something's come up, spot of bother. I may have to go back.'

'Something to do with Charles's death?'

'Certainly not. Well, not as far as I know,' he added unconvincingly. 'You never know how one spot of bother's linked up with another, do you? But I think I can say pretty definitely not.'

'How long do you need to go back for? If it's only a day, I suppose that could be managed.'

'Afraid not, old man. Fact is, I think the fuzz here may want to have a chat, and I'd just as soon not talk to them.'

'Steph's not mixed up in this, I hope?'

Colin was indignant. 'Of course not. Spot of smuggling, everybody does it, but things seem to have gone wrong. I think life might be easier at home than in Italy just for the moment.'

Colin, Derek thought, was thick. The marvel was that so many people had at different times thought otherwise. 'If they do want to talk to you there's no use running, they'll bring you back. You'd better tell me what it's about. I don't care what you've done, as long as it doesn't affect the firm or Steph.'

Colin told him.

Back at the table Gerda said to Jason, 'Do you know anything about dead bodies?'

'Dead bodies?'

'When they are released? Charles has a sister named Eileen. I have spoken to her on the telephone, and she is flying out today, but nothing can be done until the body is released. You do not look well, Jason.'

'I had an awful shock yesterday. And afterwards I drank too much.'

'Ah, yes, as you did in Headfield.'

'I was poisoned there. Or drugged.' His hand went to his bow tie. 'Gerda, I do not think you should talk so matter of factly. It gives a wrong impression, as if you didn't care about Charles or what happens to him.'

She smiled sweetly. 'But that is true. I don't mind where he is buried, in Venice or Headfield or anywhere else. Eileen can make what arrangement she chooses. You should not screw up your mouth like that, Jason, as if you had eaten something you disliked. It makes you look like an old woman.'

Jason got up, went out of the room. When Derek returned and asked about him, Gerda said she thought he felt unwell.

In the afternoon Derek went to see Morvelli. Elsa let him in, and told him Guido was very upset.

'I daresay. So am I.'

Husband and wife were sitting in the patio drinking coffee. Elsa wore a dress of blue and white towelling, Morvelli a loose shirt that concealed his bulk. He greeted Derek with open arms.

'I am desolated by the tragedy of our old friend Charles. What happens now, my dear Derek, that is what I ask myself. Or rather, what I ask you.'

'What has happened is that I'm in danger of being arrested. Thanks to you.'

Morvelli placed a hand on his heart. 'You cannot mean what you are saying, it could not be.'

Derek's blue eyes sparkled with anger as he gave them an account of his interview with Farinella.

'Since then he has been on the telephone. It seems Charles had a heart condition, did you know that?' Morvelli shook his head. 'Neither did I. Of course Gerda knew it, but she says he did not like it mentioned, he liked to seem tough. He had a heart attack when he entered the water, and died of it.'

'Then nobody is responsible.'

'Perhaps somebody pushed him. Luckily for me, the times don't fit, they have fixed the time of death as just about when I left the party to look for him. But they still think I might have had an associate who acted for me, and a lot of this is thanks to you. Why did you say we had no firm agreement about the shares?'

Elsa thought as she watched him that she had rarely seen a more handsome man, and wondered why she did not find him more attractive. Guido was too fat, a gambler, untrustworthy, she suspected him of keeping a mistress, yet he drew her like a magnet. Now he was wagging his head in apparent disbelief.

'Derek, my friend, I thought it could be damaging for you if I said such things. Francesco might then think, "Ah, he has been plotting behind his partner's back, it would be convenient for him if the partner were dead."'

'You know we had an agreement.'

'An arrangement rather. It had not been signed.'

'That was a formality. You would have been doubling your money by signing a piece of paper.'

'That was certainly what we talked about. But then I might have thought I could – how shall I put it? – make four times the amount, not twice. You know my deep need of money.'

Elsa said, 'I told you last night you should be careful when you made any arrangement with Guido.'

'That's dishonest.' Derek looked from one to the other of them. 'You mean you'd have tried to blackmail me?'

'Ah, that is what you call the public school spirit.' Morvelli shook with laughter, then wiped his eyes with a silk handkerchief. 'Your little plan to take control through the shares, that was all right, quite above board?'

'It was altogether different. Charles stood in the way of our development, you know it yourself.'

'English morality, I like it very much.' Elsa went indoors, returned with another pot of coffee and a plate of sugared bon-bons. Morvelli ate one and then another, talking as he did so. 'You are not logical, my friend. If Francesco suspects that you were in some way responsible for Charles's death, our little arrangement is of no concern to him. But I think you have no cause to worry. Francesco loves the limelight, he would like to be the great detective, but also he is lazy, if things are not easy he gives up. In Italy an investigation of this kind starts with publicity, all kinds of excitement, but in a day, a week, at most a month, there is something new, the Red Brigades, the P2 lodge, a new sex scandal. Two Englishmen dying here in Venice, that is interesting, but not for long. When I asked what happens now, I meant what happens to our firm? Will the lovely Gerda play a part in running it, will she sell to you, is there a chance that Guido Morvelli might be considered as a buyer or an equal partner? The arrangement we made with Charles must be void now he is dead, but if there is a chance for me to buy in I should like to know.'

'Where would you find the money?' Elsa made a gesture in the direction of the twisted iron statuary. 'Sell some of these?'

'When the investment is good, money is always available.'

'I haven't spoken to Gerda,' Derek said. 'I don't know what she will do.'

'I have heard something of anonymous letters.'

'They are absolutely untrue.'

'Of course. You are a faithful husband. You have a devoted wife.'

Derek stood up. Again he would have seemed to Jason like an actor, delivering rather self-consciously a parting speech. 'In spite of what you say, Guido, I think you behaved very badly, and I want you to know it. I would have kept to the arrangement we made with Charles about the shares, even though nothing was signed. Now I shall have to think about it.'

When he had gone Elsa said, 'You handled that stupidly. If you wanted a share in the business, that is. I am never sure what you want.'

'I want money, my love. Derek is an English prig, and they bore me.'

'And his wife, what is she like?'

'Apparently a plain uncomplicated Englishwoman, but I am not sure of that. I have seen her only once or twice. Charles Porson said they were a contented couple. He had an eye for women.' He laughed. 'I will tell you something. If I want those shares he will have to sell them to me, no matter what he says. Otherwise I might leave PC Travel and set up a rival agency. He would not like that.'

'You'd never do it.'

'Why not?'

'Like Francesco, you are too lazy.'

17

The chief concerns of the Guardia di Finanza are smuggling, counterfeiting, and illegal entry into the country, with the first of these predominant. Lieutenant Sollima was trim in his grey uniform with yellow flashes. His shoulders were pushed well back, his hawk-like nose thin, the deep-set eyes on either side of it close together. Sollima disliked seeing policemen in plain clothes, detested Farinella's rings, thought Grado looked like a scarecrow. They regarded him as an officious booby, who talked like a computer rather than a human being.

This he did now, as he told them that the Guardia was in possession of information that might be relevant to the investigation into the death of Richard Linnet. The Guardia had been aware for some time that goods were being smuggled into and out of Venice by a Japanese group whose representative in the city was one Shunya Inoki. Other members of the group were American and English. An agent of the Guardia named Roverto had been engaged on the matter, and had recently been successful in establishing the means by which the goods were taken out of the city, and indeed out of Italy. They were ingenious. The goods went by train, taken on at Venice, and transferred when on the train by an English steward into the metal containers used for carrying ready-prepared meals. Sometimes at Paris, sometimes at Calais, they were unloaded as apparently empty containers. Some goods were destined for France, others for Britain, these latter taken over by day trippers.

Farinella yawned, took off his jacket and put it on a hanger inside the door. Grado began sucking a mint. 'Drugs, I suppose,' he said. Sollima did not reply directly, but continued.

Last night Roverto had travelled in the same *wagon-lit* as the English steward and an American accomplice, and had spotted how the trick was worked. The French authorities had been warned in advance, and all had been caught at Calais, the steward, the American, the French handlers. The Japanese in Venice had also been taken into custody. It was an admirably organised piece of work, a small model of its kind.

'What was the Japanese connection?' Grado asked. 'I thought they exported only computers, cars and TV sets.'

Sollima was sitting upright on a hard chair. He shifted uneasily. 'Not drugs. These were films made in Japan. Pornographic.'

Grado gave his choking laugh. Farinella said softly, 'Films? Your agent Roverto spent days, or perhaps weeks, discovering how some films are being transferred from one place to another? Oh, Lieutenant, what a lot of trouble the Guardia takes for a few films.'

'These were not ordinary articles of the kind. The Japanese pornographic films are quite special. A lot of money is paid for the video cassettes.'

'No doubt they show things we ignorant Venetians have never seen or heard of.' Sollima looked at the diamond and the ruby, wondered how much they were worth, made no reply. 'Or it may be that here at the *questura* we are less easily shocked than you gentlemen of the Guardia.'

'It is not a matter of being shocked. It is a question of stopping the smuggling of forbidden articles, and in particular their transmission through our city.'

'You have not yet told me of any connection with Linnet.'

'I am sorry. The English steward has named him as the chief agent involved in Britain.' Sollima looked at his notebook. 'There is also a man concerned who is a courier for the agency PC Travel The trains run by this agency have been the means of transmission when a particular steward is on board. For this reason Linnet travelled from London to Venice on the train, to make sure things went smoothly, and an American member of the group was on the train going back. The name of the courier involved is Colin Crowley.' He saw with pleasure that what he thought of as Farinella's superior smile vanished at mention of the name.

Grado asked what time the train carrying the films had left on Saturday evening.

'At twenty hundred hours. The arrests, I have said, were made at Calais.'

'So nobody on the train knew of Linnet's death. Tell us what was said about Linnet, about the man Derek Crowley, about anybody else involved.'

But the Lieutenant had told them all he knew. The steward and the American had both named Linnet as the contact man who paid the Japanese when the video cassettes were handed over. The American had given names of some buyers in Paris and London. Both Waterton the American and the steward Sibbles had said this was the third trip undertaken, and Waterton had said there was Mafia interest in the United States, providing the video cassettes could be sent by some less circuitous route. The courier Crowley seemed to be a small cog in the wheel. Neither Derek Crowley nor Charles Porson had been mentioned. The Lieutenant was thanked and departed, head high, shoulders back.

'Penny ante stuff,' Grado said when they had gone. 'The Guardia were expecting drugs, of course. But still it offers some possibilities. Perhaps the man with the cap was connected with the smuggling, perhaps Linnet was taking an extra cut for himself and this was discovered.'

Farinella shook his head. 'The man was with Porson. Linnet

was pleased or amused to see them. But we must talk to this other Crowley, and perhaps again to our friend Derek. You had better call the hotel.'

Grado sighed, looked out of the window at the tourists wandering aimlessly along outside, and crossing the bridge. 'What a way to spend a Sunday, listening to English lies. You know what my children say? Why am I never at home to play games with them like other fathers? What is this terrible *questura*, they ask, that occupies all of my time?'

Farinella said unsympathetically that he worked no more than the usual rota of Sundays. Grado put another mint in his mouth and called the Pacifico.

You had better tell them everything you know about the smuggling – that had been Derek's advice, and Colin reluctantly followed it. Farinella's sympathetic manner eased his original nervousness, and by the end of the interview he was almost jaunty. He told them that he had been approached a few weeks earlier by Chuck Waterton, whom he knew slightly, and asked if he would like to make some easy cash on the side. He had then got in touch with the steward Sibbles, whom he knew to be hard up, and Sibbles had been eager to co-operate.

'It was just putting the cassettes into the metal boxes and taking them out again, nothing really. Of course I wouldn't have done it if there'd been drugs involved, or anything like that. But films, I mean, I couldn't see there was any harm in it.'

'Forbidden films.'

'I know, but I mean to say, we're all men of the world, everyone watches them. Well, not everyone, but in England we don't worry much about this sort of thing, and I don't suppose you do either.' He was encouraged by Farinella's gentle smile.

'And you knew Mr Linnet.'

'Knew who he was, knew him to speak to, but didn't really *know* him if you get me. I met him a couple of times in London, and he'd been twice on the train. First time to make sure things went well, so he said. You know he'd been married to Sandy, Derek's wife? He was tickled pink to be using the train, getting back at Sandy in some funny way I suppose. Mind you, he'd never met Derek, he told me that.'

'As far as you are aware, neither your cousin nor Mr Porson knew anything about this smuggling?'

'Good Lord, no. They'd have gone through the roof, sacked me on the spot. Matter of fact, Derek's told me this'll be my last trip for the firm. Can't blame him, I suppose, though I was a jolly good courier, everybody said so. Seems a bit stuffy.' His jauntiness vanished. 'I say, what's likely to happen? Nothing too awful, I hope.'

Farinella allowed his smile to broaden slightly. 'So far as the *questura* is concerned, nothing at all. We are not concerned with smuggling offences, but with the deaths of Mr Porson and Mr Linnet. As for the Guardia here, and the French authorities, perhaps they will prosecute the American and the Japanese, although I shall be surprised if they end up with more than a heavy fine. For you and the steward, who played minor parts – well, you will have to give evidence. You may be fined too. If you are entirely frank and co-operative, perhaps you may not be prosecuted.'

'That's jolly cheering, old Derek was breathing fire and slaughter. I must say you've been terribly helpful. I shall tell my friends back in England that Italian policemen are wonderful.'

Grado made some unintelligible sound. Farinella said, 'You have been helpful, and it is appreciated. One more thing. You must know your cousin well. Can you give me an impression of what he is like, what sort of person? It would be most valuable.'

Talking came easily to Colin and his tongue, oiled by the Commissario's friendliness, did not fail him now. 'Derek's always been rather a golden boy, full of ideas, impresses people when they first meet him. Sometimes doesn't last, though. He's made a great success of the agency, very keen to expand, sent me to Japan scouting round for new holiday ideas, old Porson didn't approve.'

'Perhaps you made contact with Mr Inoki when you were in Japan?'

Colin looked uneasy, then decided to laugh. 'Not with him,

another Jap who helped to make the films, told me they were very artistic. Should have mentioned that before, I suppose. Anyway, back to Derek.' Grado, who found Colin extremely difficult to understand, was about to ask a question, but was checked by his colleague's almost imperceptible shake of the head. 'Seems very happy with Sandy, gets on all right with Owen, that's Sandy's son by old Linnet. Of course old Jason, Jason Durling, was Derek's great friend when he was young, used to look after him like a mother hen at school, I believe.'

'We have talked to Mr Durling.'

'He's on the trip, but not with the group. Fussy chap, bit of an old maid. He and Derek are still pretty thick.'

'Your cousin and Mr Porson, were they also pretty thick?'

Colin laughed. 'You couldn't find anybody who was thick with Porson. Shouldn't speak ill of the dead and all that, but he was a real pig, especially with women. Couldn't get enough of it from all I've heard.' He looked alarmed. 'I say, don't get the idea I had anything to do with getting rid of him. If he *was* got rid of, that is.' He looked from one of the detectives to the other, but neither spoke. 'Derek – well, Derek handled him as well as anyone, especially at first I believe. Recently he'd got fed up because Porson blocked all the plans he had for expansion, in Japan or anywhere else.'

When he had gone Grado said, 'A fool speaking some incomprehensible local dialect.'

'But, in what he told us, probably not a liar.'

'Probably not a liar,' Grado reluctantly admitted.

18

From Jason's journal, written after returning to England.

Sunday night, that last evening in Venice, now a city of memories so painful that I shall never return. In a gondola: I reclining on cushions at one end, Derek at the other. Both thoughtful, I brooding still on the indignity and humiliation I had suffered, Derek silent as he looked at the grey magnificence of stone, our gondolier also mercifully silent once we had told him we did not want the Santa Lucia, or any other song. As we passed Ca' Rezzonico where Robert Browning died, I thought of 'In a Gondola':

> *I send my heart up to thee, all my heart*
> *In this my singing!*

That was a poem ending in the death of the beloved. Better perhaps John Addington Symonds:

> *A symphony of black and blue –*
> *Venice asleep, vast night, and you*

Still not appropriate, for Venice that Sunday evening was by no means asleep, but clamorous with engine sound, noisy with tourist murmur, making one contrast once more the romantic past and the vulgar present. Yet there was still something magical about the gliding of the boat through dark water, and in this evening twilight outlines were softened so that one could almost believe in the past. It came nearer as we turned off the Grand Canal down a narrow darkened canal. Here the houses showed blind windows on either side, the plash of oars could be distinctly heard. I said something about the gondolier's tact in taking us away from the bright lights into the true silence of Venice. I confess I was jarred by Derek's reply.

'There's a route they all follow, although it varies depending whether you hire them for one hour or two. I came along this way with Sandy last year. We both know Venice as well as a stray visitor can, that's partly why she didn't come on this trip. I've spoken to her, and she offered to fly out, but I said there was no point.' I did not comment. 'Something else. Colin has got himself mixed up in some stupid smuggling business connected with Linnet. Would you believe that he wanted to clear out, go back to England and hope they'd just forget about him? I told him to stay where he was, tell them all about it. It's a damned nuisance, complicates things, but I'm not going to stay here much longer. I shall see the policeman you found *simpatico* tomorrow, and say I've got business at home that just won't wait.'

Such were the thoughts that occupied him as we glided along the water in the most romantic city in the world. Was this banal businessman the Derek I had known long ago, who had been eager to read the best in literature, and knew by heart some of Shakespeare's sonnets? I don't know what words I spoke in reply. In any case he continued, talking to me rather as if he were thinking aloud, as he had often done in the past. I suppose that should have pleased me.

'I spoke to Gerda this evening, or rather she spoke to me, just before we came out. She's willing to sell Charles's interest in the firm, in fact almost eager. Just a matter of settling the price.'

At that I did feel bound to comment. 'To discuss business affairs within twenty-four hours of her husband's death – forgive me, Derek, but I find that distasteful.'

'It's a bit hard-headed, I agree, but nobody could be sentimental about Charles. Gerda's a tough nut, but she'll find I am too, when we get down to talking money.'

At this moment the gondolier, evidently irked by our inattention, paused and told us in rapid, inaccurate but intelligible English that we were looking at the façade of the Palazzo Contarini del Bovolo, whose spiral staircase was one of the wonders of the world. He spoke at length, but in the dark evening we could hardly see the façade, and to look at the spiral staircase we should have had to land and walk around the back of the Palazzo. When we declined, the gondolier let off a small volley of Italian, and resumed his oar.

Had there not been some arrangement with Morvelli? I asked. In occasional glancing glimpses of light I saw a familiar look of exultant naughtiness on Derek's face.

'It didn't quite work out. Guido was trying to do a soft shoe shuffle.'

'I don't understand.'

'My patent slang for pulling a fast one. He's a more devious character than I thought, but he'll knuckle down when he knows I'm in control. I've said before, he's a marvellous salesman.'

Unexpectedly he asked, 'What about you?'

'What do you mean?'

'You took a hell of a knock over Cruddle. I shouldn't have been talking about myself all the time. Forgive me.' He knew perfectly well that when he spoke in that concerned way, there was nothing I wouldn't have done for him. I said that I should get over it, I should find another occupation for my leisure. He shook his head, golden curls gleaming as we went under a lamp.

'It's not that simple, and we both know it. It occupied so much of your life. There's not much anybody else can do, but if Sandy or I can help, call out.' A pause. Then he said 'Jason', and I realised – how clearly I realised, and how little it mattered – that I had received my share of emotional attention, and the conversation was about to shift to something Derek wanted. But my suspicions were not quite correct.

'What's happened here must be connected with Headfield. Those letters, the shot at Charles at the rehearsal, they must be linked with his death, even though he had a heart attack in the water. Yet it seems to make no sense. Do you have any thoughts about who sent the letters?'

'None at all.'

'They're untrue. And damaging to me.' We emerged suddenly into a wider canal, bright lights, the gondola station where we had embarked. 'I was away from Guido's party for half an hour, you know, looking for Charles. If it had been any longer I believe they'd have arrested me, on the grounds that I'd pushed him in. As it is, they think I had an associate.'

'It's a pity you left the party.'

'I'll go along with that.' The gondola was manoeuvred to the canal side, we got out. 'If you have any thoughts at all, about the letters or anything else, you'll tell me?'

I said I would.

19

Grado lived on St Elena, which is the garden suburb of Venice. The island was man-made in the nineteenth century, the architecture is modern Italian domestic, but Grado's wife Carmen had been brought up in the Tuscan countryside. She detested everything about Venice, and said that St Elena was the only place in the city to bring up children, since nowhere else could you see a blade of grass. This was not strictly accurate, but Carmen was given to exaggeration and her husband did not bother to contradict her. Grado was taken home every evening, and picked up every morning, by a Polizia motor boat. His children, a boy and a girl aged five and three, greeted him with enthusiasm, demanding piggyback rides before going to bed. When at last they had settled, Carmen cooked their supper of *fritto misto*, and he opened a bottle of Soave.

'So what about the murdered Englishmen?' she asked, as they sat in the little dining room, the french windows open on to their patch of green.

'It is not established that they were murdered. One was loaded with dope and had a heart condition, perhaps he just fell into the water. The other perhaps shot himself. Tardelli doesn't think so, but he might be wrong. What is this?'

'*Arselle.*'

Arselle are baby clams. Grado speared one, chewed with relish. 'You know I cannot eat them.'

'You would complain if they were not in the *fritto misto*.'

'True, but I shall suffer.' He forked up *telline* and *calamaretti*.

'What does Francesco think?'

'You know him, he will make a big thing out of it if he can. He hopes it will make him famous, a big man. I do not think it will happen.'

'And what do you think?'

'It was murder.'

'But you said just now . . . '

'That it is not established. I do not think it ever will be, but I have no doubt. The man Crowley, partner of the man Porson, killed them both or had them killed. First Porson, to get control of the business and to marry Porson's wife, then the man Linnet, who was perhaps in some way a witness. That is what happened. But we shall not prove it.'

'I don't see why he should kill Linnet.'

'Perhaps he had discovered some secret, who can tell? All of them lie to us. It is my belief that people lie more often when they are in another country. Francesco hopes to go to England, so that people can tell more lies to him there, but it will not happen. I shall take the last of these delicious *arselle*, these morsels of devil's food. It would have been good if the Englishmen had killed each other at home, and left a peaceful Venetian Sunday undisturbed.'

Farinella and his wife had an apartment on the Giudecca, with a view looking across the lagoon to the Lido. Lucia was florid, almost as big as Farinella, and as expansive. When he returned home she melted into his arms.

'Francesco my love.'

'Darling Lucia.'

'You look so tired. Come and rest.' She took him by the hand, led him to his customary chair, poured Campari and soda. Farinella lay back, closed his eyes, sipped, closed his eyes again. Lucia prepared their supper, a canteloupe with *prosciutto*, then sea bass with a caper sauce. Both knew that it made little difference what they ate, they would continue slowly to put on weight. At dinner they talked about the case, in a way very different from that of Grado and Carmen. Farinella described what had happened that day.

'It is difficult, delicate, yet perhaps it offers opportunities. The chief problem is that Linnet was shot with Porson's revolver, and it is difficult to see how he could have acquired it. Also, there is no apparent link between the two deaths.'

'If there is a link, Francesco will find it.'

172

'If one could prove Porson to have been a party to the smuggling – but then there is no hint of that. Everything in the case is guesswork, even the idea that Linnet greeted Porson in the bar. Perhaps it was the other man he recognised, and where is that other man?'

'My Francesco will find him.'

Farinella sighed. Lucia was an angel, but there were times when he found her admiration a little trying. He abandoned the exposition, which had been leading to the conclusion that he must find out more about Derek Crowley and that to do so it was essential for him to go to England. Instead, he said that he must make notes for the case he would present to Sostituto Rocco in the morning.

20

The posters in Morvelli's outer office showed cities on the Rhine, New York skyscrapers, the changing of the guard in London. Grado rolled gum around his mouth, and wondered why Italians ever wished to leave their own country. Morvelli came out of his office, hands outstretched.

'Come in, come in. A thousand apologies for keeping you waiting. An urgent call, a travel agent in New York wanting a hotel here at very short notice for a small party. They are desperate to visit the queen of cities.'

'Some are desperate to leave it.' Morvelli looked baffled. 'Your posters. What can be found in those places that is not in Italy?'

'Something different. It is human nature to look for that.'

'Not my nature. I should never leave Venice. My wife demands a holiday every year, I don't know why, but at least it is in Italy.'

Morvelli acknowledged this by nodding. Grado stared at him, chewing. The travel agent returned his yellow look with composure.

'Tell me the nature of the relationships in this firm, PC Travel.'

'The relationships?'

'Porson and Crowley. Did they like each other?'

'So far as I know they got on well enough. Crowley had plans for expansion, Porson did not accept them. When we spoke on the telephone I told you of Crowley's plans for gaining control, with the help of shares I was to buy.'

'He says it was more than a plan, a firm agreement.'

'Nothing is settled until it is put on paper and signed. Until then it is only words.'

'You are saying you would not have agreed to the arrangement, once you had the shares?'

'I should have consulted my own best interests, as everybody does, whether they admit it or not.'

'You understand why I ask these questions. If Crowley realised what you intended, he had good reason for wishing to be rid of Porson.' Morvelli shrugged. 'Do you think he knew you intended to . . . ' Grado chewed meditatively while pondering the next phrase, ' . . . hold him to ransom?'

'I must protest. This was a matter of business.'

'Your protest is noted. Answer the question.'

'I don't think he knew. Derek is clever. But like many clever people he confuses his hopes with the facts.'

Grado went on chewing. 'Another thing. He left your party at ten o'clock, returned at ten-thirty. You are sure of those times?'

'Within a minute or two, yes.'

'Did you know the man Linnet?'

'I don't know him, and have never heard of him.'

'What about Porson? Give me your opinion of him.'

'As a business associate I had no complaints. He knew he was lucky to have somebody like me to handle the Italian end, and he never interfered.'

'Apart from that?'

Morvelli's look of habitual good humour changed to a frown. 'I wonder no one killed him long ago.'

21

The fact that Sostituto Rocco had been appointed by the magistrate to make the preliminary investigation was not, from Farinella's point of view, a good sign. Rocco had friends among the Carabinieri, the natural rivals of the Pubblica Sicurezza. It was fortunate that the young people who saw the body had telephoned the *questura*, for it meant that the PS had been first on the scene. The Carabinieri were supposed to concern themselves primarily with political crime and offences against the State, but it was Farinella's experience that once they were on the spot the Carabinieri simply took over. However, that had not happened, the call had been made to the *questura*, the case was accordingly one for the PS. Farinella had no doubt, though, as he watched Rocco reading his notes, lips moving occasionally, mouth turned down at the corners, that this was not to the Sostituto's liking. The Commissario scratched his chin. Rocco looked up, caught the gleam of rings, and frowned. The Sostituto's hair was prematurely grey, and he wore it almost cropped, grey stubble revealing the shape of a little round skull. His voice when he spoke was, Farinella thought, like the rattle of pebbles as waves move them when rushing up the shore.

'Your conclusion, then, is inconclusive,' Rocco said. 'Porson died of a heart attack. In his drugged condition he may have fallen into the water, then suffered the heart attack. And it is possible that Linnet may have shot himself. Correct?'

What a dreary, mean little man you are, Farinella thought, but his habitual slight smile did not change, and he replied with unruffled urbanity that this was not quite so. He had thought it right to mention the accident in one case and suicide in the other as *possibilities*, no more. The whole weight of argument in his notes, he went on, was to stress the *probability*, no, the overwhelming likelihood, that crime had been committed, that

Porson had been pushed into the water with the intention he should drown, and Linnet had been murdered. He had gone on to show in detail why the affair could not be cleared up in Venice but called for a visit to Britain, collaboration with the police in that country. He became uncomfortably aware that Rocco was clicking his fingernails against each other, something that set the Commissario's teeth on edge.

'You have said all this in your notes, repetition is unnecessary. You have not succeeded in tracing the man in the cap?'

'No. He may be out of the country by now.'

Rocco took out a packet of cigarettes, offered one to Farinella who refused, extracted a cigarette, tapped it on his thumbnail, lit it. The process seemed interminable.

'You name Crowley as a prime suspect. Can you make a case against him for the magistrate?'

'Not at present. Perhaps when I have made investigations in England . . . '

'There is too much "perhaps" in your report.'

'And a lot of fact. May I be allowed to observe that the bodies were found less than forty-eight hours ago.'

'There is still a great deal of "perhaps". Perhaps we should invite a gentleman from Scotland Yard here, instead of sending you to England.'

Farinella knew he was being needled. He retained urbanity with an effort. 'I don't think so.'

Rocco had been speaking with the cigarette in his mouth, the essence of bad manners. Now he removed it, and talked rapidly in his grating voice.

'I am inclined to agree. But I do not wish to send you to stir up mud in England, not unless you can replace "perhaps" with "I am sure". There is something you have forgotten.' His watery eyes, grey as the stubbled round head, gleamed with dislike as he looked at the Commissario's plump, ringed hand. 'Venice is a city without crime, or without violent crime. A few petty thieves around the Via Garibaldi, yes, a little smuggling certainly, perhaps twice a year a bank robbery, but nothing more. You know what they say? In Venice the Grand Canal is very cold, the restaurant prices are very high, but crimes of violence are unknown. I ask again, do you understand me?'

Farinella suspected Rocco of inventing the would-be aphorism. 'I fear not.'

The Sostituto sighed, an exaggerated sound, the ebbed wave being sucked back to the sea. 'Have you forgotten the date?' Then Farinella understood, and it was true he had forgotten. 'Next week begins the Biennale. The pavilions full of art, the festival of films from all countries, thousands of visitors, many American and British. Do we wish them to read in their papers that two brutal murders have been committed here, a celebrated member of our police force is making wide-ranging enquiries? They will think their own lives are at risk, they will stay away.'

'That is ridiculous.' But he said it without passion, it had been foolish to forget.

'Perhaps. You see that I too can say perhaps.' With the cigarette again in the corner of his mouth Rocco continued. 'Justice should be served, you may say, and I agree. But there is no need to present her with the severed head of our beloved city on a silver salver. Let us proceed with discretion, Commissario. You have talked to all the English people involved, talked to them in this city. You have worked speedily and well. I do not doubt you are searching industriously for this man in the cap who seems to play an important part in the story. But the English people must now be free to leave Venice, there can be no question of keeping them here.'

'If they are in England and I am in Venice, how can I continue enquiries?'

'The telephone is a wonderful instrument, and of course you will be in touch with the English police by means of it. Perhaps they will have information, perhaps it may be necessary for you to visit England because of what they tell you. Let us see what develops.'

'I should like to emphasise that there may be a strong case against Derek Crowley. He had motive, it is said he was conducting an affair with the wife of his partner . . . '

'But he had no time. You say so here.'

'We need to investigate his alibi further.'

'By all means. But you can do without his presence in the city. As for the other Crowley, the one involved in smuggling, let us leave him for the Guardia and the French police, as you suggest.'

'So I must take it that permission for me to make personal enquiries in England is refused?'

'You have not been listening, Commissario, I have not said that. You will investigate further, you will talk to the gentleman at Scotland Yard, you will talk to me again. What I have emphasised is that you should proceed with discretion.'

22

Derek, Jason and Gerda flew back together. Before they left Derek spoke to a very jaunty Colin.

'The man at the *questura* seems to think I haven't got much to worry about. Very nice fellow, I liked him.'

'If you'll continue as courier for the rest of this tour I shall be personally grateful.'

'Of course, Derek, anything to oblige. After that, finito, I quite understand, can't have PC reps blotting their copybooks. As a matter of fact I've had the offer of another job, friend of a Jap I met while I was on that little trip for the firm, Arab named Fatah. He runs an import-export business, seems to think my languages would be useful. So I'd have been turning it in anyway before long.'

'Import-export often means gun running.'

'Could be so, but I wouldn't actually see any of the goods, strictly a middle man. As I said to Fatah, I'd just be helping to move things from point A to point B, don't want to know anything more than that. I never looked at any of those films, you know, not interested. But a lot of people are, and demand means there has to be supply, isn't that true? And guns, I mean, everybody uses them. Not everybody, I know that, but governments use them, they're not like drugs. I said to Fatah I wouldn't

178

have anything to do with drugs, and he told me he wouldn't either.'

'Colin, I can never be sure whether you're as innocent as you sound.'

'Of course I am, old boy, more so if anything.'

'Anyway, thanks for carrying on here, it would have put us in a spot if you'd said no. And take care.'

'You take care.' Colin's expression changed to one of concern, that made him look more vacuous than usual. 'From what I can gather, you've got as much to worry about as me.'

They sat together in three seats on one side of the aisle, and hardly spoke. A rented car waited for them at Gatwick.

As they neared Headfield, Derek asked Gerda if she would like him to come indoors with her.

'No, thank you. I spoke to Caroline on the telephone, and she will be at the house.'

'Can I help with anything about Charles?'

'All arrangements are made. Eileen and I saw the British Consul this morning, and he was helpful. Charles will be buried on the island of San Michele.'

'Ezra Pound is buried there,' Jason said. 'And Diaghilev The church is charming.'

'I believe that is so. Eileen will deal with it all.'

They dropped her off. She kissed Derek on the cheek, but not Jason. As she approached the house the door opened, and Caroline waved to them.

'I don't trust her,' Jason said. 'She means to do you harm.'

'The harm's been done by those letters. And it wasn't Gerda who did it.' There was silence until they reached Ponsonby Court. 'I'm sorry about your problems, Jason, I said it before. But I don't want you interfering in my life, understood?' Jason got out of the car and entered the block of flats without looking back.

23

The Colonel read the story in the paper twice with care, then asked Bealby to come in. 'Seen this?'

'Yes, Colonel.' Bealby was young, deferential.

'Was Linnet doing anything for us?'

'Nothing at all, hadn't used him for three months. I'm afraid one of his private fiddles found him out.' Bealby permitted himself a faint smirk, wiped it off when the Colonel glared at him and said that an agent's death was not a joke. He said mildly that Linnet had not been an agent, more like an errand boy, and got another glare.

'I know what Linnet was, thank you. An embarrassment alive, and an embarrassment now he's dead. All right, Bealby, I'll handle it.'

The head of Rome station was Bango Rodgers, an old friend. The two had worked together years ago on the XYZ plan, which had had as its objective the replacing of Rumania's Ceauşescu by a figure sympathetic to the West. The project had collapsed when it proved that three of the people most closely involved were double agents, but neither Bango nor the Colonel felt in any way responsible for that, and failure can breed warmer friendships than success. Bango's voice was warmly welcoming.

'A spot of bother,' the Colonel said. 'Fellow named Linnet, just been shot in Venice. In the papers, you may have seen it.'

'Can't say I have, got my hands full. What was it, a plant?'

'No no,' the Colonel said a little testily. Bango should have read the papers. 'He was a petty crook we used occasionally. Had all sorts of shady contacts in a good many countries, sometimes a man like that can be a useful messenger.'

'Understood. Was he working?'

'Not for us. For himself, very likely. The department has no connection, none at all.'

'So how can I help?'

'Point is this, Bango. There are two deaths in Venice, another Englishman, chap I never heard of. He seems to have died accidentally, no problem there. I think Linnet shot himself, no question of it. We do *not* want a brouhaha, investigation, stones turned over, Linnet's connection mentioned. Can you talk to somebody?'

'Of course, glad to help. No chance the department was involved, I suppose?'

'None in the world. Linnet was nobody, a grain of sand on the beach. Nobody would have worried about him.'

They finished with mutual expressions of goodwill. Bango read the story in the English papers, then put wheels in motion.

24

Sandy told Owen what had happened before Derek returned. To her surprise and distress two tears rolled down his cheeks. She took his hand, and said there was no need to worry about Derek.

'It isn't that. He was my father, and I liked him. I'd not seen him for years, and now I shall never see him again.'

'You won't be missing much. He was fun to be with, but he was never much good.'

'I know he was a crook, but he never hurt anyone or had them hurt, did he?' She shook her head. 'I wish he'd asked me to have lunch with him or something like that. Do you think Derek killed him?'

'Of course not. You shouldn't think of such a thing. How was the James Joyce conference?'

'All right, except that there was some chap who went on and on about the parallels with *Ulysses*, which was pretty boring. And lots of linguistic stuff. Mummy.'

'Yes?'

He shook his head, took off the large glasses, wiped his eyes.

'Darling, don't worry. Whatever happens, we'll be together, I promise.'

When Derek got back she said that Owen was upset. Derek replied that Owen was not the only one. He got them both a drink, then sank down in the plush armchair. There was silence between them. Silence was alien to Derek, and made him feel uneasy. He asked what was wrong, and she did not reply. He passed a hand through his curls.

'For God's sake, Sandy, what's up? I've just had the worst forty-eight hours of my life, the Italian police more or less suggested I'd killed my partner but they couldn't understand how, and you don't say anything, don't ask a single question. Has something happened I ought to know about?' She shook her head. 'Something you're not telling me. Sandy, we don't have secrets from each other, do we?'

'You know the first thing Owen said when he heard about it? He asked if I thought you'd killed his father.'

'Look, darling, I'm sorry, but I don't care what Owen said or what he thinks.'

'If Owen asks a question like that, other people will too.'

'The only thing that interests me is what you think.'

'I don't know.'

'You *don't know*.' As always there was something actorish in his reaction as he got up and walked about the room, stopping to straighten the picture that might have been a Pollock reproduction, running a hand again through his curls. 'What reason could I possibly have for killing Linnet? I'd never met the man.'

'I don't know,' she repeated. Then after a pause, 'You had reasons to kill Charles.'

'I didn't have time, even the Italians admit that. And in any case nobody killed Charles, he took some drugs and fell into the water and had a heart attack. In any case I had no reason, you know that. I'd made an arrangement with Morvelli that would have given me control.' An idea struck him. 'You've not had another of those letters, you aren't thinking about them?'

'No, I've had no more letters. But yes, of course they're what I was thinking about.'

'You don't mean to say you believe them, you can't?'

'Can't I? If I said I didn't, that was before Charles died. I'm not sure what I believe, or how long I can go on. Or if I want to go on.' She had been looking down at the floor, but now raised her head. 'I shall never be sure, Derek, you must see that.'

'Never be *sure*,' he said incredulously. 'We've always been sure of each other, haven't we? I wasn't having an affair with Gerda, I swear to you I wasn't. Do you want me to go down on my knees and swear it?'

'Of course not, don't be ridiculous. You don't understand what I've been saying, you haven't really listened.'

'I understand you're worried about the letters. I think I know who wrote them.' She looked at him, her freckles more obvious than usual. 'It's obvious, when you think about it. He's just a little crazy in some ways. I've told him to stop interfering in my life. Think what he's like, and you can't be surprised. Jason.'

She put a hand to her mouth, and for a moment he was unsure of her reaction. Then he saw that the hand had been placed there to check what proved uncontrollable laughter.

25

Even to speak on the telephone to Scotland Yard excited Farinella. He envisaged that great organisation as a perfect machine. You made your request for information, your plea for help, and the wheels began to spin – no, the computer brain began to spill out paper – and the answers came in minutes to questions that might occupy another police force for weeks or months. Of course some Italian police forces used computers, there were intelligent policemen in Italy and Francesco Farinella was one of them, yet there could really be no comparison. Scotland Yard was unique.

His experience was at first discouraging. He was put on to somebody named Turnpike. He could not fathom Turnpike's rank, but he had apparently been assigned to deal with Farinella because of an alleged fluency in Italian. His use of the language was so nearly unintelligible that they turned to English, and

Farinella was pleased to be complimented on his accent. It was disconcerting, however, to be told that any conjectural crime would not be Scotland Yard's affair.

'Headfield's outside the Met area, comes under Thames Valley. Mind you, if that Linnet character lived in London we might be able to give you some info on him, but we can't just go poking about in Headfield, wouldn't be appreciated by the locals. Mind if I give you a bit of advice?'

'On the contrary, I should value it.'

'Whatever crime's been committed, and I gather from you you're not sure whether there's been one or not, it happened in your parish.'

'I beg your pardon?'

'Sorry, should have said in your area. It's strictly for you, not our business. Unless you're asking for us to take over, but you're not doing that. So all right, we'll co-operate, but you got to understand there are limits. Give me some questions about this Porson and I'll put 'em to the Thames Valley boys, and ditto about the geezer who was shot, but you're liable just to get answers to what you ask, you read me? If you want any real digging you or somebody else will need to come and do it yourself.'

'Precisely,' Farinella said with enthusiasm. 'I entirely agree. I shall represent your view most strongly to Sostituto Rocco, who is in charge of the preliminary investigation. I am most grateful to you . . .'

He paused in the expectation that his interlocutor would identify himself as Inspector, Superintendent, even Commander. Instead he said, 'Bill Turnpike.'

'Thank you. Commissario Francesco Farinella.'

'Right. Now, you tell me just what you want, Franny, and I'll do my best to come up with something.'

If there was something lacking in dignity about this form of address, it was no more than three days before Turnpike, in his own words, came up with something. His cheerful voice said that he would be putting this stuff on the telex, but he thought Franny might like to have it straight from the horse's mouth.

'First of all, Porson. No police record, bar one conviction for drunken driving seven years ago when he managed to con the magistrates into letting him keep his licence. Got a reputation for chasing anything in skirts – Joe Hardcastle, who told me, used a coarse phrase which I won't repeat.' He then repeated it, and laughed. Farinella, who did not understand why anybody should want to make love to a pig in knickers, laughed too. 'Chairman of the local shooting club, got a shooting gallery attached to his house, collects revolvers, often carries one. Married this German piece much younger than himself, nobody knows where she came from, lots of rumours. But you know what the English are, for them wogs begin at Calais. Begging your pardon, Franny.' He laughed again.

'Then, his partner Crowley. No police record, everyone likes him, supposed to be the live wire behind PC Travel, which is doing pretty well. Rumours are he doesn't get on well with Porson, but seems to be nothing more than gossip. His cousin Colin, nothing there either, or nothing much. In and out of jobs, said to be unreliable, gets mixed up with girls, at the moment dating Derek Crowley's sister. Seems to be on good terms with Derek.' Turnpike broke off. 'There's a lot of seems to be, and rumour has it, which is why I wanted a word on the blower – the phone. Been a few whispers about the anonymous letters, but nobody Joe Hardcastle talked to had received one, which doesn't mean too much. The Thames Valley boys haven't spent a lot of time on it and won't, this came easy. I said before if you want to dig deeper you have to do it yourself.'

'You have told me. And thank you.'

'About the letters, all it really means is nobody's reported them, and if they're not reported they don't exist, get me? Now Linnet, Richard Arthur. Here we do have something. Prison record – convicted of false pretences, put on probation, twelve years ago sentenced for fraud, two years, then eight years ago a five year sentence for fraud and forgery. Said to be a bit of an artist, passports a speciality. No record of violence, and as far as we know he's kept his nose clean since he came out, though it seems unlikely. Shacked up for the last couple of years with an ex-ballet dancer turned nightclub stripper, name of Nancy Nelligan.'

Farinella said that was immensely helpful, thank you, Superintendent. There was another laugh. 'Sergeant.'

It was not very much, as the Commissario said to Grado, but the very littleness of it made the case for an investigation on the spot overwhelming. Grado had made an unencouraging discovery of his own. Jose, the barman who had told the story about the drink and the man in the raincoat, had a string of convictions for theft and fraud, and had got the hotel job on the recommendation of a man closely linked to a Mafia family.

The Commissario tried to view this cheerfully. 'That can have nothing to do with the case. Why should Jose invent such a story? It draws attention to him, and if he was put in the hotel to steal or to pass on information, that is the last thing he would want.'

Grado took out a piece of gum and stuck it under his chair, one of his more disgusting habits. 'I didn't say he'd been put in to steal. Suppose the man Linnet is trying to cheat somebody, picks the wrong person, it is a Mafia killing. This little story about a man in a raincoat would be quite useful, eh? You can look as hard as you like for the man, he never existed.'

'But Jose sticks to his story?'

'Of course.' Grado put in another piece of gum, and added that timings, carefully carried out, had failed to reveal any way in which Derek Crowley could have left the ghetto, reached either the Emperor Napoleon where Linnet had been shot, or the fondamenta near the Fenice Theatre where Porson had been found, and return in half an hour. The most experienced dodger through Venetian byways could hardly have done it on foot and a journey by vaporetto both ways, with an accompanying walk at either end, would also have taken too long. The only possibility was use of a private motor boat, and stringent enquiries had failed to reveal the use or hire of any such boat. They had investigated the possibility that Morvelli might have been in collusion with Crowley, but although Morvelli owned a motor boat there was no doubt at all that it had been tied up the whole evening.

This was not cheerful hearing, but the Commissario still felt that he could make a good case, perhaps even an overwhelming one, for the usefulness of personal enquiries in Britain.

In the meantime telephone bells had been ringing. They rang in the Public Prosecutor's apartment in Rome, in the office of Giudice Istruttore Calvino, whose duty it was to decide whether and how the investigation should proceed further, in the little room where Sostituto Rocco was preparing the *verbale* on which Calvino would make his decision.

Rocco might not have moved since Farinella had last seen him a week ago. A cigarette was stuck in the corner of his mouth, he was hunched over his desk, his eyes had as little animation as his voice when he asked what further developments the Commissario had to report. Farinella outlined what he had learned from Scotland Yard without mentioning that he had been dealing with a mere sergeant, and stressed, perhaps indeed overstressed, what Turnpike had said about the vital importance of on-the-spot investigation. He made a casual mention of Jose's criminal record, but said nothing about the apparent alibi of Derek Crowley.

Rocco listened without interrupting him, then said in that voice which was like dice rattling in a cup, 'We are no further advanced than when we last talked, do you agree?'

Not at all, Farinella said, spreading out his jewelled hands in protest. The reports from Scotland Yard opened up all sorts of possibilities that should – must – be investigated further. He was aware of a sound like a mouse in a wainscot, realised that it was the Sostituto's clicking fingernails, and lost the thread of his argument.

'Is it right to say you are no nearer making a case against any individual than you were a week ago? You disagree, but present no evidence. In the meantime there has been a development.' He removed the cigarette, stubbed it, looked at Farinella with watery grey eyes. 'It has been decided that Linnet's death was suicide.'

'But Tardelli . . . '

'You will find that Dottor Tardelli has changed his mind. He now agrees that the circumstances point to suicide.'

'The man in the cap . . . '

'As you have said, Jose is a crook and a liar. There is no proof that such a man ever existed. Even according to your own story, he left the bar with Porson and so presumably had no part in Linnet's death.'

'How did Linnet get Porson's revolver?'

'You have told me that Linnet was a criminal. It is possible Porson was mixed up in Linnet's crooked deals, learned that the smuggling operation had gone wrong, perhaps other things had gone wrong as well. Porson gave Linnet his revolver, then decided that the game was up too, took the drugged drink. He laughed when the drug was put in because he knew he was finished.' As if in a sudden flush of modesty, he looked down at his desk. The clicking began again.

'That is preposterous.'

'Perhaps. Nevertheless, it has been decided that Linnet shot himself. That will be the effect of my verbale.'

'I shall protest to Giudice Calvino.'

Rocco nodded his grey bullet head. 'You may do so. It would be unwise.'

A thought occurred to Farinella. 'Do you mean this is a political affair? You are recommending that the investigation should be passed to the Carabinieri?'

Rocco's laugh was like breaking glass. 'No no, my friend, not the Carabinieri. I am saying that, in regard to Linnet, he shot himself. Finis. Investigation closed.'

'Then it is political.' Rocco shrugged narrow shoulders. 'What about Porson?'

'In regard to Porson . . . ' There was a pause, more nail clicking. 'Investigations may proceed. Providing it is understood that the affair of Linnet is not drawn into it.'

'That is impossible. There would be no point in my making further investigations in England if I have to ignore the death of Linnet.'

The watery eyes looked steadily at him. 'Nevertheless, Commissario, I assure you that is what must happen.'

In effect that, for Commissario Francesco Farinella, was how it ended. He knew that there would be no good outcome when he spoke to Tardelli, and the pathologist said that he had perhaps been too dogmatic, these things were a matter of opinion rather than fact, in the matter of Linnet suicide was a perfectly reasonable possibility, perhaps even a probability. Investigations continued for a few more days, but Grado found nobody who had seen Porson after he left Morvelli's party and before he appeared in the bar of the Emperor Napoleon. The man in the cap – for whose existence there was only Jose's word – remained a mystery. The film smuggling business, which was in any case not the affair of the PS, fizzles out in a few fines, with the Guardia di Finanza congratulating themselves on their own watchfulness.

In short, the affair died. Farinella was unable to share Grado's view that he was lucky not to have been sent to England, since the English were all liars and would have enmeshed him in the webs of deceit they spun. He felt, as he said to Lucia, that this was the kind of chance for glory that came only once or twice in a lifetime, and that it had been snatched from him. Lucia wanted him to go above Rocco's head, and make a protest to the Giudice Istruttore. He considered the idea but rejected it, since the directive that Linnet's death should be treated as suicide plainly came from some more important source than the Sostituto. To complain would merely be to make trouble for himself. One had to accept reality, and he reported to Rocco that although the circumstances of Porson's death remained suspicious, he was unable to present evidence that would justify the arrest of any individual. He added that something further might be done if he were allowed to pursue the matter in England, or if the British police were invited to take up the case with his assistance. Rocco replied to this last suggestion, which he no doubt recognised as a face-saving rider, that the Commissario had done everything possible, but had not produced sufficient evidence to justify a perhaps lengthy and expensive investigation abroad, and that the British police had shown no interest in the case.

Some months later the *Sunday Banner* story appeared.

PART THREE

The *Sunday Banner* story concluded

. . . The first unusual thing about these anonymous letters is that they lasted such a short time, and were identical in their message. Most anonymous letter writers begin with mild accusations, which build up to a crescendo over a period of weeks or even months. Here, however, the message was the same in every case, although the wording varied. The first letter we have traced was sent ten days before the death of Charles Porson in Venice, and was received by TV producer Norman Dixon and his wife Caroline. Members of the Crowley family and others received letters within the next two or three days. All the letters said that Derek Crowley was having an affair with Charles Porson's wife Gerda. Porson and Crowley were partners in PC Travel, a well-regarded and prosperous Headfield travel firm. With Porson's death the letters ended – almost, one might think, as if their object had been achieved.

We asked Derek Crowley whether he thought this was a possibility, and also why neither he nor Porson had gone to the police. Crowley is a lively, handsome man, who is in his late thirties but looks younger. He talked readily, but showed signs of strain. These were not surprising, in view of the rumours circulating in the town.

'We didn't go to the police because everybody concerned knew that the accusations were absurd. If they'd gone on for several weeks I suppose we'd have done something. As for achieving their object I think that's just nonsense.'

We asked Crowley for his own view about the letters.

'There are two possibilities. The first is that they were written to damage the firm, the second that they were written by somebody jealous of me.' But he could not think of any commercial rival, and refused to speculate on the identity of any individual who might have sent them.

Some of the rumours in the town concern the strained relations said to exist between the partners. Crowley refused to admit any strain, although he agreed that they had arguments. Porson's former secretary Julia Nettleberry, however, spoke of frequent quarrels between the two men, most of them because Porson objected to what he called 'lunatic projects' for expansion advocated by Crowley. Miss Nettleberry also said that it was something of a joke among the staff that no girl should ever be left on her own with Porson because he was certain to make a pass at her. Had she suffered personally?

'I couldn't count the times. More than once I've smacked his face. He didn't seem to mind, rather enjoyed it.'

There was general agreement that Porson was a difficult man to like. Another woman member of the staff called him the perfect embodiment of the male chauvinist pig, and even members of the Headfield Shooting Club invited to the specially built shooting gallery at the rear of his house found him arrogant and boastful. Major 'Metty' Metcalf, who took part in some of the shooting matches organised by Porson at the gallery, said that he could be extremely sulky if he lost.

'He was a good shot, better then me, but thought he was unbeatable,' Major Metcalf said. 'If I happened to beat him he'd say he was feeling off colour, or that he'd been out drinking and his hand wasn't steady. But he had a passion for guns, no doubt about that.' This passion extended to having a special pocket made in his suits to accommodate his gold-plated Beretta revolver. Everybody we spoke to agreed that he carried this for show, not because he feared attack. It was the ultimate in male chauvinist piggishness, the woman already quoted said, adding that he produced it as though showing you his sexual organ.

There is an odd feature about one letter sent to the Dixons, which named the address where Crowley and Gerda Porson were said to meet, a flat in West Headfield. This proved to be a false lead, and when we talked to Pat O'Brien, caretaker of this rather dingy block of flats, he told us that he had received an envelope holding thirty-five pounds in notes, and a typewritten request that if anybody should ask whether Mr Crowley or Mrs Porson had recently rented a flat in the block he should say that they had. He did so when Mrs Dixon made an enquiry of this kind, but subsequently became nervous about what he had said, and retracted it. He had not kept the typewritten note enclosing the money.

O'Brien's story makes it seem that somebody was trying to blacken the reputations of Crowley and Mrs Porson. They have had some success. Friends of the Crowleys agree that before the letters arrived Derek and Sandy were a very happy couple, but Sandy Crowley has now moved out of the family house with Owen, son by her first marriage, to a flat in the town. She has obtained a secretarial job in London, and in the brief interview she gave us said that she thought the separation from her husband might be permanent. She added that when her son left school at the end of the term, she would probably leave Headfield.

Derek Crowley said that he hopes Sandy will return to him when the rumours have died down. They have certainly not been checked by the fact that Gerda Porson has sold her husband's shares in the travel firm to Derek Crowley, so that he is now sole owner. Mrs Porson sold the shares against the advice of Porson's lawyer, Mr Carter, who said to us that she could certainly have obtained a higher figure for the shares. She told him, however, that her prime concern was to get rid of them and put the whole affair behind her.

There seems little doubt that in the week after the letters began to arrive, at least one and possibly two attempts were made to kill Charles Porson. The first occurred at the rehearsal of a play done by a local amateur dramatic society. Porson and Crowley were both members of the society, although Crowley was not present when Porson was nearly shot by a property revolver into which one live round had been placed. In the course of the play this revolver had to be fired by Mrs Crowley at Porson. Fortunately she missed. In fact it is most unlikely that he would have been hit, although the person who inserted the live round would not have known that. We were able to borrow this property revolver. A gunsmith reported to us that it was so much out of alignment that if aimed straight it would certainly have missed any target.

It is more doubtful whether the second incident was a genuine murder attempt. Porson was extremely fond of the drink Bloody Mary (vodka and tomato juice), something well-known to his friends. At a party a friend of Crowley's named Jason Durling took a Bloody Mary, the only one on that drink tray. The effect was to make him semi-conscious and apparently extremely drunk. It is probable, although not certain, that the drink was meant for Porson. If so, the attempt that misfired in Headfield succeeded forty-eight hours later in Venice.

The play rehearsal was held on Wednesday, the party on the following evening. On Friday a PC Travel party set off by train for Venice. It included the two partners, along with Jason Durling and Derek Crowley's cousin Colin, who acted as courier to the party and also, we learned, engaged in a smuggling enterprise of his own relating to the import of Japanese porno films. Such trains are rarely fully booked, and one of the travellers on it was Richard Linnet, first husband of Sandy Crowley, although they had been divorced for some years. Linnet's presence on the train was not a coincidence. He was involved in the smuggling operation. Our researches have convinced us that neither Derek Crowley nor Porson knew anything of this.

Linnet is an enigmatic figure. He had served prison sentences for fraud and forgery, but had apparently also been engaged at times on work for some Government intelligence agency. We talked about him to Nancy Nelligan, who had lived with him for the past three years. Nancy, a vivacious redhead in her thirties who had a previous career as a ballet dancer and has occasional small parts in TV sitcoms, said he had been fun to live with.

'Dicky Bird was always cheerful, whether he was flush or nearly skint. Far as I knew he was on the straight and narrow, but I never asked questions, and of course I knew he had things going on the side.' She was vague about what those things might be, although she said that he had more than once tried to involve her in smuggling enterprises. She had always said no. He had once gone so far as to produce a forged passport for her in a false name, but she had refused to use it. 'I said, what are you trying to do, Dicky, put me inside, and I burnt that passport page by page. It was the only time I saw him angry, and I was sorry afterwards, it was so beautifully done it was really a work of art. Dicky was very clever.'

She added that he had done work for the Government, but she had been told not to talk about that. Who had told her? She refused to say. She did not know that he had been married, and he had never mentioned the names Porson or Crowley. After the burning of the passport he had never tried to involve her in any of his business affairs. We asked what she would do now. She said that she had a little pension, she didn't say from what source, but that Dicky Bird hadn't left any money. ('You wouldn't expect it really, it was easy come, easy go.') She would be looking for work.

(The next section of the article is omitted, as it recounts in detail the events relating to the deaths, Morvelli's party, the discovery of the bodies, and the story of the bartender Jose.)

We talked to Commissario Farinella, who was in charge of the case, in the little *questura* building at the end of the Fondamenta San Lorenzo. He was co-operative and friendly, but made it clear that he thought a solution to the various puzzles highly unlikely. He made a careful differentiation between the two deaths.

'It has been decided by the authorities that Signor Linnet shot himself. Dottor Tardelli, our expert pathologist, has agreed that this was likely, and the case is officially closed. Signor Porson's death is another matter. It is true that he had a heart attack when he entered the water, but my belief is that he was drugged, taken to the dark place where he was found, and pushed into the water.'

The Commissario thinks that the person who pushed him in knew that Porson suffered from angina, so that a heart attack was a possibility, but would have been prepared if necessary to stop him climbing out of the water. In his drugged, semi-conscious state Porson could have made little resistance, and would quickly have drowned.

Who knew that Porson suffered from angina? The only people who have admitted knowledge are Gerda Porson, and Julia

Nettleberry, who had seen him take little pills which he kept on his desk, and had once been told by him that they were for a heart condition. Derek Crowley was emphatic that he did not know of his partner's condition.

The Commissario can offer few hard facts to back up his theory. He has no explanation for the movement of Porson's Beretta out of his possession into that of Linnet when the two men had met only in the hotel bar, nor about the identity of the mysterious man in the cap who was apparently responsible for drugging Porson's drink, and even more remarkably appears to have done so with his compliance. The Commissario believes that the departures from Morvelli's party were highly significant.

It seems likely that Porson left to keep an appointment, and he could easily have made the journey from the party to the Emperor Napoleon by vaporetto. He was not seen to do so, but it is unlikely that any traveller on the vaporetto would be particularly noticed, and from the San Marco stop it is no more than five minutes' walk to the hotel. The police enquiries, which we were convinced have been extremely thorough, have concentrated on the possibility that somebody followed Porson from the party, and it is plain that the person they have in mind was Derek Crowley, who was absent for half an hour. They have proved conclusively that it would have been impossible for Crowley to leave the party, meet Porson at or near the spot where he entered the water, and return within the given time. When we suggested that this proved Crowley could have had no connection with his partner's death, however, the Commissario merely shrugged his shoulders.

In their concentration on Derek Crowley's alibi, however, the Italian police paid less attention that they might have done to the man in the cap, and because of this they have missed evidence that poses the problem of the Guest Who Never Arrived. On the assumption that the man in the cap might have arrived in Venice that day (several flights arrived from a number of countries during the afternoon and early evening) we checked on all hotel and pensione bookings and arrivals on Saturday, with a surprising result. Our investigator had with her photographs of

Porson and Crowley, and at a little pensione called the Eros the picture of Porson was recognised. He had come in on Saturday morning, and had booked a room for that night on behalf of a friend who would be arriving later. He gave the name of the friend as Mr R. Jay.

The Eros is a shabby little place. It is in an alley no more than five minutes' walk from the Emperor Napoleon hotel, but to reach it you would pass the dark little fondamenta near which the body was found. The owner of the Eros, a Rumanian named Antonescu who has lived in Venice for twenty years, was positive in his identification of Porson as the man who booked and paid for the room. It was never occupied, however. Mr R. Jay is the Guest Who Never Arrived.

If Antonescu's identification is correct, the discovery raises further questions. Was Jay the man in the cap? And does the booking provide a link between Porson and Linnet? Linnet called himself Dicky Bird when introducing himself to Jason Durling. Is the fact that Jay's name is that of a bird significant, or merely coincidental?

Mr Durling's name has been only briefly mentioned, but he was a recurrent presence on the scene, and an important source of information. He knew Derek Crowley at school and university, and remains a close friend. He also travelled to Venice with Linnet. He expressed the view that too much had already been said and suggested, too many rumours spread, but he eventually agreed to talk to us. Mr Durling is small and dapper, his manner gentle but sometimes gently ironic. He is a civil servant in a Whitehall ministry, and has lived in Headfield all his life. He told us that he has an affection for the town, but regards it as a hive of sometimes malicious gossip. He said that Derek Crowley was a brilliant personality whose career and marriage were being affected by rumours without any factual basis, and added that Derek's stepfather Xavier Crowley had been greatly upset by them. Xavier Crowley, who was also the recipient of an anonymous letter, is now in a nursing home, and was not well enough to be interviewed.

We asked Durling about the Bloody Mary he had drunk at the

party in Headfield.

'At the time I thought I had been poisoned, but I believe now that the drink was meant for Porson and I took it by mistake. It had a very powerful effect. Within minutes I had lost all sense of time and direction. If Porson had the same drug put into his drink in Venice he would have had little idea of what he was doing.'

He denied that he had been drunk at the Headfield party, but admitted drinking too much on the fatal Saturday night in Venice, saying he had suffered a deep disappointment about something quite unconnected with the case. Dolores Makins, cashier in a Headfield bank, who was with Durling early in the evening, confirmed taking him back to his room, where she would have thought him likely to 'pass out'. Durling told us that he knew nothing of what had happened until wakened by Derek Crowley after the deaths.

We had been told stories – which, it should be said, were at secondhand – that Derek Crowley had been in trouble of some sort in his youth. Durling refused to comment on these suggestions. Colin Crowley also refused to talk to us about this, or about the smuggling offences for which he, along with others involved, was heavily fined.

Within a month of Charles Porson's death his widow left England. She paid a brief visit to Germany to visit her parents, then rented a villa on the island of Elba. When we first contacted her she refused to be interviewed, but later changed her mind. To use her own words: 'I may as well say it all now. Then it will be done with. I shall refuse to give any other interviews, and hope I will be left alone.'

We found her in a small rented villa near Bagnaia, a few miles from the island's capital Portoferraio. She said that she was there alone, and we saw no sign that anybody else was staying at the villa. She is using her maiden name of Rieger, because she does not wish to be reminded of the past.

Even though we had seen photographs of Gerda Rieger, we were surprised by her youth and beauty. This is not of a classic kind, but she is an almost perfect example of an exuberant

Teutonic blonde. It was late September when we saw her, the weather was still warm, and she wore shorts and a halter. She talked readily, in a slightly accented voice, with only occasional flashes of impatience. One of our first questions was whether there had been any truth in the letters.

'None at all. But that did not stop people from believing them. I like Derek, but if he has kissed me it is on the cheek. I do not think I have ever been alone with him.'

She said she had no idea who sent the letters, or why. 'But there were people in Headfield who did not like me. I was young and pretty – you see I don't mind saying it – and a bloody German. For some people that was enough. They said that I married Charles for his money, and that was true. I never pretended to love him, and he knew it. I did not like the life I had in Germany, as a nightclub hostess. I was happy to leave it.'

Why had she left England so suddenly? 'There was nothing sudden. I did not want to play a part in the business, why should I stay? I was advised that the price offered was a low one, but I did not care.'

We asked if she was the sole beneficiary under her husband's will. When she understood the word 'beneficiary,' she agreed that she was. It was when we suggested that it was strange to come and live alone on Elba rather than staying with friends that she showed impatience.

'What friends? I have no friends. I wanted to get away from hints and sneers, do you understand? So I come here, I rent this place, I look for a new life. Perhaps I shall stay here, perhaps when the season is over I leave, I don't know. I shall do what I want, for the first time in my life.' When we pursued the point about possible loneliness she became annoyed. 'Perhaps you do not believe I am alone, you think a man must be here? You are free to look. In six months, perhaps less, there may be somebody else in my life, but for now I wish nothing except to forget.'

But since she had not loved her husband, what was there to forget? 'Some say I had his partner as lover, some say I had him killed – oh yes, I have heard that. I can tell you that there is plenty to forget.' We said we had heard that Charles Porson pursued women. 'I knew that, everybody knew it. But I did not care. He could have had a dozen women a month, it would not have worried me.'

What did she think had happened? 'I do not know, I was at the party. I do not know, and I will be frank with you and say, I do not care.'

There are question marks round the title of this article. At the end of our investigation we have the strong impression that not one, but two murders may have been committed – for we believe that there was an intention to kill Porson, even though he died of a heart attack.

At the least it must be said that the present state of affairs will be profoundly unsatisfactory until four questions are answered. Here they are:

(i)   Who wrote the anonymous letters?
(ii) Who was the man in the cap?
(iii) Was he identical with the man 'Jay' for whom Porson booked a room at the Pensione Eros? And in any case, what happened to him?
(iv) How did Porson's Beretta pass into Linnet's possesion?

We believe Derek Crowley knows – or thinks he knows – the answer to the first question. If we are right, he should speak out. And we think the present article provides good grounds for Scotland Yard to open a file on what we boldy characterise, without any question marks, as *The Venice Murders*.

EPILOGUE

The *Sunday Banner* sold a lot of copies in Headfield on the week that the colour magazine carried the article on '??? The Venice Murders ???'.

For the next month it was the chief subject of town gossip. Some people said that Derek would really have to do something about it, others that nowadays papers could print anything and get away with it. But nobody outside Headfield – that is, nobody in a position of authority – paid much attention to it. David Devonshire and Sally Simpson, who was what he called his live-in girl friend, had only middling journalistic reputations. He was a reject from *The Sunday Times* Insight team, she had worked in TV, radio and women's magazines, but never for long.

The article was read at Scotland Yard, where it was quickly decided that conjectural crimes taking place in a foreign country, even though they involved British nationals, were not their pigeon. The Colonel read it, and thanked the Lord that Linnet's red-headed bint knew which side her bread was buttered, and hadn't opened her mouth too wide. At the same time, she shouldn't have opened it at all, and he sent Bealby to tell her that if she wanted to continue receiving the modest sum of money that wasn't called a pension, she should remember that.

'About Linnet, sir. I suppose he *wasn't* terminated by the Department?'

The Colonel glared at him. 'Of course not.'

'Then what happened?'

'Some petty private business, I suppose. I don't know and don't care. Just tell Miss Nancy Whatnot to keep her mouth shut in future.'

Nancy was, and did.

In Venice Farinella read the article, and said to Grado that they should have checked the hotels. Grado shrugged, and said it could be of no importance, he knew Antonescu who would do anything for money, no doubt the English journalists had bribed him to say what he did. Farinella did not believe this, but he knew that the case was a lost cause. He consoled himself with the sympathy of Lucia, who repeatedly told him how badly he had been treated.

In Headfield Derek smiled and smiled, and said he knew who his friends were, and did not care about what was hinted in a scandal sheet. His deepest regret was that Uncle X had been told about the article in his nursing home, and had somehow got hold of a copy of the paper. Reading it, Derek believed, had brought on the stroke after which he became more or less a vegetable, one that consumed solids and liquids but was almost unintelligible in speech and cloudy in mind.

Sandy did not return to Derek. She left Headfield, and was said to have some job in London in the public relations department of an electronics firm.

Jason wrote to Derek, assuring him that he did not believe a word of the hints and sneers in the *Banner* story, and had told them nothing at all about the past. He received the briefest of notes in reply.

And then, slowly, Headfield forgot the affair. The deaths in Venice had no public solution.

In the three years that followed, several things happened to the major and lesser characters involved.

PC Travel (the name remained unchanged) expanded, not in the Far East but in the United States. With the enthusiastic co-operation of Guido Morvelli, who became a partner, Derek devised unusual tours under the general heading 'The Old World and the New', embracing both Italy and the United States, with particular attention to artistic festivals in both countries. The fact that the tours were extremely expensive was regarded as one reason for their success. Derek returned from one of the trips to the States when he was setting up the tours accompanied by Debby Morton, who settled in at Philip and Elizabeth Villa. Debby was in her late twenties, a lively extrovert who had worked as copy editor for a New York publisher. She offered avocado and guacamole dips as hostess at cocktail parties that were agreed to be delightfully American, American as the uninhibited conversation in which she said the most amusingly original things. The seal of Headfield approval was set on Debby when Eldred Bruce-Comfort came, saw, and said she was a charming young creature with a true feeling for art and literature. Derek filed for divorce from Sandy on the grounds of desertion, and Headfield opinion agreed that she had behaved very badly in abandoning her husband when he was in trouble.

Norman Dixon made a docufict about Indians and Pakistanis in Wolverhampton, intercut with scenes showing British colonial rule in India. The fict part of this was written by the young novelist Biffy, and soon after it had been shown to considerable critical acclaim, Norman left Caroline and went to live with Biffy. Their house was sold, and with her part of the proceeds Caroline started a dress shop in town, living in the flat above the shop.

Colin Crowley's activities as middleman for gun runners lasted only three months, ending when he was beaten up by an Iraqi who said that a consignment of automatic weapons were not the brand new guns paid for, but ancient relics from World War II. He spent three months in a Syrian hospital, and returned to Headfield much chastened. He was quietly married to Steph at a registry office, and re-engaged by PC Travel as office manager. In that position he was a great success, liked by everybody. Within a year the couple had a son, who was called Colin Xavier. The Xavier was in memory of Uncle X, who had slipped out of life soon after Colin's marriage. He could not be present at the wedding, and although Mary did her best to explain it to him, she could not be sure that anything got through the fog clouding his mind.

Xavier's funeral was impressive. Many Headfield people remembered him as editor, businessman, sportsman, figure in town affairs. There were dozens of wreaths, and nearly two hundred mourners followed the coffin. Jason was among them, properly funereal in dark suit, dark grey overcoat, black bow tie. As they left the church he spoke to Derek, whose only concession to convention was a black tie. It was a fine day in winter, and the wind ruffled his curls. Jason said they had not seen each other for months, and Derek replied that he had been busy.

'I think you've been avoiding me.' He paused, but there was no contradiction. 'Derek, I've had a lot of time to think about what happened in Venice, and why. I believe I know almost all of it now.'

206

'Do you?'

'I think we should talk about it.'

Derek's eyes flashed with what might have been genuine, or (as Jason preferred to think) simulated anger. 'I've had time to think too. Whatever you know, or think you know, keep it to yourself.'

'You remember that evening in Venice, in the gondola. It seemed to me, when I thought about it, that you were hinting I wrote those letters. You can't think that.'

'Can't I?'

'There are things I've worked out . . . '

Derek's pale face was distorted with anger. 'How dare you come and talk to me like this when Uncle X is being buried. I don't want to hear anything more.' His voice was raised and Mary, a yard or two in front of them, looked round in surprise. 'Whatever you know, whatever you think you've worked out, keep it to yourself.'

He went forward to join his aunt. They did not speak again.

It was true that, with his constant occupation of research into Cruddle's life and works at an end, Jason had had plenty of time to think about the questions posed at the end of the *Banner* article. What had at first been an interest, pursued to fill a gap in his life, became a passion after what he felt to be his rejection by Derek. He filled pages of his journal with facts, conjectures, possible explanations. He bought two large albums in which he pasted everything that had appeared in the press about the affair, together with such things as his correspondence with British Airways, and at the end a typescript setting out the conclusions he had reached.

In this typescript he analysed what had happened from the beginning, considering all that had occurred before the tragedies, the letters, the revolver shot, the Bloody Mary. Each of these was given a separate section, and at the end of each section he summarised what might be deduced from the individual incident. When he linked these summaries up with what had happened in Venice, the man in the cap, the addition to Porson's drink, the hotel booking, there seemed one inevitable answer. There were gaps in his knowledge, areas that remained speculative, but some of these gaps were filled. The British Airways correspondence provided one piece in the jigsaw, and another dropped into place at a retrospective show of Max Beerbohm caricatures. He was tapped on the shoulder, and a voice said, 'Jason Durling, isn't it?' He would not have recognised the tall youth in a bottle green velvet suit, but for his large spectacles. Owen said that his mother was well and that he was marking time, waiting to go up to Oxford. What was he reading? English.

'Specialising in James Joyce?' Jason asked playfully. 'The last time we met you were going to a Joyce conference in London.'

'Not London – Manchester. And we have to start with Anglo-Saxon still, or at least I am. Anyway modernism's played out, I'm into Kingsley Amis.'

'He's much more straightforward, certainly.'

Owen shook his head. 'There's a lot of symbolism. A man named Conquest wrote an article called "Christian Symbolism in *Lucky Jim*". Very instructive.'

'Do you ever hear from . . . ' Jason had been about to say ' . . . your stepfather', but substituted '–Derek?'

Behind thick lenses Owen's pale blue eyes were hostile. 'I don't wish to. That part of my life is over.'

Jason became so absorbed by the new quest that the old one was almost forgotten. He was left surprisingly unmoved by publication of *The Genius They Forgot: the Life and Work of D.M. Cruddle*, by Dwight Eidelberg, although he read with pleasure the dismissive reviews, like that which wound up: 'Mr Eidelberg's unintended achievement is to convince us that no faded flower of the period was ever more completely withered than D.M. Cruddle.'

He sent a letter to Gerda's solicitors asking for her present address, but was told in reply only that his communication had been sent on to Fräulein Rieger. The letter remained unanswered. A quest begun should have an end, however, and it was in pursuit of such an end that he went to Elba in early October. A taxi took him from Portoferraio to the tiny resort of

Bagnaia. There he asked questions, found the villa that Fräulein Rieger had rented, but was told by the English couple living there that she had left two years ago. Where had she gone? Somewhere on the island, they believed, not back to England or her native Germany, but where? One or two letters had come for her, they had had an address, but perhaps it had been destroyed. Or perhaps, the retired Major said to his wife, perhaps it was in the jumble box where they kept all kinds of things that just might conceivably be needed one day. And the jumble box revealed a strip of paper and an address: Villa Appiano, Poggio. That was where Fräulein Rieger had been, two years ago. And, yes, they said with obvious surprise at the question, when they had seen her at Bagnaia she had been living alone.

In Portoferraio he rented a little Fiat. Elba is a small island, and the roads, many made recently for tourists, are good. In little more than an hour he was at the fishing village of Marciana Marina, and had turned off the coast road inland and upwards, the road at first rising gently through fields and vineyards, then more steeply. He drove through thick chestnut woods, a board said 'Poggio' and then he was among narrow streets that curled round on themselves like a sleeping cat. He parked the Fiat in a little square and looked for the Post Office. The air was deliciously cool, the steep narrow streets showed vistas of flowers in pots outside houses.

In the post office he produced the paper with its name and address, and tried to explain in stumbling phrases what he wanted, but was met with a shrug of the shoulders. Bystanders were curious to see the paper, then shook their heads or murmured 'Non capisco'. He returned to the street and sat on a bench. For some reason it had not occurred to him that, once arrived in Poggio, he would be unable to find anybody who knew Gerda. Nor had he seriously considered that she might no longer be here.

'Excuse me. I couldn't help hearing you a moment ago. The Italians can be so brusque, can't they?' The voice was English, the accent ladylike, the speaker a middle-aged middle-class woman who smiled at him from beneath a wide straw hat. She sat down beside him.

209

'I thought I really *must* speak, I mean out of sympathy. You see, my cousin Geoffrey was in the Foreign Office. Not in an important post, although he made it seem so in conversation. You can see it was a surprise.'

'Did your cousin know Fräulein Rieger?'

'No, why should you think so? Not so far as I am aware, that is, although in these days one never knows. Certainly I have never heard of her.'

An arch look came sidewise under the hat. Jason was painfully reminded of Dolores Makins.

'I'm afraid I don't understand.'

'Surely you were asking for the Villa Appiano? Dear Geoffrey used to spend his holidays there years ago, and I always came out for two or three weeks, sometimes longer. And Tom, of course, Tom used to say . . . '

Was Tom, now deceased, husband or brother? His occasional questions bounced off her discourse like arrows from a shield, but he eventually learned that the villa was outside Poggio, on a track leading off the road to Marciano Alto. He refused her suggestion that she should come at least part of the way to guide him (she was staying with her daughter and son-in-law at Marciano Marina, but had taken the bus up to Poggio because, she said, she longed to be alone), thanked her, and broke away. She remained on the bench looking after him. He did not dare to turn back and wave, in case she rose in pursuit.

The road to Marciano Alto wound further upwards, then corkscrewed round so that he almost missed the dirt track leading off to the right. It had been bright on the road but he moved now into the shade of woods, thick branches of chestnuts hiding the sun. The track narrowed, the day seemed to grow darker. He stopped the car, got out, walked on a few yards and saw nothing but dense forest on either side, heard no sound. For a moment he knew again the terror of his nightmare. The trees seemed to press in on him, he felt the sense of confinement that always preceded the struggle to escape. If he could have turned the car and gone back he would have done so, but the narrow track led ineluctably ahead. He said aloud 'I fear the stillness', and as if the words had been a signal, that stillness was broken by the reassuring resonance of an axe striking wood. Shivering a little, he returned to the car.

A hundred yards on, the track turned almost at a right angle. On the left the chestnut forest ended, and the land dropped sharply to reveal a panorama of ordered fields, a sprinkling of tiny cottages, and beyond them the hard brilliance of blue sea. Still the track coiled and twisted, so that he almost missed the man-made break in the trees on the right, and the small board that said 'Villa Appiano'. Here there was an asphalted path opening out on to a patch of rough land where a Range Rover stood. He parked the car beside it, and got out. The valley lay below him like an opened fan.

Jason was not particularly susceptible to the beauty of landscape, but he stood entranced for several moments beside the rough stone wall that served as a brake before the steep drop into the valley. To his right was another low wall broken by a gap, past which he saw the villa white and gleaming in the sun. In front of it was a terrace with chairs and a marble table. From this terrace, as he walked through, he could see past an open sliding window into an untidy living room. This was the back of the villa, and it occurred to him suddenly that if Gerda had left, the occupant might not be pleased to see a stranger peering in. He had turned to walk round to the other side of the house when Gerda came out on to the terrace. She said, 'Jason hallo, what are you doing here?'

Her reaction was so natural that it surprised him, yet what had he expected? He said something incoherent and ridiculous, about being in Elba and meeting somebody who had said she lived here. Gerda smiled and nodded, they sat down. She took in his seersucker suit, his bow tie, his reversed calf shoes, and said that he looked just like himself. She was blooming, golden hair slightly bleached by the sun, golden skin faintly fuzzy. She wore a dark blue shirt and shorts, with a thin white jacket covering her shoulders.

The sound he heard had ceased. Gerda smiled, put her head back and closed her eyes, as if the remark about his appearance

211

had exhausted her conversational capacity. Jason moved uneasily on his chair.

A man appeared at the other end of the terrace, carrying a basket of logs. He wore shirt and trousers, and a cap was pulled down over his face. He disappeared round the other side of the house. Jason looked at Gerda. She opened her eyes, smiled at him, closed them again.

The man reappeared without the log basket, came towards them, took off the cap. It was Sandy, her hair cut short. Jason sighed. She sat down.

'In my working clothes,' she said. 'Chopping up logs for winter. The person you expected?'

'The person I expected.'

'Gerda's solicitors sent on your letter, we thought you might turn up. Though we're not sure why.'

'I know it all, Sandy. I've spent the past three years working it out, and I think I know it all.'

'My my. Then you'd better tell us.'

He found no difficulty in doing so, for this was a scene he had rehearsed many times in his mind, so that now when he translated thought into speech the ideas came out in the right order, and he was able to admire his own clarity of expression, his admirable shaping of the tale. He had reflected sometimes in the past that this shaping and ordering should have been given to the biography of Cruddle rather than the solution of this different puzzle, yet the exposition still pleased him.

'The first thing to understand is that the object of the exercise was to kill Charles Porson, and that no consideration was given to the possibility that his death might be regarded as an accident. Why should he die? So that Gerda might have the pleasure of his money without the pain of his company. But when one partner in a marriage is murdered the other is almost automatically the chief suspect, and this is much more likely to be so when the potential suspect is an attractive foreigner with a dubious background. How does one divert suspicion? Why, by the daring way of emphasising it. Since people think Gerda may be a slut, accuse her of having an affair, but make the accusation obviously falsc. Hence the anonymous letters, the first step in carrying out the plan, which said that Gerda was having an affair with Derek. The conspirators thought nobody would believe them since Derek was known to be happily married, nor of course was anybody likely to think Gerda had played a part in sending them out. By "the conspirators" I mean you two, and I have no doubt that Sandy was the prime mover, Gerda the consenting partner.'

Gerda looked, a little nervously perhaps, at Sandy, and received a reassuring smile.

'The letters were meant to create an atmosphere of suspicion. They succeeded almost too well, because everybody loves a scandal. It was perhaps a mistake for Sandy deliberately to murmur "That bitch" so that I could hear it, and to set Caroline Dixon on a wild goose chase for a lovers' hideout which didn't exist. However, the atmosphere was certainly created. It was emphasised by the apparent attempt to kill Charles at the rehearsal. Of course, there was no intention to kill him. Sandy made sure the shot went wide, and just in case it remained unnoticed she drew attention to the fact that the vase had been broken.'

'The revolver was out of alignment,' Sandy said.

'I think you knew that. In any case you fired so wide that the shot could not possibly have hit Charles. The right effect was achieved, it was established that somebody would like to see Charles dead. At the same time you were careful to avoid a police investigation, which was the last thing you wanted. The attempted shooting was played down as a practical joke, and Derek refused to go to the police about the letters. He would have been guided by you about that, Sandy, he did what you wanted.

'Then we come to the incident of the Bloody Mary at the Bruce-Comforts' party, drunk by me. I thought at first I had been poisoned, then realised I had taken a drink meant for Charles. I think this was an experiment, to see the effect of a strong drug, and I served as guinea pig instead of Charles, that's all. Where did the drug come from? I remembered that at the party I heard the dentist you call the Extractor talking about the merits of something called chorambazine, which he said made a patient almost but not quite insensible. Sandy was his receptionist, and would have had access to the drug.' He paused, but Sandy said nothing.

'So the scene is set for Venice. There Charles is to be drugged, and when almost insensible pushed into the water. It was part of the plan to make clear that Gerda could have had no direct connection with his death, and no more could Derek, because he would be at a travel agents' conference in England. I think there was clearly no intention to involve him. You couldn't know that Charles would have a heart attack, and were prepared for the case to be treated as murder, a murder which would remain a mystery. The plan was persisted in even after you knew that Derek would be in Venice during that weekend. It was too good a chance to miss.

'But how was it to be done? To understand that we must look at Sandy's character, and at that of Charles Porson.'

A pair of dark glasses lay on the marble table. Gerda picked them up and put them on. Sandy said 'By all means tell me about my character.'

'The person we knew in Headfield was the Sandy who had been for six years Derek's apparently happy wife, but before that she'd been married for eight years to a crook. Not just for eighteen months, but eight years.'

'If I'm to be talked about like this, I'd sooner you said "you" and not "she". I am here, after all.' She put a hand on Gerda's arm. 'Not that it matters, darling. Whether Jason says "you" or "she", it's just talk.'

Jason frowned like a scientist whose demonstration has been interrupted by an awkward student.

'Married to a crook,' he repeated. 'And one whose speciality was forgery. His mistress Nancy Nelligan told how he had forged a passport for her, so beautifully done that she was sorry she'd destroyed it. I'll come back to that. The point I'm making now is that the Sandy who married Derek had lived quite a different life when she was Mrs Linnet. And she'd been Mrs Linnet for a long time.

'And what was Charles like? We all knew that he liked to . . . '

his lips refused to form the coarse word '. . . go to bed with women. Any women, all women, but he was especially pleased to cuckold the wife of somebody he knew, like his friend Jack Sanderson. Can you imagine what enjoyment he would have got from bedding the wife of the handsome partner with whom he was so much at odds? And for it to be done in Venice, under Derek's nose as it were, when he thought Sandy was safely tucked up in bed at home, that made it perfect. At some time Porson made a pass at you, Sandy, as he did to all attractive women, and to his delight you responded. That was why he left the party. To meet you, and go to bed with you.'

'Perfectly true that Charles made a pass, it was automatic, but not that I said yes. In any case, I *was* tucked up in bed at Headfield.'

'I agree the idea seems outrageous. What put it into my mind? Why, the incident in the hotel bar which was never explained, and really was extraordinary. Just consider. Porson saw the man in the cap empty the phial into his drink, saw it, and *laughed*. Why should he have laughed, what could possibly have amused him about the emptying of a phial into his glass, what did he think it contained? In the end I found the answer: an aphrodisiac. I think I decided then, Sandy, that you must have been the man in the cap.

'When I gave that answer, so many balls fell into the right slots. I understood Porson's look of complacency, remembered that Sandy was a tall woman, recalled Derek saying you both knew Venice well. And it explained why Porson had booked a room in a shabby little hotel. Then I thought of the passport Linnet had forged for Nancy Nelligan. Wasn't it very likely that he had forged another for the wife who had lived with him for eight years, the woman who must have known about his frauds, and perhaps was his confederate when needed? And to forge the passport in the name of Jay, so that there were two dicky birds, was just the sort of joke to please Linnet. I found out from British Airways that a Richard Jay had flown from Gatwick to Venice on a plane arriving at eight-thirty that Saturday night. There's no direct flight back from Venice to London late at night, and it took me some time to discover that Mr Jay had travelled back by an Air France midnight flight to Paris, then flown from Paris to Heathrow. I have the correspondence with British Airways here if you'd care to look at it.'

Sandy shook her head.

'Very well. Now here is the reconstruction of what happened. Charles left the party at nine o'clock in expectation of sexual pleasure. He'd arranged to meet you, Sandy, I don't know where but in some well-known place, perhaps Florian's in the Piazza San Marco. You'd have told him that for safety's sake you'd be dressed as a man. No doubt when you met he wanted to go at once to the Eros, but you had no intention of running the risk of possible identification later on, slight though it was. When the plan was first made you mus: have told him about the aphrodisiac, and said it took a little while to act, so you had a drink on the way to the Eros, at the Emperor Napoleon. It all went as you intended, the drug affected him as it had me, and with your knowledge of Venice it was no problem to lead him to a dark place and push him into the water.

'For a long time I was puzzled by the question of Owen. He lived at home, and so would have known of your absence that Saturday night. But that problem was solved when I learned that the James Joyce conference he'd attended was in Manchester, not London, as I'd assumed. So there it was, a perfect murder in which the conspirators couldn't possibly come under suspicion. Gerda knew that she should make sure she was in company that evening. You were supposedly at home in Headfield. And again I think you meant no harm to Derek, you couldn't tell that he would leave the party in search of Charles, get lost, and come under suspicion. You just wanted to leave Derek for Gerda. It's a feeling I understand.' He lowered his eyes in embarrassment.

'But you've never come out of the closet.'

He ignored the remark. 'If the crime was not perfect, it was because you had a piece of bad luck. Something happened that you couldn't possibly have foreseen. Linnet was in the hotel, in the bar, recognised you. Of course he wasn't deceived by the man's clothes, and it was you he greeted, not Charles. But you're nothing if not resourceful. Before you pushed Charles into that cold Venetian water you took his revolver. Then you rang the hotel, spoke to Linnet, said you wanted to talk, perhaps even said you'd consider going back to him. He sent away the girl in his room, you went back, and you shot him. After that a water taxi to the airport, and Mr Richard Jay was in comfortable time for the flight back to Paris. When Derek called you on Sunday morning, housewife Sandy was home again.'

Sandy whispered to Gerda, who got up and went inside the house. She stuck out her trousered legs, and examined the shabby espadrilles she was wearing. 'And what do you intend to do about it?'

The question took him aback, even shocked him. The quest had been an intellectual exercise, taken up in despair and pursued with increasing fervour, but it had never occurred to him that it might have a practical end. It was a kind of game, a puzzle to which he had provided an answer. He said, feeling the inadequacy of the words. 'I want to know the truth.'

'The truth,' she repeated. The sun was moving from the terrace, half of it was now in shadow. 'The truth is that after a couple of years life with Derek bored me. All that little boy acting, that swagger, the pretence that he was daring and then crying out when he was hurt, wanting to be comforted, it bored me. And Gerda – well, I knew what Gerda wanted the second time I talked to her. So here we are.'

'If that was all you wanted, to live together, you could have done it in Headfield.'

'In Headfield! My dear man, you don't know what you're saying. In Headfield without money, with women like Caroline sneering at me behind my back, and saying she'd always known I was butch and Gerda was my tart. You can't be serious, Jason. Could *you* settle down in Headfield, even with Derek? In London yes, but then what would we have done for money? And we didn't want the kind of life you get in London, just enough to live on comfortably. So, yes, Charles's death was lucky, we're very comfortable here in Elba. You might call us a contented couple.'

'I'm not sure I understand. You deny all I've been saying.'

Her gaze was candid under the wide brow. 'Why should I bother? It's all the product of an overheated imagination.'

'Why did Charles laugh when something was added to his drink, if it wasn't an aphrodisiac?'

'I haven't the slightest idea.'

'Why did you say "that bitch" at the luncheon party, deliberately so that I could hear it?'

'I said nothing of the kind. You misheard or imagined something. I told you so at the time.'

'When I told Derek I knew what had happened, he hinted that he knew too, but said I should keep it to myself. Why would he have said that unless he knew or believed you were implicated?'

'I can't be responsible for what Derek said, you must see that. Ah, Gerda.' Gerda had removed her dark glasses and changed into slacks. She carried a tray. On it were two tall glasses holding what looked like a fizzy lemon drink, and a third that shone fiery red as it was caught by the setting rays of the sun. 'Your favourite Bloody Mary.'

Jason looked from the drink to the two women. Both were smiling. It was Sandy who spoke.

'If there was any truth in what you've been saying, this drink might be laced with whatever knock-out drops we keep handy. Drink it, and within a few mintues you'd feel muzzy, in no condition to drive your car. The track you came down is slippery, dangerous if you're not careful, somebody had an accident there last year. It would be easy to miss that right angle bend and go off the track, over and over, down and down. Poor Jason, we should say, what a pity we never saw him.'

He stared at the tomato-coloured drink, speechless.

'Or say the Bloody Mary is just straight vodka and tomato juice. Gerda's been away long enough to tamper with your car. I believe draining the brake fluid is quite simple, and on a slope very effective.'

Now the sun had disappeared altogether behind the house. As it vanished darkness came down, softening shapes and blurring outlines, so that he could see the women's faces but not define their features.

'All that might be so if we were what you think us,' Sandy said. 'But none of it's true. You are quite safe, you could stay and eat local fish for supper, we can even put you up for the night. The truth is that Charles took some drug or other and fell into the water, my little dicky bird played one trick too many, couldn't see a way out, and shot himself. Or perhaps the man in the cap truly was a Mafia executioner, and took Charles's revolver. Anyway, it had nothing to do with Gerda or with me. You've woven fantasies, Jason, woven them out of your longing for Derek, and if Derek said you should keep your ideas to yourself he meant he wanted no more to do with you. Confess it now, didn't you always want to go to bed with him?'

Jason stood up. He was trembling. 'Oh, you are vile, both of you, vile.'

'You've never dared to face reality, or to take chances. Now here's reality in front of you, in the shape of a Bloody Mary. Reality, Jason, not fantasy. Are you going to accept it, just once in your life?'

He stretched out his hand towards the drink.

From *The Times*

ENGLISHMAN'S DEATH ON ELBA ECHO OF VENETIAN TRAGEDIES

The death has been reported of Mr Jason Durling, an official in a Whitehall ministry, while on a visit to Elba. It is thought that he took a sharp bend too fast in his rented car, which turned over down a steep hillside. The car caught fire, and Mr Durling was trapped inside it.

The tragedy carries an echo of the mysterious death three years ago of Charles Porson, an English businessman on a visit to Venice, who died from a heart attack after taking drugs and falling into an offshoot of the Grand Canal. Both men lived in Headfield, Mr Durling was in Venice at the time of Porson's death, and at the time of the accident was on his way to see Mrs Porson, who has reverted to her maiden name of Rieger and lives on Elba. The body was so badly burned as to be unrecognisable, and identification was first made when Fräulein Rieger became anxious at Mr Durling's failure to arrive, and notified the authorities. Later she and Mrs Crowley, a friend from Headfield staying with her, were too upset to comment. Sir Robin Bruce-Comfort, a colleague and friend of Durling, said he had done much valuable work in the Ministry, and would be greatly missed.

The little-used track is a danger spot that demands very careful driving round the bends. An accident occurred there last year, and consideration is being given to the erection of a fence and warning notices. The Elban police confirm that there is no suggestion Mr Durling's death was anything but a tragic accident.